KINETIC REBIRTH

a KINETICS novel

C. McDonnell

FOR JESSICA

my ultimate beta reader, my partner-in-crime,
my best friend.
May you fly high in the clouds
and continue to live on in my writing,
as my best source of inspiration.

ACKNOWLEDGEMENTS

To start, we need to follow a friendship that lasted over five years. Through mutual friends at my college, Jessi and I met via forum-based roleplaying. It started out where we would be the only people online all the time. We were rarely in the same scenes, so we'd chat back and forth while awaiting the friends we were waiting on to return to that creative, glorious portion of the interwebs. After a few months, Jessi and I created characters that ended up in a relationship, so we could interact more than via Facebook chatbox. That summer, we started hanging in person, and continued to roleplay long after that forum fizzled out, utilizing Google Docs to our advantage. We created a good number of roleplaying documents, and loved every single moment.

As of this book's release, it will have been six years since that first day of active forum roleplay. Since that fateful day, we had created eight Google documents with different storylines and varying characters and even started writing a book series together. In our personal lives, I graduated college and published my debut novel, THE PROTEKTOR'S REALITY, as well as four short story prequels as eBooks. She went on to get married to the love of her life, and they were due to have a child in August 2017.

I start this section like this, because she was the most major source for this book series. When she died, I was distraught. I still am. She didn't deserve what happened to her, nor did the people she left behind. They say death is always harder on the living, but she wouldn't want us fixated on her death. She was the brightest ray of sunshine I ever had in my life, and I'm proud to call her my closest, dearest friend. This series uses all characters pulled from our various roleplays, and mashed together in a singular universe.

All but one.

When I say Jessi was my most major source of inspiration, it's also because I have inserted her into this series, writing the character as accurately to real Jessi's personality as I could manage. I hope I'm doing her justice.

Now, for other people to get the spotlight.

There are a good number of people I need to thank, for this book wouldn't have been possible without them. First off, my fellow writers from the Smoky Mountain writer's retreat. Half of this book was written through that retreat, and the support from all of you just weeks after Jessi's death helped me push on through. I look forward to this retreat every year, and look forward to the wonderful people that make it such a fun, creative time, even for someone as socially-awkward as me.

Next, my editor, Kat Howard. Her feedback made the editing process a bit weaker of a blow to the gut. She also gave me the greatest compliment I think I will ever receive, and it was pertaining to Jessi's character: "*I know you mentioned she was based on and in tribute to a friend of yours, and I really think that she is a beautiful tribute – she's the character in the book I'd most like to know as a real person.*" Thank you, Kat, because that comment made me cry tears of joy. I wish you could've met her.

Also, shoutout to Designed by Starla, who has created amazing covers for me for this series and my debut novel. If you need a kick butt cover for your book, she's the best you could ever hire!

To my family and friends, for supporting me through the good times and the bad. I'm not going to specifically name anybody, as this section would be as long as the book, but you all know who you are. I couldn't have created this ultimate dedication without having such an amazingly wonderful group of people behind me.

And, lastly, to you. The reader. The one who picked this book to read. You readers who like my stories are one of the best sources of motivation I can have. As long as people will read my stories, I will continue to write them. Well… I'll be writing regardless, but if it gets beyond a Word Document, we'll know when we get there.

To conclude, thank you for picking this story out. Jessi will live on in spirit, in the hearts of those who cared about her, and in the imaginations of every one of you readers, who can hopefully see how bright and amazing my best friend was. Here's hoping I did her justice.

Enjoy the Ride, everybody. And, welcome to Majora.

- C.M.

Chapter 1

Keyboard keys tap-tapped all around Jaden Walker. She ripped her gaze from her computer screen to gaze around the competition room. Her spot sat in the second row from the back, with about ten rows of students and computers in front of her. Supervisors scattered around the rows, keeping an eye out for cheaters. Jaden didn't see the point in that, as every competitor's test had been randomized out of a pool of questions. In order to cheat, you'd either need a camera and earpiece or be an idiot. That first option screamed "Idiot" to her too, to be entirely honest.

After a quick sweep of the testing room, Jaden locked gazes with one of the Supervisors. His burning amber hair stuck out like a sore thumb as he smiled crookedly at her, as if he knew something she didn't. That look pointed out the obvious, as he – being a Supervisor – already functioned in an aspect of the business world and obviously would know more than college freshman Jaden Walker. Rolling her eyes, she directed her attention back to her test. Despite the beaming talent surrounding her, she knew she would wipe the floor with them.

About twenty minutes later, she closed down the testing browser, grabbed her coat, and scooched her way down the narrow walkway to get out of the square of competitors. Right as she reached the edge, she ran right into somebody, quickly dismissing the sudden static shock that zappd her. "I'm sorry-"

"Shhhh…" the man whispered, "Others are still testing."

Jaden nodded. "Sorry." She kept her voice hushed as well.

When she looked up at the Supervisor, she recognized him as the red-headed man who'd made her feel annoyed earlier. "May I ask your name?"

Scoffing, she replied lightly, "Like you need to know."

The smallest of smiles crept onto the man's face, his green eyes gazing down at her as if analyzing her every move. "I'm sure I'll know it soon enough."

"Riiiiiiight…" A chill shot down her back, which she shrugged off. As she turned around to leave, she felt his eyes on her the whole walk to the back exit. As the door shut behind her, she relaxed, releasing a heavy sigh.

"Sooooooo, how'd you do?"

Jaden spotted Lukas, her closest friend, leaning against the wall with one foot flat against the tan wallpaper. "I hope you're not leaving a shoe print on that wall. The convention center staff might not take too kindly to that."

Removing his foot, he smiled. "Avoiding the question, I see?"

Shoulders dropping from exasperation, she snapped lightly, "How should I know? I won't know until the awards ceremony tomorrow night."

"Jeesh, just asked a question. No need to be harsh."

Rolling her eyes with a small smile, Jaden walked down the testing hallway. Her eyes skimmed the walls, all plastered with promotional "BS" related to this Phi Beta Lambda national conference. She won first place in two state competitions and second in a third, which gave her admittance to the national level of testing. Even placing in the top ten would be amazing.

Plus, it looked impressive on a resume when she would graduate in a few years. She'd just finished her final test, so all that was left of her agenda involved networking with business professionals (in her wording, schmoozing the big wigs) and tomorrow night's award ceremony at Six PM.

Lukas suddenly appeared at her side, matching her step by step, completely in sync with her pace and speed. "So, no weird people in there?"

"Well there was one guy, but I think other people saw him, *so* not a figment." The term "figment" referred to the hallucinations she'd had since she was a child. At first, her parents blamed it on an over-active, childish imagination. Once she'd reached high school and still saw people and animals who weren't there, her parents worried deeply for their daughter. They employed the help of a shrink, who, for each session, she'd humored with breathing exercises and repetitive mantras and meds until she bolted out to go home and read a book. Rather quickly, she masked her diagnosed schizophrenia from the world, instead diving deep into her studies and avoiding as many social situations whenever possible.

"You trust your sight yet?"

Heaving a heavy sigh, Jaden responded, "Not entirely. You're still here."

"Hey!"

After whacking him lightly on the back of his head, she finally cracked a smile. Lukas had been her friend since third grade and stuck like glue to her side. In fact, he went everywhere with her. Weirdly enough, he'd frequently show up out of the blue during personal trips and vacations, insisting he wanted to surprise her. At first, his surprises did shock and elate her, but after a couple years of it, it became pretty predictable. His parents tended to be lenient toward him and his antics, and they somehow had the money for him to follow her pretty much anywhere. Part of her thanked

God that he wasn't another one of her figments. People saw him, talked to him, and played with him, so he existed. Since he'd been by her side for so long, she confided her mental handicap to him early on, and only him. Outside of him and her family, no one knew, and she wanted it to stay that way. She'd thought it was strange with how accepting he was with it. He didn't freak out or get depressed or feel worrisome. He'd pretty much shrugged it off, like seeing imaginary people everywhere was as normal as pizza on a Friday night.

Lukas rubbed where she whacked him. "Um, *ow*!"

Her smiled widened slightly as she shoved him with her shoulder. "That didn't hurt and you know it." She knew it too, because he possessed a "high pain tolerance", as he'd reminded her on countless occasions.

With a light chuckle, he shoved her with his shoulder like she had to him. "Good, you remembered." Then, he froze, stopping in his tracks. His icy blue eyes locked on something ahead. "Uh, oh…"

Her eyes followed his line of sight and easily spotted two teenagers making a beeline for them. Or, rather her, because she went to address Lukas to discover he'd vanished. Again. He'd done this frequently in her life, and it always annoyed her. He didn't up and poof away in a puff of smoke, but he always picked the perfect moment to disappear on her, usually moments he didn't want to deal with. "Freaking kidding me, Wolfe!"

The two kids stopped about three feet from her. The girl waved and greeted, "Hi!" Her personality bubbled with childish excitement, like a kid stuck in a sixteen-year-old's big boned body.

Jaden stared at her for a moment before weakly raising a hand as well. "Hi?"

The boy with her rolled his eyes. "Jess, you're freaking her out."

The girl's eyes widened slightly. "I'm so sorry! I didn't mean to startle you."

"Not startled," Jaden replied slowly, "Just weirded out. What can I do for you two?"

The girl and boy looked at each other briefly before turning attention back to her. "My name's Jessica, but most people call me Jessi. My twin brother here, Kiran, usually calls me Jess or JV, just randomly picking between four different variations of my name. It's a good thing I'm used to being addressed with all four throughout my life."

Kiran's head rolled back as he sighed, "Jess, diarrhea of the mouth again. I honestly don't think she cares about your millions of nicknames."

Shaking a hand at him, Jaden said, "It's fine. I don't mind. My sister's the same way sometimes. So, Jessi, Kiran… Can I help you with something?"

The two teens exchanged looks again before looking back at her. Jessi told her, "We think someone might be looking for you."

Raising an eyebrow, Jaden responded, "Probably my parents. They've been wandering around this Gaylord center every time I have mandatory events. I'll find them eventually, I promise. Now, if you'll excuse me."

She walked around them, but only made it two steps before the two kids stepped into her path. Holding up a hand, a "STOP" gesture, Jessi told her, "No, not your parents. Someone else. Someone bad."

In her mind, Jaden could only call them crazy kids with overactive imaginations. Right when that thought crossed her mind, she recalled that being her parents' initial reaction to her seeing the figments. These two probably have been dealing with the same stuff she had her whole life, and she felt a pang of empathy for them. "Look, I'm sure security around here will be able to pick him up like a sore thumb."

Jessi shook her head, her sandy brown hair flying around at the rapid, overly-excited speed she swung it. Jaden caught scattered blonde highlights in the strands of her bob-like haircut. "No, they can't, because no one can see him. Nobody but you."

Jaden's heart started pounding in her chest, her skin chilled with goosebumps. Did these two kids, strangers at that, really know that she was a schizo? Shaking her head slightly to snap out of her worrisome, panicked thoughts, she replied, "I have no idea what you mean by that. Plus, I've got a seminar at four that I can't be late for."

This time, Kiran spoke up, "Which seminar?"

She hesitated. Clearly these two needed help, or at least needed to stick with their guardian or chaperone. But, she really didn't see the harm in sharing. "'Budgeting for Needs and Wants'. Since I'll be coming out of college debt-free, thanks to my dad's military benefits, I need to figure out how to budget once I don't have my parents to help. I graduate in about three years, so it's better to be prepared, you know?"

Kiran's eyes lit up, his irises a blue-green that reflected the color of the ocean. "Oh, cool! That sounds like fun! Mind if we tag along?"

As much as Jaden wanted to get as far away from these unhinged children as fast as she could, she bit back her stress and told them nonchalantly, "Yeah, sure, that's seems okay with me. You can join me. Make sure you have a notebook handy. I've heard the speaker is amazing and gives *tons* of good advice."

Kiran's mouth widened into a huge smile. "That's sounds awesome! Sold! C'mon, Jess, let's go learn about finances."

Jessi stared at her brother for a few seconds before sighing heavily. "Alright, Mr. Studious Crazy, I'll come too. Take notes for both of us though. I don't want to zone out and not have the *amazing* knowledge this strange businessman has to offer."

Jaden recognized the slight sarcasm in the girl's words, but Kiran's excitement blocked him from identifying it himself. "Great! Lead the way..." He faded off, biting his lip. He glanced at her and then at his sister.

Mentally rolling her eyes, Jaden filled in the missing blank: "Jaden. Jaden Walker."

With a smile, Jessi responded, "Nice to meet you, Jaden. I hope we won't slow you down much."

As she held back a laugh, remembering a ton of times that Lukas had said that to her in jest, she told her, "Trust me, I've dealt with worse. Okay, I believe that seminar is in room 2B."

"Excellent!" Kiran rubbed his hands together, during which Jaden thought she saw sparks flying out. Trying to snap herself out of those thoughts didn't work at first.

First figments, and now I'm imagining electricity popping out of a kid's hands. Don't tell me my problem is branching out more...

"Let's go!"

Kiran's shout of excitement shocked her out of it. Her head snapped up from where it had been angled at the floor to find the two teens halfway across the atrium. Kiran waved at her excitedly. "C'mon, slowpoke! Thought this was your panel choice."

Her face cracked a small smile at his eagerness. As she walked to catch up with them, a question ran through her head that worried her.

Did they know?

Followed by a second one:

How?

Chapter 2

The next day, Jaden woke up to pouring down rain. She flicked on the TV, a talk show as the predetermined channel. After skipping a few shows, a weatherman appeared on the flat screen. "Nashville is right on the edge of a storm, but by midday should clear up. The humidity, however, shall remain at a high level throughout the day."

She muted the television, not needing to hear anything more. "Great," she grumbled aloud, "My hair poofs when it's humid. Just my luck on the day of the awards ceremony." She sat up on the bed of her hotel room, kicked her legs over the side, and stretched, a huge yawn escaping her mouth. As she rubbed her eyes, she walked into the bathroom. She washed her face, wiping and scrubbing away the sleepiness. Once she was done, she caught her reflection in the mirror. The pixie cut hairstyle had long been awaited when she was a little girl, when she had a slightly unhealthy obsession with the singer P!nk. Finally, as a high school graduation present, her parents allowed her to mimic the singer's style. She used her own twist and kept most of it black, but bleached the tips of each strand in homage to the pop-rocker. Sighing, she quickly got some gel through her hair, spiking it up. Her hairstyle choice reflected some badass chick who plays by no rules, but that assumption took a one-eighty to her true personality. Jaden Walker felt compassion and empathy, helped anyone who needed it, suffered from extreme introversion and social anxiety, and had to survive arguments with her sister about facts versus fiction, as her sister, Dove, gossiped with no basis in truth.

A string of knocks pounded against the bathroom door. "Hey, my turn, pipsqueak!"

Jaden rolled her eyes. *Speak of the devil…* "I'll be out in a minute, Dove."

"Hurry up! I have to pee!"

The smallest of humored smiles appeared on Jaden's lips. "I'll try," she drawled, "But I might be in here for a while. Have a reputation that will skyrocket tonight, so I absolutely need to look professional."

Dove groaned loudly on the other side of the door. "You're such a brat, you know that?"

With a gleeful tone, Jaden replied, "Yes, I know. You don't need to state the obvious, gym rat!" She quickly brushed her teeth and applied her makeup. It took a total of about five more minutes. When she opened the bathroom door, Dove burst in and shoved Jaden out. The door slammed behind her, so loud that their hotel neighbors probably heard it. Shaking her head with a silent chuckle, Jaden headed back to the bedroom. She prepped for the day pretty fast, and within minutes, her body screamed "business professional", with a suit, dress shoes, and red dress shirt. The only glaring part of her ensemble lay draped around her neck: her convention nametag. In a similar fashion to the fantasy conventions she'd attended in the past, her name stood out in bold and all caps, and her school and state in tiny letters underneath.

Tugging on her suit jacket, she smiled. "Okay, ready to go. Mom?"

"Yes, dear?"

"I've gotta go now. Meeting up with Lukas for breakfast."

"Okay, sweetheart. Be careful, okay?"

That seemed like an odd request. While her mom had always been annoyingly overprotective, she still didn't understand the need for all of them there. For moral support, her mother had insisted, but she knew they were there because they didn't think she could handle the travel and competition alone. The main reason?

Her disability, that's what.

She pondered briefly of her mother's word choice though. What dangers could possibly be lurking in a giant convention center filled with young business students and security everywhere? Shrugging it off, she replied to humor her mother, "Alright, I promise!" She grabbed her purse and left the room. The hallways in the hotel section of this place proved the fanciness of this whole property. Fancy wallpaper covered in little colored flowers. Small tables randomly placed against the walls. Lights that hung from the ceiling, rather than those built-in rectangular lights you see in most modern buildings.

Soon, she broke out into the main area. Foliage filled the interior and even had a small river weaving through it, where people could actually ride a boat through the whole place. Bridges crossed over top of the waterways in rustic stonework style. She wandered through the whole place until she reached one of the eateries that she and Lukas had picked out the day before. She stood there for a few minutes, gazing around the paths to spot Lukas. After about six minutes of looking, she pulled out her phone. She scrolled through her Facebook, reading about the summer escapades her classmates from college currently were taking part in.

Two hands slammed on her shoulders, startling her enough to almost jump out of her skin. She quickly spun out of the loose grip and discovered the attacker: Lukas. And, boy, was he hysterical. Frowning, Jaden snapped, "Not funny."

"Maybe not for you," he replied between raucous laughter. Eventually, the firm glare she continued to give him slowed down the amusement, eventually quashing it. "Geez, take a joke, Jay."

"Do you understand how wired my nerves are right now? I took three *national* business competitions, and I have to wait another ten hours to find out if I did well enough to place. These awards are BIG leverages on a resume and put me ahead of a lot of other prospective job hunters my age."

Lukas lifted a hand, and opened and shut the fingers and thumb, a gesture that always means, "Blah blah blah," and made Jaden a bit annoyed. "Yadda yadda yadda. You've explained that tons of times. I don't need a repeat lesson, teach. Sorry not sorry."

Holding her head with a hand, Jaden groaned, "Why do I hang out with you again?"

"Because I'm your foil. My Batman to your Joker. My nuts to your chocolate. My peanut butter to your jelly."

Jaden made a disgusted face. "Fluff. Marshmallow fluff. Jelly is gross."

Smiling crookedly, he told her, "Okay, you're a fluff. Sounds reasonable."

She shoved him lightly with one hand. "You really think you're funny, don't you?"

"Well, my public demands it."

Stifling a laugh, she glanced up at the breakfast eatery. "We gonna eat now, or do you want to starve today?" As if on cue, a soft rumbling reached her ears. This time, a snicker actually snorted out of her mouth. "Guess that answers my question."

This time, Lukas possessed glaring rights. "Oh, shut up."

As they got in line, Jaden still stayed on the topic of his hungry stomach. "Your stomach always sounds like Scooby-Doo when you're hungry. Remember that one time in the Accounting class, when you had to skip eating to make it to class on time?"

Hanging his head back, he groaned, "Don't remind me. That was horrible."

Nudging him with her shoulder, she asked playfully, "And what did Prof Stevens say when it rang through the whole lecture hall?"

Brow furrowing, Lukas looked down at his feet. His shoulders rose and fell with his heavy sigh. "He said, 'Everyone watch out. I think a baby lion is trying to roar'." When Jaden started cackling with laughter, he shot her a glare out of the corners of his eyes. "Oh, bite me, Walker."

They finally reached the front of the buffet line. Both grabbed plates and food faster than a homeless dog gobbling up scraps. Once the food stacked high on their plates, they made their way to a booth in the back of the seating area. The first few minutes of breakfast had them sitting in silence, shoveling food down their throat like they had since they were teens. Even at eighteen, Jaden's appetite still massively beat out her sister's. Both were born with slim figures, but Jaden had a bit more muscle and meat to her, which matched the amount of food she ate. Every time her family went out to eat, Jaden rolled eyes at Dove's suggestion of Panera or Tropical Smoothie Café, while her sister did the same to her requests of Five Guys, Texas Roadhouse, or CiCi's Pizza. What could she say? Food just doesn't feel right when it advertises it as healthy or low carb. Kinda off-putting to be honest.

When Jaden's plate reached half-empty status, a clang of silverware made her look up. Lukas leaned back, his hands behind his head and his plate completely cleaned of any trace of food. "Ah!" he said, "That hit the spot."

With a snicker, Jaden commented, "Shaggy, you were definitely hungry. You been starving yourself?"

Rolling his eyes as an obvious mocking technique, he replied, "I'm just a simple guy with simple needs. Just feed me, let me get six hours of sleep, and let me watch my TV, and I'm set."

Cocking an eyebrow with a teasing smile, she asked him, "A simple guy who just devoured a plate of food stacked half a foot high? Furthest thing from simple."

As Lukas stuck out his tongue, a familiar voice called out, "Jaden!"

A chill shot down her spine again. Lifting her gaze to look across the dining area, she spotted Kiran and Jessi hurrying toward their table. Again, apparently, just her table alone, because Lukas had vanished yet again. Under her breath, she mumbled, "I look away for a second…" When the teens reached her table, she plastered a smile on her face. "Hey there, long time no see." As they slid into the bench that Lukas had been in just seconds before, she said, "Yeah, feel free to join me." She'd said it with sarcasm, but their minds seemed to be oblivious to it.

Kiran stared down her plate in a similar fashion to how Lukas had when going through the line. Jessi, on the other hand, stared at the tablecloth for a few more seconds before looking at Jaden. "Did you sleep okay, Jay?" she asked.

"Um, yeah, I guess…" Jaden gazed around a bit, trying to see if there were any adults that looked anything like these two kids. "Hey, where are your parents?"

Very bluntly, Kiran responded, "Not here."

Jaden's brow furrowed. "Like, not out of the hotel room, or not staying here at all, or…"

"No, like not in town."

That screamed trouble in Jaden's mind. What kind of parents would drop off their children for a business student convention in a new city and let them fend for themselves? Jaden filled the awkward silence by eating two more pork sausage links. Wiping her mouth, she spoke up again, "So, what tests did you guys take?"

Kiran's head cocked, clearly confused. "What tests?"

Jaden just stared at him, red alert going off in her head. "The tests that all participants come to compete in? Don't tell me you guys aren't with the National Leadership Conference for college level FBLA?"

Kiran shook his head. "Nope."

"Then why are you two here? I know this is a hotel for any travelers, but you're two kids with no parents in town. Seems a bit odd, you know?"

As Kiran ignored Jaden, his sister told her, "We know it sounds strange, but we're here for a very specific reason."

Thinking back to yesterday, Jaden asked, "Is it something to do with this bad somebody you guys mentioned yesterday? The one only I can see?"

Jessi smiled and nodded. "Yep."

Resisting the urge to roll her eyes, Jaden couldn't help but think there was something seriously wrong with these kids. Plus, with these kids seeming to possess a bunch of problems, their parents ditch them in a strange city, openly knowing their children had handicaps? She could empathize with them, but empathy only went so far. The fact that these two had latched on her with their messed-up fantasies just made her more annoyed.

Jaden looked around the whole restaurant, trying to find Lukas to help her out of this mess. When she couldn't locate him, she sighed, knowing she'd need another excuse to get away from these kids. "Hey, I just remembered I have a chapter meeting I need to get to."

When she started scooching out of her side of the booth, Jessi asked, "What about the rest of your plate? You must be hungry to have that much piled on."

With a three second glance at her plate filled with egg whites, bacon, and toast, she felt her introverted worries tackling her hunger to the ground, grabbing it, and twisting. "You guys can finish it if you want. Suddenly, I'm not as hungry as I thought." As she walked toward the exit, she could feel something a bit odd about those kids. They definitely had issues, but, for some reason, the empathy she felt seemed to be morphing into understanding and connection.

Shaking her head, she walked through the doorway and out into the massive interior garden. People hurried this way and that, crisscrossing through crowds. She lifted her arm and looked at her FitBit. While she had said she had a chapter meeting, that wasn't for another hour and a half. Gazing around, she saw a sign of arrows, directing people to various spots in the Gaylord. One of them caught her eye: "Library".

With the smallest of smiles, she followed the direction of the arrow, hoping to lose herself in a fantasy book, where the things that just happened to her are entirely normal and spanned so many different titles. At least the events in fantasy books were fiction, whereas those two kids are as real as real could get. All she could do was hope that her life was not turning into a fantasy novel. Still, if her life did take that turn, she humored the idea that she'd be able to handle anything that might happen. Since reading fantasy and paranormal had been a staple for her since elementary school, she'd be better prepared than the characters in said books. All the research she'd accumulated over her love of books would prove useful in the long run, wouldn't it?

Her smile twitched bigger at that thought. Now, that was a ridiculous idea, wasn't it? While a world of magic and adventure might be a dream to most avid readers, Jaden was content where she was. Reality could be tough sometimes, but definitely better than being attacked by magical villains and avoiding blasts of fire or water. No, if given the choice, her fantasy world would remain in the written word.

Chapter 3

After her chapter meeting, Jaden followed her itinerary to one of the board rooms, where the schmoozing of business professionals would take place. We're talking presidents, project managers, CFOs, CEOs: from every spectrum. The intent of this event was to make connections in the business world. This helped when all the students attending would graduate and be looking for a job; they can reach out to the professionals they met here for possible opportunities.

She rounded a corner and almost ran smack dab into Lukas. Staggering back a few steps, Jaden clutched her heart. "Damn, Lukas, you almost gave me a heart attack."

Cocking his head, Lukas thoughtfully replied, "That's statistically unlikely. Eighteen year olds have a slim chance of that, whereas those adults twice your age-"

Groaning and rolling her eyes, she walked around him, continuing her path to Board Room 3B. He quickly caught up though, snapping, "That was rude."

"Sorry, Wolfe," Jaden apologized, picking up the pace. Her tone, however, was the furthest thing from repentant. "This networking thing could boost-"

Lukas did the "Blah Blah Blah" gesture again, opening and closing his hand like a duck. "Could boost your chances of getting a job after graduation compared to other college grads. It seems that every event here has that as an excuse to ditch me constantly."

"Um, one…" Jaden held up a single finger, "This trip is for my benefit, not a chaotic, "The Detour"-style vacation." She caught the twitch of humor on her best friend's face, obviously because he liked his TBS Originals. "Secondly, because *every event here* has that for a reason. We are at a business conference after all. Totally professional gathering. No room for crazy partiers."

Lukas raised an eyebrow and drawled, "Right, and that's why the opening ceremony had dancing, blaringly loud pop music, cheering, singing, and chanting, plus confetti. I feel a bit sorry for the janitorial staff after that. Confetti is hard to get off carpeted surfaces."

Her usual habit of eye rolling happened yet again as she told him, "Well, we may be professional-bound, but we are still college students. We do need unwinding time, you know."

"Yeah, yeah, yeah, I get it."

Soon, Board Room 3B came into view, with a few students dolled up in suits making their way inside. Turning to her friend, she asked, "What's on your agenda while I do this?"

With a shrug, Lukas responded, "Dunno. Maybe take one of those boat tours and flip the vessel, so everyone on board ends up in the water. Or, maybe go to the top floor and drop water balloons onto people on lower levels."

While she knew he was joking, she still had to tell him, "How about you stay away from any bit of water, so you don't get kicked out?"

Giving her a salute, he replied, "Aye Aye, Captain. Now, get to schmoozing."

The smallest of smiles cracked Jaden's lips as she nodded silently. Then, she turned back around and entered the board room. There were tons of people in there, either wearing a blue sticker or a neon green sticker. She received her green sticker from a table near the entrance. The woman explained that the blue stickers signified business professionals, while green meant PBL student. After that, she wandered around, trying to find any business professionals that weren't already talking to someone else. Trying to insert herself into an already in-progress convo usually spiked her anxiety levels and terrified her introversion. After about five minutes, she felt her stomach growling. As she clutched it, she remembered she hadn't finished breakfast, thanks to those twins, who had unknowingly brought back the nausea she'd been struggling with until a few years ago: nausea stemming from her unease as a schizo. She walked over to the snack table off to the far side of the room. After grabbing a small plastic plate, she grabbed a handful of M&Ms, some mini hotdogs, and a few crackers with a proportionally correct amount of cheese. Everyone knows that the cracker-to-cheese ratio was 2 to 1.

"Wow, did they go all out, hm?"

She glanced to her left to find a businessman scooping some ranch onto his plate of veggies. "Is that sarcasm, Sir?"

The man smiled, chuckling softly, "Veiled contempt, actually. I mean, how can you have a networking gathering without strawberries and a chocolate fountain. Ridiculous, if you ask me."

Jaden couldn't help but giggle. "Yeah." She found this man easy to talk to, made her feel relaxed. Hadn't expected any one of these stiffs to be that laid back. She'd known that businesses were formal and serious settings, and her personality matched quite nicely. However, she didn't declare management as her major for the dull Christmas parties or personal cubicles. She picked it because it felt right. And now, with this guy being so casual and lighthearted, she at least felt a bit of a glimmer on the horizon of her planned future. Guess not all business execs were black and white.

The man glanced at her and set down his plate. “Oh, where are my manners?” Holding out a hand for her to shake, he greeted, “My name’s Griffin Valentine, President and CEO of ArmsWorth.”

“Jaden. Jaden Walker.” She gripped his hand as her Communications professor had taught them and shook.

Griffin’s eyes widened slightly as he commented, “Wow, that’s quite a firm grip for a young female.”

Jaden shrugged. “What can I say, I’m a strong girl.”

Chuckling, Griffin picked up his plate. “You wanna get a table? No use in standing here and blocking people from this *amazing* smorgasbord.” After the businessman rolled his eyes, she definitely for a fact knew she liked this guy. They reached a tall table and sat in the high chairs, setting their plates down. “So, Jaden. Why is it you are here?”

“Well, I’m a business major-”

Shaking a hand at her, he clarified, “I mean, besides the obvious. You obviously learned business tactics very easily, putting you ahead of the crowd. Why do you need a trophy to prove your knowledge?”

Aiming her gaze at her lap, she responded slowly to watch what she said, “Well, awards look good on a resume.”

Griffin nodded in agreement. “Yes, they absolutely do. But, so do real world experiences. Tell me, have you ever taken a risk in your life?” When she didn’t look up, he continued, “I know your type. Studious, introverted, keeps to themselves, focuses on school work rather than her social life, likes her fantasies inside of a book instead of getting out in the world and living them. Now, don’t get me wrong, being that conservative is not always a bad thing. However, it might benefit you greatly to take some risks every so once in a while. Watching someone ride a motorcycle is completely different from riding on the back of one."

Jaden replied softly, "I just… I have some complications in my life, let's just say that."

"All of us do, Jaden Walker. But, if you don't fight back or put yourself out there, you lose in the long run." Standing up, he rolled his shoulders. "Unfortunately, I have to head out. Speaking in a panel in ten. But, here." He reached into his inside jacket pocket, pulling out a business card. "I like you, Jaden. You seem pretty strong. Call me if you need anything. Employment, advice, money, guns and ammo."

Cocking an eyebrow, she asked, "You say guns as a joke, right?"

With a small smile, Griffin told her, "Nope. ArmsWorth is centrically focused on guns and gun safety, and anything relating to it. If you need a hitman, I can point you in the right direction." After he winked and she just stared blankly at him, he chuckled, "*That* was the joke, Jaden. But, like I said, for anything."

Jaden nodded. "I'll keep that in mind, Sir."

"Good." He stood up, walked around the table, and patted her shoulder as he walked by. "Nice meeting you, Jaden. Hope to hear from you again sometime."

As he walked away, she watched him the whole time until he left the board room. She continued to stare at the door for a few more minutes, replaying the conversation she'd just had. Aloud, she muttered, "Did he actually just offer me guns?"

"Yes, yes, I believe he did."

Her head snapped back to find that annoying redheaded Supervisor sitting in Griffin's old seat. "Who asked you?" she snapped.

His eyes widened into shock. "Is that how you talk to a business professional? You won't make it far in that field if you keep that attitude."

Frowning, she nodded. "I'm sorry, Sir. I apologize."

He waved it off. "No worries, Jaden. I've got a thick skin." Holding out his hand, he said, "My name is Skylar Meisyn. I work for a chemistry lab."

"That sounds interesting," Jaden commented thoughtfully.

"Yeah, it's fun," Skylar told her, "We have holdings and experts in every field of science. There's a big rumor that we perform Summonings and other magical sciences, and we laugh over it. It's quite fun to talk to someone about your job and casually mention your current project is to unleash the Anti-Christ."

Jaden snorted and laughed. "That sounds hilarious!"

With a wide smile, he replied, "Yeah, it's a blast! Now, should I pull my hand back, as you seem to be germaphobic?"

She glanced down at his hand, realizing her rudeness. When she took his hand, sharp pain shot from their grip straight up her arm, almost like lightning. She yanked back, clutching her arm tight to her chest. Her eyes widened when she realized her mistake. She hadn't felt that shock in years, simply because she'd avoided touching them since high school. But, that feeling of a shot of electricity through touch filled tons of her memories as a child. Her eyes skimmed his suit, and her heart started pounding when she realized he wasn't wearing a blue sticker.

He was a figment.

Jaden practically fell out of her chair and stumbled backwards, keeping her eyes on him at all times. Skylar's eyebrows drooped in pity. "Something wrong, Jaden?"

"Y-y-you aren't r-real…" she stuttered.

Skylar's mouth broke into a wide, sinister grin. "No, dear Jaden, I'm as real as real can get."

"N-no, y-you aren't."

Dropping out of the high chair, Skylar took slow, menacing steps toward her, like a cheetah on the prowl. "Calm breaths, Jaden. You're creating quite the scene."

Her wide, terrified eyes swept the room, recognizing every gaze locked on her. Cringing, she bolted out of Board Room 3B. After running down a few halls, she found an empty conference room. She quickly dashed into that room, shut the door behind her, and locked it. Her body pressed against the door by her back and slowly lowered to the ground. Once sitting on the floor, she felt tears welling up. Usually, she can tell the difference between a real person and a figment. Why couldn't she now? Maybe this was just a fluke. Yeah, just a result of anxiety from the competitions. That had to be it. Luckily, her figments were a one-and-done thing after she touched them. Thinking about it, though, reminded her that this man had been in her testing room. She'd seen one boy in the fifth row make eye contact with him, which is why she assumed he existed. Maybe that kid just happened to look toward an empty space, because there was no way in existence that another sane person could see the figments her mind created.

"Aw, still think I'm not real."

Her head shot up at Skylar's voice, eyes widening. Sure enough, Skylar sat in a rolling chair only about five feet from where she sat. Holding up a hand as she backed up alongside the wall, she breathed, "Get a-away f-from me."

Making a hissing noise between his teeth in a disappointing fashion, he stood up. " 'Fraid I can't do that, Jaden. See, I need you to help me with something."

Eyes twitching between wide and narrowed, she replied, "I c-can't help a figment. You're j-just in m-my head."

"Breathe, Jaden," Skylar ordered gently, "I'm not going to hurt you."

"Y-You can't hurt m-me. Y-You d-d-don't exis-st."

Cocking his head, he asked, "Then how did you feel what you felt when you took my hand?"

That was an excellent question. She'd just assumed her brain tricked her into that feeling to supplement the paranoia of her condition. But, now that she thought about it, that theory seemed a bit off. If it had been a trick of the mind, it probably would have just been that shock. Then, after breaking contact, she'd be fine. How was it, then, that her arm ached for hours after making contact with a figment of her imagination?

"Ah, that was a good question, no?" Her gaze snapped back up to Skylar, who was about seven feet away and blocking the door. "Now, are you understanding enough to hear me out?"

Jaden took a few deep breaths, then asked, "H-How is that possible? I made you up. My brain is messed up, and makes me see people that don't exist."

"Yes, that is true, to an extent. However, the one glaring error in that description pertains to my existence. I am very much real, just on a different plane."

Her brow furrowed, trying to figure out what he was getting at. Things had calmed down slightly, so she was able to speak without stuttering: "I don't understand."

Right as Skylar opened his mouth to say something, a loud "Kyah!" sounded outside of the conference room, and the door broke off its hinges and slammed into him. He went flying, slammed onto the long table, slid all the way across it, and fell off the far end.

Two figures ran into the room, sporting identical goggles that looked extremely reminiscent of ones you'd wear in a science lab, but blacked-out. One of them ran up to her and held out a hand to help her up. Since Jaden was still in shock, she just stared at this person.

The person groaned and slid the goggles down to rest around her neck, revealing that person to be none other than Jessica. "Looks like you don't have a leg to stand on." Since all emotional control was out of reach, Jaden couldn't help but smile at the lighthearted joke. "Okay, up and at 'em. We gotta get out of here."

Jaden finally grabbed her hand, grateful for a familiar face. Together, they got Jaden to her feet. Patting her on the shoulder, Jessi smiled, a gesture that helped Jaden relax a little bit. "Just breathe, okay? It would be bad for you to stop breathing."

"Yes," Jaden replied, "That would be bad."

As the two girls grinned at each other, Kiran, the other goggled person, called out, "When you two ladies are done with the jokes, we should probably get out of here."

A groan sounded across the long room, and Jaden recognized the tone as coming from Skylar. With Jessi's hand patting her on the back, Jaden ran out of the room, the twins close behind.

As the three ran down the hall, Kiran glanced back. "Uh, oh."

Jaden looked behind them as well to find four men in suits pursuing them. One pulled a gun from his inside jacket pocket and aimed it their way. "Oh hell!"

"Jay, get on the other side of me." Jessi's voice sounded urgent, so Jaden moved around her. Right as she left her old spot in their formation, a bullet narrowly missed her. Her heart pounded faster. Did this teen girl somehow predict the path of a bullet before it left its barrel?

Kiran moved to run alongside the left wall. As he ran, he let his hand slide across the wallpaper. Sparks flew from his trailing fingertips, reminding Jaden of what she'd seen before. Guess that hadn't been her imagination after all. Then, one by one, the ceiling lights blacked out, shrouding them in a cloak of darkness. Those men with guns shouted, apparently losing their trail.

Chapter 4

Continuing through the labyrinth of halls, they reached the guest room area. Recognizing room numbers, Jaden realized they were near her family's accommodations. She slowed to a quick power walk, skimming room numbers as she did. Finally, she reached Room 131. Knocking on the door, she called out, "Mom? Dad? You guys there?" When she got only silence as a response, she frowned. "That's odd. They were planning on staying in the room to binge-watch Big Bang… Why the heck didn't I have them give me a room key?"

Kiran stepped in front of her, startling her enough to make her yelp and jump back. With a wicked grin, he drawled, "Watch the master at work." He placed his hand over top of the key mechanism and closed his eyes. Within five seconds, the whirring of the machine sounded, followed by a click. Kiran turned the door handle and pushed it open. "Cake."

Jaden ran past him, but came to an abrupt stop. Her eyes looked at every detail of that hotel room, but there was no sign that anyone had lived there, even for a day. All the beds were crisply made, not a single wrinkle or crease out of place. All the suitcases, including Jaden's, had vanished. Running into the bathroom, she saw an empty vanity, where just hours before had been covered in Dove's 'products', such as hair gel, body splash, and who knows what else. But, every bit of it, including the shaving cream that had coated the sink, had been wiped from existence.

Slowly walking back into the main room, she stared at her feet, almost in a haze. "Wh… Where are they? And what happened to my stuff? I had a CD and hat signed by Peter Hollens in my suitcase for luck!" While trying to maintain calm breathing, she stared wide-eyed at the carpet, shaking her head in disbelief. "I… I don't understand."

"We do."

Jaden whipped around to find Jessi and Kiran inside with her, door shut. "What happened to my family?" Her eyes stung a bit, though she didn't know why. She'd always told herself the second she could escape her parents, she would. So, why was her lip quivering at the idea of them being gone and her being on her own?

Kiran rubbed the back of his neck, grimacing. "They were a substitute family."

Brow furrowing, a million more questions joined the collection that already flew around in her head. "What the heck does that mean?"

Jessi walked up to her, wrapped an arm around her shoulders, and led her to the couch. Once both were sitting down, Jessi let out a heavy exhale. "Okay, now, this might seem crazy, so bear with us a bit. The people you thought were your family… They essentially took on a job to let you live a normal life. Your real family sent you away for that, to protect you."

Her mind filling with more and more questions, Jaden snapped, "Protect me from what? The knowledge of being a schizo?"

Jessi cocked her head slightly, her expression trying to comfort her. "Jaden, you aren't a schizophrenic, okay?"

Eyes stinging more, Jaden cringed, angling her head away. "Like I'd expect you to pick up on it. My meds help me so I can be normal like everyone else."

"Do they really help? Or did you just think they helped?"

With a small sniffle of a runny nose, she thought Jessi's words over. Sure, she'd seen a shrink and been on medication since high school. But, though the figments lessened in appearance, there hadn't been much difference. They still showed up, and she still had adverse effects when touching them. In fact, there had been a few instances when she'd touched one and gotten more consequences than just a slight static shock. In those few instances, she'd get dizzy, shaky, nauseous, and a bunch of other random maladies. What Skylar mentioned made her think something strange, so farfetched that she couldn't wrap her mind around it: what if her figments weren't imaginary?

What if they were real?

Swallowing past a lump in her throat, Jaden replied weakly, "I… I don't know. They said it would help, and it felt like it did."

Kiran scoffed, "Please. Those pills are placebos. Only pure full-blooded humans would use schizophrenia as the reason, and medication as the solution. That's only because they don't understand us or how we work."

"Understand us as what? Who exactly are we, and why does that lunatic of a red-head want me?" She was tired of asking all these questions when their answers beat around the bush. Her short fuse burned out, and her fingernails digging into the palms of her hands were barely felt. Couldn't someone give her direct answers?

A loud groan turned her attention to Kiran. "Look, I'll rip off the Band-Aid. We are Kinetics, as are you, and one of your skills is seeing ghosts."

Jaden crossed her arms, but clutched them close to her torso to hide the slight tremor. Okay, maybe not *that* direct. "Excuse me, but I'm a what-now?"

Jessi quickly added, "Kiran, don't overload her, okay? She's probably really confused right now, so we need to take it slow." Then, her head snapped up, staring into space. Jaden noticed her eyes gloss over for about two seconds before restoring to their beautifully rich blue. Grimacing, she corrected, "On second thought, we can overload her on the bus. We've got company coming."

A string of knocks pounded from the door. "Jay, you in there?"

Jaden's heart raced. "That's Lukas…"

Kiran arched an eyebrow. "Who's that?"

"My best friend. I gotta let him in." As she went to stand up, Jessi's arm shot out and knocked her back down. Looking between both twins, she snapped, "Why can't I let him in?"

Jessi stared down at her hands, which had started a sort of nervous twiddling. "You can't trust anyone, Jaden. We've learned that the hard way."

"Oh, that's bull. She can trust me." Jaden's head jerked to the bedroom doorway to find Lukas leaning in the frame. "The question is, why should she trust you?"

Jaden leapt up and ran into Lukas's arms, holding him tightly. "Lukas!"

He rubbed her back with one hand, held her skull close to his chest with the other. "I'm here, Jay. And I know everything that's happened."

"Wait, what?" Jaden ripped free of his comforting grasp and took two steps back. "How do you know that? And how did you get in here?"

Lukas stared at his feet. "Um… Long story, no time." Looking back up, he glanced between Jessi and Kiran. "You two are like her, right?"

Jessi nodded. "We had to find her before Skylar did, or else the result would be… catastrophic."

Jaden's friend narrowed his eyes, repeating firmly, "You are like her?"

The twins exchanged looks before directing their attention back to him, both nodding. Then, Jessi's expression brightened. "I get it now! You're her paladin!"

"My what?" Jaden's gaze snapped back to her so-called friend. "What does she mean by that?"

Lukas met her eyes, and she could see the apologetic look in his. "It's… complicated."

"Um, guys?" Jessi called out, garnering everyone's attention, "I think we're running out of time to get out of here, so we really should bolt."

"Agreed," Lukas replied, "We need to get to a safer location to discuss this."

Kiran nodded. "We've got one downtown. A bus leaves in five minutes headed there."

Jessi got off the couch and powerwalked to the door. Opening it, she yelled, "Run like you stole something!," and then took off.

As Jaden and Lukas flashed a sideways glance at Kiran, the twin shrugged. "She's complicated. I deal with it in my own way: Going along with it." Throwing out a hand toward the door, he said, "Follow the leader."

Jaden and Lukas looked at each other, the former scared and the latter comforting. Lukas placed a hand on her shoulder. "I'm sticking by you. No matter what happens, I will always protect you."

After she nodded, she turned toward the door and followed Jessi's path toward the lobby, with Lukas right behind her and Kiran bringing up the rear. When they reached the main atrium, her stomach twisted, causing cramps in her abdomen. She clutched it, coming to a complete stop. Lukas slid to a stop past her and came running back. "Jaden, what's wrong?"

Her breathing picked up pace, shuddering with the chills that accompanied all the sickening feelings. *Damn, this hasn't happened in years...* While broken breaths choked out of her throat, she glanced up at the second-floor balcony. When her eyes met Skylar's, a prickling pain poked at her left temple, making her wince. With one hand pushing against her forehead and the other arm pressing tight to her stomach, she started running again. Her pace matched that of an injured gazelle, almost a hobbling, staggering stride. Finally, they exited through the sliding doors. When they slid shut, all the pain and cramping vanished, sending Jaden into a heavy fit of coughing breaths.

Lukas patted Jaden on the back as she bent over, hacking up a lung. Man, she sure as heck didn't miss this torture! "C'mon, Jay, onto the bus."

Nodding fiercely, she looked up to find Jessi and Kiran already on the bus, waving at them to hurry up. With weak, staggering steps, she walked onto the bus and into the back rows, practically collapsing onto the bench seats. She attempted to slide into an upright position next to the window, but her head felt like a giant weight on her shoulders, bobbing this way and that.

Lukas slid in next to her and fixed her into a position where she leaned on him, her head resting on his shoulder. In that position, she felt comforted. It was like none of that crazy ever happened. It all had to be a dream, right? Surely everything that she just went through was an extension of her schizophrenia creeping into her dreams.

Chapter 5

"Jay, are you okay?"

Her eyes shot open at Jessi's voice. The girl's head blocked most of her vision, being only inches from her face. When she nodded slowly, Jessi smiled. "She's awake!"

A distant voice shouted, "Knew that already! I'm her paladin for a reason, you know."

"Lukas…" Jaden mumbled, still slightly disoriented. Her head fell to her right, cushioned by a pillow under her cranium. Her surroundings subtracted a city bus and added a dingy warehouse-type place. Not as huge as a business warehouse, but with the rusty metal and high beams above her, it was a nice guess.

When she tried to sit up, pain shot through her chest. Jessi's hand blocked her progress and gently pushed her back onto the mattress that she now laid on. "Easy there, cowgirl. You need to relax and breathe, okay?"

After a single nod, she gazed around this place they were in. Her mind both registered and didn't register any bit of her surroundings. Through her haze, she heard Lukas say her name, but didn't comprehend her friend's existence in that warehouse until his face came in to view next to her. "Hey, Lukas…"

The side of his mouth twitched, a micro-expression of happiness. "Hey yourself. How ya feeling, slugger?"

"Better, I guess." Her gaze scanned the room again, trying to snap out of her current mental haze. She vaguely heard an exasperated groan as footsteps grew closer. In a flash, icy water froze her face and torso, effectively soaking her hair and clothes. Her body snapped upright as she gasped for air. Her eyes landed on Kiran, who stood at the foot of the bed with an empty glass. "What. The. Heck." Each word came out enunciated and firmly pissed.

With a shrug, Kiran simply replied, "You needed to snap out of it. I knew a quicker way."

Jaden's glare made him flinch. "Watch yourself, Sparky. I'm one shock away from pummeling you."

Staring at his feet, he muttered, "Sorry."

A hand touched her shoulder, and she turned her head to lock eyes with Lukas. "Are you sure you're okay?"

She realized that the indoor water park Kiran had just blasted her with had shocked her back to functioning state and nodded. "Yep, all better." As she turned and slid off the bed, the floor under her feet surprisingly comforted her. Once she steadied, all the craziness from earlier flashed into her mind's eye. The prickles in her head came back, and she braced herself with the mattress behind her. She squeezed her eyes shut, trying to force out the irritating sensation in her temple.

Arms wrapped around her waist. "Breathe, Jay."

Jaden bit past the pain, growling through a tightened jaw, "Stop saying that!" The grip loosened slightly, but Jessi's arms still remained wrapped around her hips. After a few more minutes, the sensation faded, and the shaky breaths returned, her butt falling to the mattress. She heard someone inhale and snapped, "If you tell me to breathe one more time, I swear someone's getting punched."

Jessi huffed softly. "Fine." The body sitting next to her stood up. "Kir, I'm gonna go wander town to find the supplies we need. You stay here with Jaden and Lukas, just in case."

"Will do."

Silence filled the air, aside from Jessi's leaving footsteps. Creaking sounds pierced the air, maybe from rusty hinges. It made Jaden wince until the sounds vanished, filling the warehouse with silence once more. Sighing, Jaden pried open her eyes and looked at Kiran. "Did I upset her?"

Kiran stared at his feet again, fidgeting slightly. "Well, you didn't exactly roll out the thank you wagon. Saving you was our mission, one that JV volunteered us for. According to her, it would have ended up with us saving you anyway, but volunteering would save a good number of lives."

Cocking an eyebrow, Jaden asked, "What lives?"

A few silent moments passed before he lifted his gaze. When she met his eyes, she could see the grim truth in the teenager's expression. "The lives of the others who would attempt to save you. JV estimated about thirteen people would have lost their lives if we didn't volunteer up front. Our… community is a giving one, and we look out for each other. Granted, Jess shouldn't take action on her glimpses – she's been warned of altering the future – but her loyalty to our friends and family let her take this risk. She chose to save you and save our… citizens, rather than lose another dozen lives while everyone waited for us to make up our minds. It was always supposed to be us. It just mattered how soon we decided to embrace it."

Jaden shook her head and hands at him. "Hold on. What do you mean by all that? Why did you guys need to 'save' me? How did she know all this? And, most of all, what were you saving me from?"

Kiran blinked, expression blank. "From Skylar Meisyn, of course."

"Wait, my figment?"

He shook his head, pressing two fingers to his temple. "I thought I was clear enough." Lifting his eyes again, Kiran explained, "You are not a schizo, okay? You are like us: a Kinetic. Kinetics are gifted individuals, believed to be a superior mutation of humans, who each possess two psychic abilities of the dozens that exist. One of yours is Channeling, which allows you to see the dead."

Jaden stared at him for a few more seconds. "Wait... What? Are you trying to tell me all the people I thought were imaginary people actually were ghosts?"

Nodding, Kiran replied, "In a sense, yes. At least, you can see ones stuck in Limbo, which is a plane closer to reality than Heaven or Hell. Heaven is for most individuals, while Hell is for a select few who wasted any chances at forgiveness. Limbo is a voluntary option for people that die. The ones stuck in Limbo have a wish or desire that keeps them tethered to this world. Only Channelers can see them without equipment." He tapped the lens of the weird blacked-out science goggles that sat around his neck.

A towel whacked her in the face, and she spun to see Lukas at the other end of it. "Well, Channelers and their paladins. Dry off, and I'll explain."

Yanking it free from his grip, she ruffled her soaked hair with the towel. "Spill."

Lukas leaned back against the headboard. "Well, I'm your paladin, which is a fancy way of saying protector. I protect you, as well as keep your abilities in check, so your powers don't go out of control based on emotions. I came into being right when you were born, and have been by your side your whole life."

"How is that possible?" Jaden asked, eyeing him curiously, "We didn't meet until third grade."

Wagging a finger at her, he corrected, "You didn't meet my *human* form. However, my true appearance takes a different form."

She raised an eyebrow. "What kind of 'form'?"

Sighing, Lukas hung his head. He slid off the bed, crouching down on all fours. His body encased in a white glow, changing shape. While Jaden attempted to watch the whole thing, the brightening light put black spots in her eyes. She squeezed them shut, trying to shake them away. When she opened them, Lukas had vanished. "Lukas?" she called out.

A fluffy shape leapt up onto the bed from behind her. *You called?*

She spun around and came face to face with a Husky, who wagged his giant, fluffy tail. Gazing deep into the giant dog's icy blue eyes, she knew instantly who this was. "Kohei? You were Kohei?" Her smile widened as she ruffled the fur around his neck.

Yes, I was. And I took care of you, didn't I?

Puckering her lips, she replied in baby talk, "Yesh, yesh you did, Kohei. Yesh you did."

Kohei glared at her. He probably would have rolled his eyes if dogs could willingly do that. *Scrap the baby talk. You know who I really am, and that tone is demeaning.*

Recoiling, Jaden sighed, "Sorry. Guess nostalgia got the better of me. But, I thought Mom and Dad told me you'd died when I was eight."

No, their exact words were that I "went to a higher place." Which, essentially, was the truth. I upgraded my Kohei form to my Lukas persona. Quite the promotion, if you ask me.

With a nod, all Jaden could muster was an, "Uh, huh. Sure." Her smile widened again as she remembered all her memories of Kohei. The two of them had grown up together, since… birth… *Back this train up…*

Her gaze shot up, staring at Kohei with a cocked head. "What you told me… about being created when I was born… It's starting to make… a bit of sense…"

Kohei lifted a paw and placed it firmly on her leg. *It's a lot to take in, I know. Just take your time.*

Jaden responded by grabbing the large dog and latching onto him tightly. After a few moments, she whispered, "Thank you."

A sigh rang through her head. *You're welcome, princess. Now, would you allow me to change back?*

Nodding, Jaden pulled back and wiped a tricky tear that had snuck out from her right eye. "Yeah, go ahead."

Kohei's form shone white again, and yet again, Jaden had to shut her eyes once the brightness reached her limit. When the glow vanished behind her closed eyelids, she opened them to find Lukas sitting on the bed where Kohei had been, except now he sported a white tee and red tracksuit. Smiling at her, he cocked his head and asked, "Better?"

Jaden leapt a few feet and hugged him hard. "Much better."

Lukas squeezed her tightly. "Good. Glad to have pleased you, Princess. And I'm not going anywhere."

For a brief moment, she pulled back and looked him right in the eyes, ones that matched perfectly with Kohei's. "Promise?"

With two small, slow nods, he answered, "Promise."

She grabbed him in a tight hug again. She lost track of time as she remained in her best friend's grasp. He really had been her lifelong best friend, whether she knew at the time or not. First, he'd been her loyal canine companion, guarding her from vicious mailmen and tricky squirrels. Then, he'd matured enough to walk at her side as a human. Or, at least as human looked to the outsider. She may have struggled with the faith her parents raised her on, but she had to thank God for putting Lukas in her childhood to protect her. If He hadn't, then her life would have not only been duller, but also more dangerous. After all, he had been girl's best friend. What would have happened if he hadn't always been there – she didn't have the energy or want to think about. The point was, he did exist.

And thank goodness he wasn't a figment.

Chapter 6

Sounds of the door creaking open and shut made Jaden pry her eyes open. She had fallen asleep holding Lukas, whose chest she still lay on. Rubbing the sleepiness from her eyes, she recognized Kiran's figure. Kiran walked silently to the bed, quieter than any sixteen-year-old boy she'd ever met. His gentle, quiet footfalls made him actually seem mild. Based on her interactions, however, she knew his movements contradicted his true personality.

As Kiran reached out a hand, Lukas' hand shot out and grabbed Kiran's wrist. The kid cried out at the split-second attack, eyes wide and breathing heavily. Lukas' eyes glared at him, his face in a tight snarl. The expression softened just a tad as he yanked Kiran closer, until only a few inches remained between their faces. "Never," Lukas snarled, "Do. That. Again. *Capiche*?"

Kiran nodded, still looking terrified. "Yes. Understood." Then, his brow furrowed. Squeezing his eyes shut, he ripped his arm free and staggered back. After glancing at both Jaden and Lukas, he dropped the shopping bag on the floor. "Jaden, I got you some new clothes. Figured your business getup has seen its last legs."

Jaden glanced down at her soiled, torn dress shirt and slacks, running her fingers down the frayed edges of her blazer. With a slow nod, she said, “Yeah, thanks.”

With a soft huff, Kiran took slow steps backward. “You’re quite welcome. Now, if you’ll excuse me…” He spun around with the grace of an ice skater, his back now to them as he walked through a doorway leading to a smaller room. She had no idea what was in that room, but she also didn’t really care.

She looked at Lukas with slight contempt. Whacking him lightly with the back of her hand, she snapped, “You just scared the crap out of him!”

Lukas’ eyes narrowed at her now. “I was just doing my job! If I knew he was there before he reached out a hand, that all would’ve been avoided. Didn’t sense him coming either, which is quite odd…”

“Twit.” Hitting him again, she slid off the bed. Grabbing the shopping bag Kiran had deposited on the floor, she peeked inside. “Interesting choices…” With a shrug, she walked into the bathroom and changed her soaked attire to the dryer ones. After about five minutes, she stepped out. The skinny jeans fit tightly to her hips and legs. Black and red sneakers adorned her feet, while a skin-tight, black tank covered her torso, her breasts held tightly in place with a midnight sports bra underneath.

A whistle reached her ears, and looked up to find Lukas laying sideways across the bed, a sly and teasing expression plastered on his face. “Sexy.”

Scoffing and rolling her eyes, she walked over to the bed, grabbed her wet shirt from inside of the shopping bag, and slapped it over his face. As he yelled, she smirked. “Don’t wish for what you don’t want.”

After balling up the soiled tee and throwing it aside, Lukas sat up and scowled at her. “Funny. Very, very funny.”

The door creaked open quicker than usual, and the loud slam that accompanied it made both of them redirect their attention to Jessi, who dashed across the large space. "They know!"

As she ran toward the room Kiran had gone into, Jaden asked, "'They know what? And who exactly are 'they'?"

Jessi replied hurriedly, "They know we're here, and they're coming. Get ready to bolt again."

Face starting to heat up, Jaden snapped, "Who. Are. They?" The warmth in her cheeks burned hotter as Jessi ignored her outright and headed to the small, interior room.

Once she'd run into that room, both teens' voices sounded muffled, so Jaden couldn't make out coherent words. After about two minutes, Jessi powerwalked out, arms crossed as she glared at Lukas. "You scared my brother. That's not okay."

Lukas looked at his lap. "I said I was sorry, alright?"

Keeping that glare still firm, Jessi pointed at him, and then at the open doorway leading to the back room. "Go apologize. Now."

Raising an eyebrow, Lukas asked softly, "You're kidding me, right?"

Angling her head down made Jessi's glare even more scalding. "Does it look like I'm kidding?"

Sighing, Lukas got off the bed, muttering, "Kid needs to get a backbone. Or grow a pair."

After her friend had gone into the room, Jaden sat down on the mattress, closed her eyes, and sighed deeply. Someone sat next to her and patted her leg. Opening her eyes, she met Jessi's slightly comforting expression. "Penny for your thoughts?"

Shrugging, Jaden replied, "Not many rational or logical thoughts, to be honest."

"Thoughts don't need to be rational or logical," Jessi told her, "They just have to have someone willing to listen." The two girls exchanged half-hearted smiles. Jessi was starting to grow on her. Until the teen's eyes glossed over again, staring into space and almost as if blind. "Um, boys?" she called out, "Wrap up that apology with a bow and move on. We don't have much time."

They filed out of the room, Lukas pulling on a zippered jacket as he walked, while Kiran threw a backpack onto his shoulders, hiking it up. Once all four of them stood near the bed, Jessi's eyes returned to solid, rich sapphire. "They're about four blocks away. We've gotta get to Garland and Jakob's ASAP. Kiran, what's the quickest way?"

Kiran slid up his long sleeve covering his right arm, revealing a contraption of some kind that covered half of his lower arm. When he pressed a button on the side, the device beeped. An instant later, a bright blue image of lines, shapes, and squiggles flashed up above one of the screens on the device. The surprise shocked Jaden enough for her to recoil back, falling flat to the mattress. Kiran snickered, but after a "Stop that!," from his sister, he stopped and cleared his throat. "Well, we're here in downtown Nashville, about ten blocks away from the Bridgestone Arena." Jaden sat up finally. "Garland and Jakob's portal is hidden in the back of the Parthenoooon… here!" He pointed at a section of the mashup of blue lines, which, upon closer inspection, looked like a grid layout of a city. Meaning, a hologram of downtown Nashville.

Today just kept getting weirder and weirder.

Kiran pressed the button on the side again, and after another soft beep, the holographic grid of the city vanished. "Well, then, who's up for a long walk?"

Rolling her shoulders, Jessi complained, "Do we have to walk? Couldn't we take a bus? Or one of those bike-drawn carts? Those look like fun!"

With the shake of his head, he answered, "We're safer on foot. There's tons of crowds around us, and I don't think Skylar is desperate enough to cause a scene."

Jessi huffed a sigh. "I hate it when you're right." As she stood up, she muttered only loud enough for Jaden to hear, "The bike ride would've been cool though…"

Kiran clapped his hands together, saying, "Alright, let's get going!"

They all walked toward the creaky front door when Jessi came to a screeching halt. Jaden noticed first and stopped as well, turning back to check on her. "You okay, Jessica?"

Jessi's eyes had glossed over again, but she took slow, staggering steps back. When color returned to them, she swiped a hand from her right side to her left. When a loud clang echoed through the medium-sized warehouse, Jaden's eyes snapped back to the front doors to find a bar locking their way out.

Kiran yelled in shock, "What the heck, Jess?"

"They're on our block," she answered, "They'd see us if we walked out there now."

Groaning, Lukas cracked his neck. "Well then, we're in for a fight."

Jaden stared at the ground, lost in thought. She rifled through her memories of the past two days, trying to find a trick or loophole or fact that could save their butts… Then, it hit her. Her head snapped up, meeting Kiran's curious gaze. "You okay?" he asked, slight sharpness to his voice.

"Am I correct in assuming one of your abilities has to do with electricity?"

Straightening slightly, Kiran puffed out his chest, his expression confident and full of himself. "Yep. An Electrokinetic."

Lukas flashed Jaden a sideways glance, but soon sported a playful, cunning smirk. "I know that look. You have a plan."

Grinning from ear-to-ear, Jaden responded, "Of course I do. Now, everyone listen carefully…"

Chapter 7

The door creaked open, no longer having the bar sealing the warehouse. The whole structure had been plunged into darkness, thanks to Kiran using his electric abilities to blow out the power. An almost demonic darkness appeared to swallow the whole room, similar to a black hole.

The four had split off into separate corners, Kiran with Jaden in the left corner closest to the door and Lukas and Jessi to the right. They'd split Jaden and Lukas, because then, if one was found, the other could attack.

Figures brandishing pistols and revolvers crept into the dark space, supposedly searching for them. Then, after the handful of soldiers made it to the center of the room, a single man walked into the doorway, stopping right in the way of their exit.

Jaden cursed under her breath. The plan should have drawn all the trackers to the center or further back in their search, leaving the door open and free for them to bolt out of without notice. She glanced at Kiran, who held a finger to his lips. She nodded, signaling understanding.

That one figure stood out from the others. The soldiers prowling around the warehouse dressed in all black from their helmets to their sneakers. Since he stood in the lit doorway, Jaden could see him clearly. He stuck out like a sore thumb compared to his men. His getup included a bright white suit, a red dress shirt underneath the blinding jacket, and black dress shoes that weirdly complemented the rest of the outfit. She spotted dark auburn hair, the color so dark that she wouldn't have noticed the red if the light from outside didn't shine on him. His sky-blue eyes skimmed from one corner to another, while his mouth twitched ever so slightly.

"Guys, I'm not going to hurt you," he said, taking two slow steps further into the room. Jaden knew that if this man walked a few more feet in, their getaway path would be clear. If he stepped more than that, their escape would less likely be noticed.

Jessi's voice echoed through the warehouse: "We already know that's a lie, Shalbriri!"

Jaden smiled at the confusion on the soldiers' faces. Apparently, another skill of Kiran's was something called technopathy, which meant he could manipulate technology. He got the intercom system running again, and Jessi, apparently being telekinetic, placed the speaker high in the rafters. The echo and amped volume made it so they couldn't hear Jessi's regular voice. The speaker overshadowed it completely.

Shalbriri's head jerked this way and that, and a smile crept onto Jaden's face at his confusion. Clearly, this man led the others, and satisfaction from his confusion filled her body with tingly, adrenaline-filled warmth. "And I know that's you, Jessica. Is your brother here as well?"

"Nun'ya business, jackel!"

Shalbriri sighed, shoulders dropping. "Look, Jessica, Kiran, can't we just discuss all this? I think you've been misled astray, and I want to clarify things for you." He took three more steps into the room, glancing around again. Jaden's heart pounded. *So close...*

Jessi scoffed, "You think we'll believe your twisted truth, Bri? You had your chance, and you gave it up."

Shalbriri's eyes narrowed, sending chills down Jaden's spine when it met her gaze. He stared directly at her for a few seconds, mouth twitching up, as if forcing back a smile. When his gaze started scanning the black hole of a storehouse, she relaxed again. He hadn't seen her.

She hoped.

"Alright, guys, I'll explain how things are going to happen. Either you come out willingly, or I'll use my skills and catch all four of you by myself."

Jessi didn't respond, but she met Jaden's eyes across the room. Thanks to the multi-use goggles Kiran had supplied them with, she could see her with clarity. And, boy, did the man's threat rattle the girl.

Shalbriri hung his head, sighing, "You two are not making things easier for yourselves." He took some more steps forward. *Just a few more...*

Three.

Two.

One.

Jaden hopped out of her crouch in the corner and dashed for the door, Kiran close behind. She spotted Lukas and Jessi bolting out of their corner too. When they reached the doorway, they rounded the opening, Kiran taking the lead, Jaden and Lukas in the middle, and Jessi bringing up the rear. Something didn't feel right, so Jaden screeched to a stop. Twisting around, she saw Jessi pressed against the brick wall, just two feet from the open doorway. Waving her hand, she mouthed, *Let's go!*

Jessi shook her head, the falling sun amplifying the blonde highlights throughout her hair. With a roll of her eyes, Jaden thought, *Hope the boys notice we're not following...* Sighing, she jogged back to Jessi. When she reached her, Jessi pointed back at the interior of the warehouse and then her ear. Easy enough gesture to understand: *Listen.*

Shalbriri still hadn't realized they'd gotten out, and he was rambling to pretty much nobody. "I know you two have a vendetta against my family, and you have every right to be frustrated. However, my family has a plan, one that will change all the dimensions. But, to make them happen, I need the girl's help." After a brief pause where Jessi's expected response never came, he sighed, "Fine. That's how you want to play this little game… Let's play!" Those last two words came out in a taunting snarl and sent a chill down Jaden's back.

Jessi's eyes glossed over for about two seconds before color returned. "Run!" As the two girls leapt away from the wall, the bricks exploded, scattering rock shards everywhere. There were a few shrieks from passing tourists. Jaden stumbled to her feet, taking off as quick as she could. As she trailed after Jessi, she risked a glance back. Her scared gaze locked with Shalbriri's, more unnerved by the small, sinister smirk that crossed his face. Shaking her head, she directed her attention forward again.

They rounded a corner about five blocks later and stopped running. Both girls gasped for air. Jaden swallowed saliva in an attempt to soothe her burning throat. It scarcely helped.

A water bottle entered her vision, being held out by Jessi. Gratefully, Jaden grabbed it and took three swallows. Her throat stopped burning, almost as a thank you for the liquid. Wiping her mouth, she handed the bottle back to Jessi. "Thanks."

Between breaths, Jessi smiled slightly. "You're most welcome, Princess." As she mockingly bowed, Jaden snickered. Jessi's eyes glossed over once more, and after a few moments, her rigid shoulders relaxed. "They're not pursuing. We're in the clear."

"Why did we stop in the first place, Jessi?"

Jessi huffed a sigh. "I was hoping to hear why he seems to hate us now. It didn't used to be that way…"

Before Jaden could open her mouth to ask another question – one she probably wouldn't have gotten an answer to anyway– a familiar voice called out:

"Jess!"

Both girls snapped upright and saw Kiran running toward them, Lukas hot on his heels. Once they reached them, Kiran hugged Jessi tightly, with Lukas holding Jaden the same. Lukas nuzzled her head with his own, muttering, "Don't scare me like that again."

Jaden nodded, murmuring back, "Promise."

Everyone released their grips, glancing at everyone in their group. While they'd avoided danger, even just barely, no one relaxed. "Okay, the Parthenon replica is only a few blocks away now. I've already contacted Jakob, and he's ready when we are." When everyone nodded, he added, "Good. Let's go."

Jessi grabbed his shoulder as he went to continue toward their destination. When he twisted to meet his sister's eyes, Jessi whimpered, "Bike cart?" Her eyes drooped, welling with tears in the best puppy dog face Jaden had ever seen.

Hanging his head back, her brother groaned, "Fine. We'll take the cart. Just, quit that look, okay?"

Expression flipping one-eighty to a gleefilled grin, Jessi squealed, "Yay! Bike cart, bike cart…" She continued to chant those two words all the way to the main road.

As Kiran waved down one of those biking trolleys, Lukas spoke softly, "Something's not right."

Jaden cocked her head and looked up at him. "What's wrong?"

Shaking his head, he apologized, "Sorry, don't worry about it. My brain's kind of in a haze. Everything's happening so fast."

Slipping her hand into his and squeezing tight, she smiled faintly, "We'll get through this. We always do."

With a soft, weak chuckle, he ruffled her hair, his way of being affectionate. "Look at you, Miss Optimist."

Rubbing the back of her neck sheepishly, she replied, “Trying to stay positive is the only thing keeping me sane.”

Kiran walked back to them, frowning, with Jessi trailing after him. Lukas’s mouth twitched. “Couldn’t grab one, I see?”

“I’d like to see you do better, jackel.”

Lukas grinned, “Do better, I shall.” He walked to the edge of the road, waved a hand, and whistled sharply. When a bike cart pulled over to him a mere ten seconds later, he twisted back to them, grinning smugly. “Better, I did.”

With a soft groan, Kiran growled, “Show off.” The four of them got into the back of the cart. Jessi and Kiran sat in the first bench, while Jaden and Lukas took the second. Yawning, Jaden rested her head on Lukas’ shoulder. Her friend wrapped an arm around her, pulling her in closer. Paladin or not, at least she had him.

While she wished that the crazy fantasy worlds had just stayed in their stupid books, at least she had him.

Chapter 8

The jerk of the cart stopping startled Jaden to the point she almost fell out of the bench. Lukas grabbed her around her waist, keeping her from hitting the pavement. "Okay there, trooper?"

Nodding, she stood upright. "Yep. Right as rain."

The two of them slid out of the back bench and gazed at the distant structure. The Nashville Parthenon stuck up in the middle of the setting sun. God, a day hadn't gone by yet? This little adventure felt like an eternity! Kiran jogged ahead, already halfway across the lawn. Jessi had stopped a couple dozen feet away, waving at them with the energy of seeing a long-lost friend. Jaden groaned. She bounced back quick, didn't she?

Sighing, she walked to Jessi, Lukas following and watching her six. Jessi's wide smile dispelled any anxiety she currently felt. "No worries, Jay. I wasn't gonna leave ya here. Neither would Kiran, but he's too proud of a boy to admit attachments."

As the three walked side-by-side, Jaden asked, "What do you mean by, 'attachments'?"

"Well…" Jessi explained, "My brother tends to latch on to people he empathizes with or wants to help. You're currently in both categories, so it's easy enough to see him trying to both latch onto you and stay away from you at the same time. It's really confusing to him, so don't talk to him about it. He's had enough troubles in his life, and he's pretty broken."

Jaden and Lukas exchanged looks, Lukas voicing what both were thinking: "Are we talking romantic attachment here?"

Jessi snorted. "Romantic attachment? My brother? Goodness no!"

"Then what kind of attachment? Seems just like a sped-up friendship complex."

Sighing, she replied, "More like over-protective, over-eager attachment. It's complicated. It's almost unnatural, both in the short amount of time it takes to become attached, to how strong he feels the bond is. It may just seem like a quick bonding emotion, but somehow it's more complex and confusing than that, even for me. And I've known him since we shared a womb." She tucked a strand of hair behind her ear. "He's always needed something or someone to protect. It's just that almost everyone he latches onto like that ends up gone."

"Gone in what way?"

Jessi grimaced. Shaking a hand at them, she stated, "Never mind that. It's not important. What is important is getting us safely out of here."

They rounded the corner of the massive structure, a place where security couldn't see them. Kiran ran his fingers along the stone base, feeling for… something. "C'mon, c'mon…" he murmured to himself.

Jessi crept up behind him and tapped him on the shoulder. Kiran leapt a few inches in the air, spinning around to face his sister, who cracked up. "The look you're giving me is priceless!"

Scowling, he replied, "The look I'm giving you means 'Buzz off'!" Then, he went back to rubbing his fingers all over the base, this time more hurriedly. "Jess, call Jakob. I can't find the Source."

Rolling her eyes, she replied, "Of course you can't. I should have figured you wouldn't."

With a soft groan, he snapped, "Quit the peanut gallery remarks and call him."

"Now?"

Glaring at her out of the corners of his eyes, he replied through gritted teeth, "Yes, now would be nice."

Smile widening, she taunted in a sing-songy tone, "What do you say?"

Kiran's face burned red, his jaw tensing. Then, he snapped away from the stone and snatched the cell phone from his sister's clip-on case. "Fine, I'll do it. We're in a hurry. You make things too difficult, you know that?"

Grinning, Jessi replied, "Yes, yes I do."

"Act your age, dummy."

Grin turning teasing and smug, she added, "And the answer was 'please'."

"I know what the answer was!" Kiran barked, lifting the speaker to his ear. After a few seconds, Kiran brightened. "Jakob, my man! Hey, so I can't find the Source to get us to you guys. Any way you can tell me where you've moved it?" Nodding as the person on the other end talked, he continued, "Yes, yes, I know that already, but where's…" He stopped abruptly, hanging his head a few moments later. "Can't you be a bit more specific than that?" A soft growl rumbled from deep down inside Kiran, as his grip on the phone tightened. "Of course, I know, but we've got… No, you listen here! We found her, idiot!" After a moment of silence, Kiran shook his head, as if the man on the other end could see them. "No, I'm not joking. Send Pixel if you want to be sure, but it's her. Skylar located her first, but we won that battle." He puffed out his chest again, making Jessi cover her mouth with a hand as she snickered.

~Okay, Macho Man, exhale that fake muscle.~

Jaden looked everywhere for the sound of that slightly electronic voice. Then, a blue blur flew in from behind Jaden. She yelped at the sudden appearance. Once she'd regained her wits, she registered the blur as a blue sphere with a digital screen that had pixelated eyes. Kiran brightened. "Pixelator! How you holdin' up?"

~As well as any AI servant can do. Now, where is she?~

Kiran pointed at Jaden. "The poor girl you terrified out of her jeans."

Scowling, Jaden snapped, "I was not terrified! Startled… maybe." Her cheeks flushed hot, and she averted her eyes, staring at the amazingly kept grass under her feet.

~Miss?~ When she glanced up out of the corners of her eyes, that orb floated about five inches away from her, eyeing her up and down. *~My name is Pixel. I am the Kalea's Artificial Intelligence software. May I ask your name?~*

Jaden huffed quietly, but drawled back, "You can ask, but whether I'll give it is another story entirely."

As the robot recoiled a bit, she thought that its eyes laughed. Whether at her or not, this robot at least possessed a humor chip. *~Yep, definitely Cabrera's girl. No mistaking that attitude.~* Before Jaden could open her mouth to retort, the orb flew back over to Kiran. *~Two inches North and Five inches East, where the sunset and the Earth go meet.~*

Kiran's shoulders dropped. "More riddles? Seriously?"

Jaden stared off into space, the words the robot spoke coming to her from distant, forgotten memory, where a gentle woman's voice sang as a lullaby:

Two inches North, and Five inches East
Where the Sunset and the Earth go to meet
And when Darkness has had its hold on the realms
The pattern will repeat, with the new day's sun at the helm

"Um, Jay?"

Her head snapped up, meeting everyone's gaze. All three of her companions appeared to be both confused and intrigued. "What?" she snapped, tone coming out more sharp than she had meant.

Lukas smiled first, turning back to the twins. "Doesn't remember her childhood that far back, and yet she still remembers Keira. Do you remember those verses?" When the two kids shook their heads, Lukas continued, "Of course you don't. It went out of style hundreds of years ago. The only families left that know every word of it are the Meisyns, Bellaroses, Kaleas, and Cabreras. It's verses from "*The Circle of Livings and Meanings*", created back when written word had yet to be developed. Quite ancient."

The orb moved up and down, in apparent agreement with him. *~That is correct, Master Kohei. Very impressive you should remember as well.~*

With a shrug, Lukas responded, "Her memories share with mine, remember?"

~Of course, Master Kohei.~

Jaden tugged on Lukas' shirt. When her friend turned to look at her, she hissed, "What the bloody Hell is happening here?"

After a quick glance back at the twins and mechanical annoyance, Lukas rounded the corner, dragging her with him. Now safely out of earshot, he whispered, "Look, I know this is all overwhelming, and I can understand how confused you are. But, you have to trust me now, okay? My job, my wish, my life; I only exist to keep you safe and protected. And that's what I'm going to do, alright? Hold your questions until we are a dimension away from Shalbriri and Skylar, and we'll answer them, I promise."

With a slow nod, Jaden could only say, "Uh huh."

Satisfied, Lukas walked back to the others. Jaden followed him… to find the other three had disappeared. They jogged around the back to find Kiran and Jessi bolting down the other long wall. Jessi turned to them as they ran, waving them to join in. Groaning, Lukas commented bitterly, "So, running again, huh? This is getting old."

They dashed off after the twins, who had just rounded the corner to the front of the structure. When they turned the corner as well, they saw the kids dashing through the crowds on their way up the white stone stairs. As they hurried to catch up, the wide eyes and exclamations from tourists they pushed past didn't slow them down. "Subtlety would've been nicer, don't you think?" Lukas asked as they dashed past the shocked people.

Jaden raised an eyebrow. "You think we have time for subtlety? Because the twins don't seem to think so."

Hanging his head and shaking it, he sighed deeply, "When did I become a babysitter of three?"

They reached the top of the steps when something bright blue whizzed right past her head. Shards of stone shattered where it hit, making Jaden close her eyes. When she opened them, she turned around to look over the park that lay before them.

And spotted Shalbriri with a hand stretched in their direction.

When a blue light shone in the man's palm, Jaden ripped her eyes away from his confident and taunting gaze and shouted, "Run!"

The two of them dashed inside the structure. Once in the main lobby area, they didn't see Kiran or Jessi anywhere, until Jessi peeked around a bookcase in the gift shop and waved them inside. Once they had joined the female twin, they found her brother pacing in a short line, muttering unintelligible words to himself.

"Is he okay?" Jaden asked, maybe just a tad concerned.

Jessi waved dismissively at her. "No, that's how he puts pieces together. Jakob gives riddles for one particular reason: keeping people out. Kiran usually likes the challenges presented by them, but his want to get you to safety trumps his own amusement."

"Yeah," Lukas chimed in, "Especially because Mr. Ginger Energy Blaster is hot on our trail."

"Wait… You mean Bri's here?"

Lukas nodded. "Incoming across the field of tourists. Almost took Jay out from close to a couple hundred feet away."

Jessi's face turned pale. When she tugged on Kiran's sleeve, his expression snapped instantly to murderous. His breathing turned rapid as the fire in his eyes dimmed. "You know… Not to… Do that…"

"Bri's coming, Kir. We don't have time for an elaborate plan. We need a simple one."

Kiran gave her a condescending glare. "If there was a simple one, would we still be here?"

"Oh, there's one you didn't consider." As all three stared at her, she grinned. Then, she bolted out of the gift shop, past the ticket desk, and into the exhibit. Kiran, Lukas, and Jaden all groaned in sync and chased after her. Once in the exhibit, security guards shouted out, pursuing them. The four filed into a single exhibition room, and Jessi shut the door. Pressing her hand to the surface, a loud thump echoed to Jaden's hearing. *She must've locked it somehow…*

The exhibit they were in appeared to have an African or Lion King-esque theme to it. Photos and painting of sunsets and sunrises littered the walls. Their goal didn't appear to be those beautiful paintings, however, as Kiran and Jessi hovered over a globe in a glass case. Lukas sauntered over, gazing at it as well. "Is that… What I think it is?"

Kiran nodded. "Yup. A Transporter. In other words, our ticket out of here. They've stepped up their game, haven't they?" Pulling a short stick out of the pack on his back, Kiran slammed it against the glass, effectively shattering it. Instantly, alarms blared and red lights flashed.

Jaden covered her ears and shouted to them, "What now?"

Lukas gently took her hand and guided her over to the globe. When Kiran nodded, he and his sister placed both of their hands on the surface of the old, golden sphere of a map. Jaden glanced at Lukas, and when he gestured toward the map with a nod of his head, she put both of her hands on it as well, her friend copying a second later. Wind suddenly whipped around them, so fierce she slammed her eyes shut. Lights flashed behind her close eyelids, all different colors. Then, just as quickly as it had come, the wind dissipated, and the strobe lights vanished.

A gentle hand touched her shoulder. Her eyes shot open to find Lukas standing next to her, smiling. Gazing around, she breathed, "Whoa..." They had been deposited in a lush rainforest, rivalling the beauty of the Amazon, which she'd only seen in pictures. Oddly, some trees had different colored leaves, and not like fall back home. Like leaves and plant life that should be green, but instead are black, red, purple, blue, grey, and everything in between. The fauna beat out the Amazon too. Blood red foxes dashed around. Bright pink and black birds sung their songs on branches of dark blue trees. Copper and silver scaled fish hopped into the air from a pond with the clearest water she'd ever seen. "Where are we?"

Lukas patted her shoulder again, replying simply, "We're finally home."

Chapter 9

The group wandered through the amazingly beautiful forest. Jaden kept falling behind, in shock and awe over all the colors and splendor surrounding her. Never in a million years could she have ever imagined a place this stunning until she'd seen it herself. Lukas stayed by her side, calling to the twins when they fell too far behind. He'd warned her at the start of their walk that getting lost in there would be easy, and only the twins knew their destination. Jaden only half heard him, her mind still trying to comprehend this forest from her dreams. So, he stuck next to her like glue, guiding her whenever she slowed or stopped.

Was this home? Part of her felt differently, while another part of her sensed the familiarity and déjà vu. It surprised her when the idea was presented. Her old home, her old life, her old family… Was all of it a lie? Sure, her parents and her never really saw eye-to-eye about anything, so the loss of them in her life only stung a bit. She never really felt close to them. Heck, she barely knew anything about their lives outside of the house. Her father traveled frequently, and for long stretches of time, while her mother stayed home as a virtual assistant and talent manager.

The one person she missed though was Dove. She and her sister had a 'special' relationship, but heck, so did most siblings. Dove could be difficult at times, but always had her back, particularly when Jaden and their parents argued. Something Dove had said when she was younger always served as a source of comfort and stability:

"I'm the only one who is allowed to upset you. Anybody else tries, and I'll kick them clear across the freeway."

When the quote flew through her mind, she choked on a breath. A weak smile appeared on her face, as a single tear ran down her cheek.

"Jay?" Sniffling softly, Jaden met Lukas's worried gaze. "Everything okay?"

As she wiped away that tear, she responded, "No, it's not. And I don't think it ever will be."

A string of loud knocks snapped Jaden's attention forward, where a small cabin overgrown with vines sat. Jessi knocked again, while Kiran sat on the front stoop, arms crossed and pouting. "Garland, it's us! Can you let us in?" When only silence answered, Jessi huffed, the strength of it seen in her chest moving up then down. "Seriously?" Knocking again, she snapped, "Gar, I'm a hungry Jessi! Open up!" Silence hovered again, turning Jessi's huffs into annoyed groans. "Gar!"

"She's not there, Jess," Kiran drawled, "Those two love their mind games and puzzles, and we fell right into one. Doesn't look like it's an easy one either. Putting the dimensional portal inside this time should have screamed 'complicated', and I didn't even notice."

Jessi scoffed, "Quit the negativity, Emo Kiree." Pounding on the door, she snapped, "Garland, this better not be another game of yours!"

~But, Miss Theron...~ A dome-like shape next to the door flashed in rhythm with the words it spoke. Seemed as though Jaden had adjusted to being surprised, because she didn't jump or shout this time at Pixel's electronic voice. Maybe she was just turning numb. *~Everything in life is a game. I thought we taught you better than that.~* The lights in the dome stopped flashing, becoming clear glass once more.

Kiran flung his head back, lying against the steps. It had to be painful, but he didn't seem to notice or care. "Please don't tell me that's their puzzle."

"Has to be," Jessi answered, "It's the only other thing that's talked besides you and your complaining attitude."

With a scowl and glare, Kiran replied, "Ha ha ha, very funny. Now, would Her Gracefulness like to solve the clue, or should I attempt it? Seems like it was aimed at you, Miss Theron."

Jessi huffed, dropping onto the stairs next to her brother. "So, *everything's a game...* That probably is a reference to us solving their puzzles, letting us know we're stuck in one."

"Genius."

Whacking him, she snapped, "Quiet, Sarcastic Charlie Brown. Your Peanut Gallery is not wanted or needed at this time." When he stuck out his tongue at her, she rolled her eyes. "Pathetic."

Jaden moved her attention to Lukas briefly. "Do they have Charlie Brown here?"

With a soft, almost silent chuckle, Lukas told her, "I assume they've spent a lot of time on the old world. Probably know more about Earth pop culture than most here."

"Okay, sooooo..." Jessi's voice brought their attention back to current events, "*We taught you better than that...* That's the part that confuses me. Neither Jakob nor Garland ever taught me anything, aside from training puzzles that were tests for..." Her eyes brightened slightly, and she leapt off the stoop. "I know who we need to find!"

"Great! Who?"

"Master Keegan, of course!" Jessi answered excitedly, "I was one of his top students until he..." Her excited expression vanished, turning instantly into a calculating frown. "Oh."

"Yeah, 'Oh' is right, genius," Kiran snapped, "Keegan died six years ago."

Jessi pointed a finger at him. "Not died! Him dying was the rumor."

Kiran rolled his head forward again, the expression on his face dark and firm, not sparing any sympathy. "Jessica, the man fell off the map six years ago, with no contact to anyone. The official announcement supported MIA status and most likely dead."

"Ah ha! 'Most Likely' doesn't mean definite, you know. Besides, he fits the riddle. Why else would Garland and Jakob have him as the answer to Puzzle Two?"

Kiran's gaze aimed at the ground. The teen started pacing in his short line again, lost in thought and muttering words they couldn't decipher.

"Jaden?" Jaden snapped back to attention, meeting Jessi's eyes. "I'm sorry about all this. Jakob and Garland like challenging people, but we figured they'd make an exception for your arrival. Guess we figured wrong."

Nodding slowly, Jaden only replied with another, "Uh huh." Yep, definitely numb now.

Lukas' arm wrapped around her shoulders again, squeezing her tightly. Planting a kiss on the top of her head, he murmured to her, "It's okay to feel scared, Jay."

Twisting out of his grip, she eyed him curiously. "Scared? I'm beyond scared, you idiot! Just this morning, I was reading about all this – magic and portals and mean dudes who can shoot blue bullets from far away – IN BOOKS. Do you understand? In. Books."

Holding his hands out in an effort to calm her, Lukas said slowly, "Calm down a little bit, Princess."

Calming maneuver: ineffective. "And now, I'm being pursued by ghosts and black-clad soldiers and flying through weird portals shaped like globes and walking through foliage I've only seen in dreams, now visible IN REAL LIFE! This can't be reality, it just can't!" Salty tears stung at her eyes, making her squeeze them shut to dull the pain.

When a few slipped down her cheek, a finger wiped them away. Opening her sore eyes, she met Lukas' calm, soothing gaze. "Listen to me very carefully, Jaden." His tone and pace were soft, calm, and gentle, just as he'd done when she was scared or hurt in the past. "Reality can be overwhelming at times." When she inhaled to counter again, he pushed a finger to her lips. "Let me finish, Jay. While you didn't ask for this, this life was the one you were intended to be in since you were born. Obviously, fate had a hand in twisting that, and you ended up where you did when you were four, memories locked up for your safety. And right now, I can see that seal slipping, and the true Jaden will shine through. You have to want it to though. You have to embrace this – all of this – or else, fear might drive you astray. You have to understand that it may be hard now, but that doesn't mean it always will. Your journey may have dark tunnels, but at the end of every tunnel always sits Light."

With a soft, weak chuckle, Jaden asked teasingly, "When did you turn into a philosopher?"

"Last night. Fury told me it was a stupid-ass decision, but I ignored it."

She snorted in a brief instance of humor, instantly understanding the Avengers references. Sniffling, she wiped her arm across her face. "Thank you," was all she could muster.

Ruffling her hair made her smile. "You're quite welcome, Princess."

"Um, guys?"

The two looked back at the cabin to find Kiran sitting on the stoop again, head tucked into the arms on his knees. Looking at Jessi, Lukas asked, "Um, is he okay?"

Jessi sighed deeply. "No, but I think reality broke him."

"I'm not broken!" Kiran growled, muffled from where his mouth currently was hiding.

Patting his back, Jessi comforted in baby-talk, "Of course you're not. No, you're not."

His hands whacked her away, while his glare sent a jolt through Jaden's spine. She recognized that look, that red color of iris. It had haunted her dreams for years now. Those unforgettable, dangerous eyes sent flashes of those nightmares, of the horrible things that happened with the shadowed owner of those garnet irises. Her body started shaking, and she started taking slow steps back, keeping her distance.

Even though the glare softened when he saw her, the terror that spread through her didn't change in strength. "Jaden, are you okay?"

Her eyes darted between Kiran, Jessi, and Lukas, so rapidly she couldn't comprehend who any of them were. She couldn't take the images of her nightmares that now flashed in front of her. After a few seconds, she spun around and bolted deeper into the forest.

Chapter 10

She didn't stop running for about five minutes. The calls from her group had faded within seconds as she took off into the forest. When she finally came to a halt, she collapsed, all energy lost. Crawling over to the side, she leaned her back against a tree. As she tried to catch her breath, she swore a chill shot down her back.

"Dear, dear Jaden."

Her head shot up. Unfortunately for her, she couldn't seem escape this nightmare.

Because Skylar stood right in front of her.

Holding up a hand as she gasped for air, she breathed, "Stay… Away… From… Me…"

"Oh, no worries," Skylar replied, sitting down on a tree stump opposite her, "I have no intention of touching you."

Her mind swam with questions, and while she wanted answers to all of them, she had a feeling he might get annoyed and change his mind. "Then… why are you… here?" Her gasps lessened and lessened, almost recovered at that point.

Skylar's mouth twitched into the tiniest of smiles. "Because you deserve the truth, and I know the Troublesome Twins back there won't tell you willingly."

She nodded curtly twice, just to show acknowledgement of his reasoning. "Uh huh. What truth?"

"Why you exist. Why you've gotten dragged into this. Why no one told you prior to my arrival." With a shrug, Skylar rubbed the back of his neck. "I can understand Seth and Dove's reasons, but to keep you in the dark seems like poor parenting."

Her brow furrowed. "Dove is my sister."

That small smile twitched ever so slightly. "Did they already tell you that wasn't your real family?" When Jaden moved her gaze to the dirt, Skylar continued, "Ah, seems like they did. I think by naming your fake sister after your mother was a tactic on Seth's part to easier assimilate you back to your true reality."

Jaden scoffed bitterly, "True reality? The reality where I can see ghosts, where kids can hack technology with their hands and see the future, and where I'm running from people without a clear, logical reason? No thanks, that Seth and real Dove can suck it. They can have that reality back, because I want nothing to do with it." She curled into a fetal position against the tree as a form of personal comfort.

"I can understand your frustration and confusion, Jaden, and I sympathize with you. As such, I know you deserve the truth, and the whole truth. And, while it might not send you back to professional testing and mundane college life, the truth might make it easier to comprehend this journey you've been forced into. By the way… Why aren't you at your destination? Last I heard, you were headed to a safe house."

Rolling her eyes, Jaden finally released her grip on her legs and stretched them out in front of her. For some reason, she felt relaxed just talking to Skylar. Maybe it was a trick, lull her into false security maybe, but she figured she'd be okay. As long as he didn't touch her again. "The people they were counting on to help have us locked in a series of puzzles, apparently."

Skylar's expression instantly brightened as he chuckled softly, "Jakob and Garland Kalea? That's their safe contact?"

She shrugged. "Appears so."

"Well, I can understand, given how close they were to their parents. But, geez, I'm starting to feel sorry for you. Those two never miss the chance to mess with people."

With another trademark rolling of her eyes, Jaden spat, "Glad someone finds humor in it."

Skylar slowed his laughing, responding, "Sorry, but that knowledge put me off guard. The twins should have used better judgement. They probably thought that the Kaleas would make an exception for this mission, right?" As she averted her gaze to the dirt again, Skylar continued, "That's what I thought. They must have made some quick decisions to try and beat me to you, and even though they were a tad late, it would have been longer if they thought their plans through all the way. Guess they figured shoddy planning that sped up their rescue time was smarter than thoughtful plans and arriving too late. Shouldn't blame them, if those were their only two choices." When he sighed deeply, Jaden looked up at him. The longer she looked at him, she noticed a sort of glimmer around his silhouette, like a blurred, shiny outline that changed as he moved. Maybe that glimmer signaled these spirits that she could see. "Now…" He clapped once and leaned forward, his lower arms resting on his thighs. "I promised you truth, didn't I?"

Slowly nodding, Jaden simply replied with the syllables she always did when she didn't know what words to say: "Uh huh."

"Okay, then let's get started." The glimmer of excitement in Skylar's eyes revealed a sort of childish happiness toward this 'reveal'.

"Your parents are very important and influential individuals. They had both inherited and earned a great deal of money and respect, and used that money and power to help the poor and weak and elderly. True humanitarians inside and out. When they had you, everyone rejoiced! The Cabrera bloodline would continue! However, over the years, your parents made many enemies. Sometime around you being three or four, they started receiving threats on your life, some with ultimatums, and others that just wanted to kill you no matter what, to ruin your parents' lives. Then, your talents started showing themselves, and your parents feared that those very gifts would be your downfall. In order to protect you from their enemies and your true potential, your parents locked up your gifts, blocked off your memories thus far, and sent you with the people you have lived with ever since. However, your adoptive parents went off the grid about three years ago, hence the multiple search parties vying for the glory of rescuing and returning you safely."

Jaden's mind swam with unanswered questions, but she took a deep breath and ordered them in her mind to make things easier. "So, my parents... my real parents… Are they still alive?"

With a nod, Skylar replied, "Very much so. And they miss you terribly. Dove regretted their decision only days after sending you away. Trust me, I should know: I was their Advisor."

Now all those questions she had before took backseat. If she really wanted to know why she was in this situation, her toddler years didn't matter. What mattered was what were they running from, and why. "Their advisor? As in… what exactly?"

"Oh, right, left that detail out. Your father is royalty in this dimension." After a quick pause, his eyes darted up in the air as a purple and pink puffy bird flew from a tall branch. "Dimension meaning an alternate world. This forest we're in right now is actually on our home dimension, Graddeous. Well, me to an extent. Limbo kinda sucks." When Jaden slapped a hand over her mouth to snicker, Skylar's eyes moved back to her. "There's a smile. You always had such a beautiful smile, even as an infant."

Clearing her throat, which had started turning sore, she continued with her questions: "So, lineage aside..." *Mainly because that's a biggie I don't want to address...* "Why are we running from you then, if you were my parents' Advisor?"

Sighing deeply, Skylar braced himself with his hands on either edge of the trunk and leaned back, looking both relaxed and tense at the same time. "It's rather complicated, dear Jaden. You've probably already learned of your gift of seeing spirits in Limbo." When she nodded, he smiled again, but ever so slightly. "When a spirit exists in Limbo, it remains tethered to the physical world, unable to go to on to the next life. Usually, an unfulfilled desire is their leash, or a violent murder they want revenge for, or just a loved one they want to watch out for. So, based on that, some spirits that live in Limbo actually desire to stay in Limbo. Downside is, once the ones they look after die, they remain stuck there, as their initial feelings after their own deaths keep them teathered. Pity really. However, there are certain people of a particular talent that can break those ties and send them on, as well as bring them back to the physical world. Well... the latter hasn't happened in a while, but I'm sure we'll see it soon enough. But, both the twins and I desire you to use that talent to perform one of those two unique outcomes."

While he was vague-booking on that, she still had so many questions for him. "Which is it you want? Obviously, you don't want to be stuck here forever."

The smirk returned to his face as he inhaled and exhaled deeply in a heavy sigh that relaxed his muscles. "No, I do not. But those answers will come soon enough, I assure you." He got to his feet, stretching his back in an arc. "However, I must be going."

"But, you promised to tell me the truth!"

A glint in Skylar's eyes reflected that look he'd given her during her final competition, the one she'd first seen him in. And, yes, it still annoyed her. Because that look screamed, *I know more than you do. Nyah Nyah!* "I didn't say all in one sitting, did I? Besides, you need time to process everything I've told you, as well as the beat-around-the-bush half-truths your adventure party has been feeding you." He lifted a hand, now gripping a fedora. As he placed it gracefully onto his head, he flashed her a smile. "I'm sure we'll be seeing each other again *plenty*." A strong wind suddenly blew through the still forest. Jaden covered her eyes with an arm, blocking dirt and other nature things from stinging them. Once the winds ceased, she lowered her arm to find Skylar gone.

With a heavy huff, she muttered, "What kind of game is he playing?"

"Kee, she's over here!"

The slightly familiar female voice ripped through the silent woods. Jaden lifted her head, scanning the forest floor both in front of her and behind her tree backboard. When someone dropped from the trees above, her body leapt where it sat and jumped backwards. The back of her head slammed against the firm tree, sending shots of numb, pressurized pain through the nerves in her skull. Her vision blurred for a few seconds, but eventually sharpened again. A girl around her age stood in front of her, arms on her hips and leaning forward a bit. Her eyes skimmed Jaden's figure, her jaw tight with a calculating scowl. Then, the girl straightened, angling her head slightly toward the sky. "Yep, it's her!"

Jaden blinked a few times, confused. This girl did look familiar, but she couldn't remember from where. Of all the aspects of this girl's appearance, it was the dark orange eyes that sparked déjà vu. It wasn't the yellow tank top, red suspenders, and torn and weathered shorts that only stretched to above her knees, nor the hi-top sneakers and mismatched socks with wacky designs. It wasn't the sandy blonde hair that cascaded down her shoulders, or the handkerchief tied around her neck. The strangest parts of this girl, however, weren't really any of that.

The strangest parts were the pointed orange ears jutting out of the top of her head, and the fluffy tail that matched the ears in shades of orange and brown.

This girl cocked her head, familiar dark irises eyeing her curiously. "Are you alright, Princess?"

When this girl addressed her as Princess, she realized something she'd dismissed so far. On occasion, Lukas would call her Princess, but she figured it was just another on his never-ending list of nicknames for her, a list in his head that she scoffed at before. If what Skylar had said was true, the name she'd assumed was a term of endearment turned out to reveal more about her best friend than she'd ever known. He'd called her that for years, almost as far back as she could remember. Was he somehow using that name as a comfort for him, while she remained oblivious? And, now that she'd been dragged into this whole mess, why hadn't he told her the truth yet?

"Kee!" The girl called out, scanning the tree tops. A heavy sigh released from her lungs. "I swear, he'll be the death of me someday." Then, she held out a hand. "Would you like some help getting up?"

With a curt nod, Jaden gratefully took the girl's hand. With strength that belied her slim figure, the young woman yanked Jaden to her feet. "There, all better!" With a soft smile, she held out a hand again, this time to shake. When Jaden took her hand, the girl said, "My name's Lana."

Exhaling a held breath, Jaden replied, "My name…"

"Is not needed."

Jaden raised an eyebrow as they broke grips. "It's not needed?"

Lana nodded. "Nope, it's not. I already know who you are. Princess Jaden Cabrera of the Five Kingdom domain. We've been waiting for your safe return for quite a while now."

"Really?" When Lana enthusiastically nodded, almost like a child hyped up on caffeine and sugar, Jaden breathed a soft chuckle. "Well, guess I'm rather important."

Smiling, Lana responded, "More than you know. Now, where is your travelling party?"

The images of Lukas, Jessi, and Kiran flashed to the forefront of her mind, and her heart started racing. She'd completely blanked out on them! Then, a flash of memory of the red eyed glare from her nightmares popped forward. She squeezed her eyes shut, shaking that cursed fright out of her mind. When she opened her eyes, Lana the Cat Eared Tree Climber cocked her head, her orange eyes from deep in Jaden's fuzzy mind gazing at her with a mixture of comfort and pity. "Are you alright, Princess?"

Nodding, she swallowed, the little bit of spit scratching up her sore throat. "Uh huh. I'm good."

With another child-like smile, Lana said, "Good!" Then, she gazed up at the sky again, mostly blocked by branches and leaves. Groaning, Lana shouted, "Keegan! Get your butt over here!"

A rustling of plants directed both of their attentions to a set of bushes to the side of this miniature clearing. When the first figure emerged, Jaden's first reflex sparked relief. "Lukas!" Then, she remembered the new knowledge she'd obtained since she'd ran off, and she held back the urge to hug him. Her thoughts toward him were laced with bitterness and left a bad taste in her mouth.

However, Lukas's expression brightened in relief. He dashed up to her and grabbed her tightly. Jaden made no move to hug him back. "I was so worried, Jay."

"What, think I can't take care of myself?"

Lukas's muscles stiffened, probably realizing the hostile attitude now radiating off her. He released her, skimming her figure. Aside from some dirt on her butt from sitting on the ground, she sported no cuts or punctures, no blood released anywhere, no slashes or rips or holes in her clothes. "Are you feeling okay?"

Jaden's gaze narrowed. "Oh, yeah, perfect! Absolutely perfect! It's not like I'm a long-lost Princess or anything, who has two teenagers leading me through hoops of puzzles for the immature amusement of their last-minute back-ups, in order to return to a home I never knew existed!"

Lukas' brow furrowed. "Who told you that? This Cat chick?" He thumbed toward Lana.

"Excuse me," Lana interjected, "It's *Wolf* chick."

"Yeah, whatever." He looked back at her, and she aimed her gaze at the ground, fingers curled into tight fists. "Jaden, who told you that?"

After a few moments of quiet, Jaden murmured, "Skylar."

"What?" Her head jerked up again to find Jessi and Kiran standing in this clearing as well, eyes wide. Jessi asked slowly, "Skylar's here?"

With disdain she didn't try to hide, Jaden spat, "Yeah, in this Five Realms Kingdom, or whatever the freak this crazy, twisted place is called." She leaned her shoulder against the tree she'd used earlier, crossing her arms and aiming her bitter glare at the dirt.

After a few moments of stunned silence, Jaden heard a small thud behind her. Someone else must've dropped out of the trees, but she currently didn't care and continued to stew. However, it seemed the others did care, maybe too much based on the reactions.

“Master Keegan!” Jessi exclaimed with the same happiness she always seemed to be wrapped in.

With a slightly shocked tone, Kiran piped up, “Um, interesting and unexpected turn we’ve taken.”

A soft voice, male, spoke from behind her, “It’s good to see you two as well. Now, I’ve spotted unfriendlies a little bit away from here. I’ve set off an obstacle, but that will only detain them so long.”

Jessi dashed past Jaden, and a loud grunt rang in the air. The man behind Jaden chuckled, “It’s good to see you too, JV. Now, c’mon, we’ve got to get going.”

As most of the others started walking, Jaden remained rooted to the ground. Before her reflexes could react, Lukas’ hand grabbed one of her arms and yanked her away from the tree. “Pity party later.” His tone seemed firm and mean, but when she looked at his face, she instantly noticed the red in the whites of Lukas’ eyes.

Her eyes cast downward again as she willingly walked beside him. She didn’t dare rip out of her friend’s grip, as she’d clearly upset him somehow. Replaying her words, she knew they sounded bitter and filled with hate, but it’s not like she insulted him directly. So, what could possibly be upsetting him?

Chapter 11

"Ugh!" Kiran groaned, "How much farther?"

There was a soft little smile on Keegan's face that Jaden almost didn't notice. "Patience, sport. We're getting closer."

"You said that twenty minutes ago! And I'm not your 'sport', *dummy*, so stop calling me that!"

"Can't I have a nickname for you?" Keegan glanced back, smile becoming more noticeable. Directing his attention forward again, he finished, "Guess not."

The group trudged through the forest as the sun slowly lowered. They walked in a line formation, Keegan leading with Lana by his side, Jessi trailing after like a happy puppy, Lukas and Jaden behind her, and Kiran groaning and moping at the caboose. Jaden looked back and saw the annoyed glare on Kiran's face. If he were in a cartoon, steam would be shooting out of his ears. That image of cartoon Kiran make her chuckle quietly to herself.

Lukas nudged her with his shoulder. "Starting to feel better now, I take it?"

Heat flushing her cheeks, she stared at the earth under them. "I'm sorry about back there. I got overloaded and didn't mean to upset you."

"You didn't upset me, Jay."

Her eyes snapped up to his, locking gazes. "But… you were crying. Or, almost crying."

Sighing, Lukas squeezed her hand. She looked down at their intertwined fingers, which had stayed locked for the last half hour. A few minutes ago, her hand started turning sore, but a huge part of her wanted and needed the comforting grip of her friend, so she'd ignored the cries of pain, shoving them to the back of her mind. "You did nothing to upset me. I was upset with myself."

She angled her head to look up at him again. "Why?" That one-word question both sounded concerned and said a lot about their friendship. It only took a single 'Why' to show sympathy.

Lukas's gaze darted to the ground. "I was created to protect you from harm, and yet, I was the biggest harm in your life. Openly revealing myself and pretending to be human might have persuaded enemies from attacking you, but it also required me to openly lie to your face and keep secrets from you. It killed me inside, but the fact you remained safe consoled me, at least a little bit. Even two days ago, when these two showed up, part of me clung to wanting to keep you safe and protected. Telling you everything and overloading you scared me. I didn't know how you were going to react, and I didn't want to be the one to make you pull the trigger." He breathed a shaky sigh. "My job was to keep you safe from harm. The description never mentioned injuries to the heart."

Jaden's eyes stung at Lukas' admission. Squeezing them shut to stop the pain was less than effective, and a single tear rolled down her cheek. A finger gently wiped it off her face, and she opened her eyes to Lukas' comforting gaze. "It's alright, Jay. I may be mad at myself, but I'm not going anywhere, okay?"

Nodding slowly, Jaden replied with an emotion-filled, "Uh huh."

His lips twitched into a shadow of a smile. "Good. Wouldn't want you to shun me or anything."

Jaden's lips cracked a small smile of her own as she shoved him with her shoulder. Their locked grips kept him from flying too far. "Shut up, Wolfe."

A little bit later, the sun lowered in the sky. The large harvest moon rose, becoming the light to guide their way. Finally, they reached a huge wall of bushes and pushed through them. When they reached the other side, everyone but Keegan and Lana screeched to a halt. Before them stood a tall set of stone structures high in the clouds... with tons and tons of stone steps to reach it. The style and designs looked like Romans and Mayans teamed up to create a stone Cibola.

Kiran finally broke through the bushes, and he groaned loudly, torso turning limp as he exclaimed, "You've got to be kidding me!"

"No kidding, Kir," Jessi replied from a few steps up, "C'mon, this is gonna be great!"

With a heavy sigh, Kiran hiked up his backpack and walked past them. "I'm comin', I'm comin'."

When Jaden moved to follow after, Lukas remained immovable, still holding on to her hand to keep her there. Eyeing him curiously, she asked, "What's up, Lukas?"

His eyes had grown dark and clearly upset. "What all did Skylar tell you, Jay?"

She blinked a few times before answering slowly, "Well, my parents were worried about their enemies killing me and sent me away with no memories of my toddler years or of magic. He also explained the concept of Limbo and the spirits that reside there, and when I asked him which type he was, he dodged the question and vanished."

Lukas grimaced, staring down at their interlocked hands. "They're playing with us…"

Jaden didn't know what to say in response, and instead looked back at the ancient temple-esque stairs. Tugging their hands forward, she said, "C'mon, they've gotten a head start."

Lukas' expression flipped into a confident, playful grin. "Whoever gets to the top last is a fainted Slowpoke!" Then, he released her hand and dashed up the steps.

She couldn't help but smile either as she chased after him. "Get back here, you crazy idiot!" Both easily passed Kiran, whose pace reminded Jaden of a turtle. Or a snail. Soon, they were halfway up, then three-quarters, the apex coming into view. When they reached the top, neck-and-neck, they fell to their knees, catching their breath. Lukas lifted his head to look at her and breathed, "I beat you."

Between gasps of her own, she laughed, "I don't think so, dog-boy. I clearly touched that top step with my hand before you reached it."

Shaking his head with a smile, he told her, "You be crazy."

As they laughed, they flipped over onto their backs. Between breaths, hiccups of laughter escaped Jaden's vocal chords. Just like old times, like nothing had happened. Back when they were racing each other on the middle school track, or rivals of running and hurdles during high school track meets. Those happy memories filled her mind, and her muscles relaxed.

Then, Jessi's face popped into her view of the black, star-specked sky. "You guys good?"

Well, that was nice while it lasted. Back to reality.

This twisted, sick reality that should have stayed in its book.

With a sigh, Jaden sat up, Lukas following suit. Clamoring to their feet, they exchanged looks and burst into laughter again. After it died down,

Jaden asked, "Is it weird we're laughing right now, in the situation we're in?"

Lukas shook his head. "Not weird in the slightest. That's actually the most normal thing that's happened in the last two days."

Two days? She glanced to the west, where an orange sun was only a sliver on the horizon. Had it been two days since that final competition test? Oddly, she hadn't felt tired for a while. Now that the length of time had been mentioned, however, she started yawning. Lukas wrapped an arm around her, but called out, "Keegan?"

The man who Jessi had affectionately called "Master Keegan" turned around. He had a hairstyle that Jaden could only describe as boy band crossed with supermodel. His dark brown and blond locks held up curved in the air, coming to a sort of messy point. His blue eyes briefly had a silver starburst in them, but faded soon after. "Yes, Kohei?"

So, apparently, Lukas' real name was his dog name. She didn't care. He still was Lukas as he stood next to her. Until he became a dog again. Then, he'd be Kohei. That logic probably had no basis in reality, but somehow it did to her. "The Princess is getting tired. Is there some place she can sleep?"

Jaden yanked free. "Oh, no," she barked, "You're not getting rid of me that easily!"

Eyebrows drooping, Lukas whispered, "Jay, you need sleep."

"I'm not going to be sleeping well enough until I know everything that's going on. You're trying to get me to sleep so you can discuss things behind my back, because you're afraid it'll upset me!"

Shaking his head, he told her, "You're exhausted. If you want to ensure I'm not talking behind your back, then I'll stay there with you for a while, alright?"

Her eyes skimmed his face, looking for any sign of a lie. "Promise?"

He gently grabbed her hand again and squeezed, his warm, caring smile instantly comforting her. “Promise.”

Chapter 12

Red glows flashed through the tunnel, the sound of distant alarms dull in her ears. She heard shouts off in the distance as well, both from behind her and in her current direction. Cautiously, she took careful, slow steps down the tunnel, heading for the moonlight glow at the end. The closer she got, the creepier this place felt. Her gaze darted to the walls she was walking between and noticed an occasional body lying in a bloody heap. Her heart pounded, but her feet kept walking. Eventually, she broke out into the cool night air, sucking in a clean breath to cleanse her body of the smell of blood and death. Then, her eyes landed on what lay before her. A single dark figure, crouched in the middle of a paved circle. Along the rim of the space lay contorted bodies, bleeding, bruised, but no longer crying out in pain. They'd died quickly, if she had to guess.

She inhaled sharply, and the figure's head snapped to her, his eyes blood red, narrowed, and murderous. He slowly rose to his feet. With the flick of his hands, two daggers slid out of his sleeve and into his tight grip. He started stalking closer. She tried to run away, but her feet stayed glued to where she stood at the tunnel's end. When he was within feet of her, his mouth formed a twisted, terrifying grin, his face and clothes caked with blood. Then, he leapt at forward, blades swinging toward her…

Jaden bolted upright in bed, breathing rapid and shaken. As she gasped for air, she observed her surroundings. She sat in a bed with sheets and a comforter, a nice amenity to have in this hell she now lived in. Now that there was lighting, she could see her accommodations better. It looked like a pretty normal room, with a dresser, desk, bookcase, and… She slid off the bed and padded over to a cracked door, looking inside. *A bathroom! Yes! I could use a nice warm shower.*

And so she did. The water warmed up surprisingly fast, and soap and shampoo already sat on the ledge. She grabbed a washcloth and towel from under the sink vanity and hung it next to the shower. When she stepped inside, a breath of relief exhaled from the back of her throat at the warm water hitting her shoulders. So, while electricity wasn't around, at least there was semi-modern plumbing. Thank goodness for the last owners of this ancient-style complex.

As she washed up, she tried to address that nightmare, trying to keep details to a minimum so she didn't dwell on the horror she'd seen. That tunnel seemed familiar, for some odd reason. Then again, she thought the Wolf Girl Lana brought déjà vu as well, so maybe her mind was tricking her. After all, none of what had happened seemed real, so why would her instincts be either?

But, that figure covered in blood, the one who would have killed her had she not woken up… She'd had this nightmare before. They had started in elementary school, which was way before she even started therapy for her apparently non-existent schizophrenia. These dreams kept coming whenever she was stressed out during the day, but never from the same stress. They happened entirely at random, which, once she started therapy, even confused her shrink. That person – the one with garnet, bloodthirsty eyes – had appeared always as a sadistic, violent murderer. Difference is, in all of her previous nightmares, she had never seen the killer's face. It always looked coated in black paint or shadows, all except for the terrifying, blood red eyes. This time was different. This time, she saw who the sick individual was.

That person had been none other than Kiran.

Now she couldn't unsee it, no matter how much she tried. Now that she'd seen that furious, blood-colored glare in real life, there was no denying it. That murderous, almost demonic person had been Kiran. She tried to compare the two. The Kiran she'd experienced up until this point was intelligent, slightly immature, and easily annoyed, but never annoyed enough to pull a blade on someone. He was completely harmless. Maybe the shock of those eyes had made her brain form a connection that wasn't there. Yeah, that had to be it. The eyes looked similar, so her brain assumed both sets of eyes belonged to the same person. But, that couldn't be true. Kiran was too sweet and innocent to hurt someone, much less kill dozens.

After drying off, she wrapped the towel around her body and stepped back into the room she'd slept in. She was both happy and surprised that a new set of clothes lay on the bed waiting for her. Grateful to whoever had done that, she quickly slipped on the new clothing: another pair of skinny jeans, tinted so dark a purple to look black, a black tank top, and a red leather jacket that reminded Jaden of the one Emma Swan wore on *Once Upon a Time*.

After slipping on the sneakers she'd been wearing before, she stepped outside. The sun blinded her for a second before her vision adjusted. The room she'd been in was one of many dwellings, it seemed. There were a few scattered across this plateau they'd climbed. Off to her right sat more intricate buildings, covered in arches, columns, and detailed stone carvings. This had to be akin to ancient civilizations back in the old world she'd lived in. Her mind touched on her fake family, briefly pondering what had become of them. Their faces appeared in her mind's eye, clear as day. Her parents vanishing stabbed just a bit, but her sister going away made her eyes sting with unshed tears. Shaking her head, she grimaced. "No…" She muttered to herself to ensure she heard loud and clear. "Don't look back. Keep forward motion. That isn't my life anymore."

The sad part?

She hadn't decided if this was any worse than before.

She casually wandered the town, headed toward the temple near the stairs. As she put one foot in front of the other, her eyes skimmed the details of the buildings. Everything from angels to animals to just abstract art had been carved into the stones. Every inch of stone had a light coating of dust, but it still appeared a superior white shade despite that.

As she neared the temple, she heard Kiran's voice yell from inside, "I'm not joking, Keegan!"

The low, full rumble of laughter reached Jaden's ears as she got closer. Once she'd reached the open doorway, she heard Keegan reply, "You expect me to believe that Jakob and Garland Kalea have locked you into a set of puzzles in order to get Princess Jaden home? And, for some reason, their latest clue led you kids to me?"

"YES!" Kiran shouted, clearly infuriated at the humor Keegan found in all this, "How many times do I have to say it? STOP LAUGHING!"

Despite Kiran's demand, Keegan refused to comply, continuing to chuckle to himself. "You have to admit it's an amusing concept. They don't know where I am, so how would they expect you two to find me?"

Jaden had walked down the main hallway and arrived just outside of the room the two males were arguing in. Within seconds, Lukas appeared in the doorway. "Hey, Princess," he greeted with a small smile that comforted her.

"Hey, yourself."

His smile turned softer the longer he looked at her, eventually becoming a concerned frown. "Is everything alright, Jay?"

She noticed her arms folded tight to her chest. Her body must have instinctively pulled them there when she heard Kiran's voice. Yanking them back to her side, she mentally prayed her brain would quit with the trickery. "Yep, never better." She grinned wide, a forced move that didn't seem to sway Lukas. Rolling her eyes, she shoved him back with both hands so she could enter the room. "Idiot." She heard a quiet snicker from behind her, and her lips twitched at the fluttering of her heart.

Upon entering, Jessi shouted, "Jay, you're awake!"

As Jaden nodded, Jessi hopped out of her seat, ran to her, and gave her a tight hug. It felt quite tight, and when she feared she'd become a broken chopstick, Jaden told her, "Jessi, don't I need to breathe?"

Jessi instantly released her. "Sorry, I just got a little excited." She wrapped her arm around Jaden's shoulders and led her to the table. "Jay, this is Master Keegan Kelly. He was my tutor and fighting instructor up until six years ago."

Keegan stood up and bowed to Jaden, which made her cheeks flush with embarrassed warmth. "It's an honor, Princess."

"I guess it is?" When he looked up out of the tops of his eyes at her, she could see a bit of humor in them. Rubbing the back of her neck, she apologized, "Sorry, no idea how to Princess. Like, at all."

Keegan's shoulders rose and fell with silent laughter as he straightened and sat back in his chair. "No worries, Princess. We knew there would be a gap for when you returned. Now, back to our old conversation…" He adjusted his seat to look somewhere behind her. Jaden heard a soft murmuring from there:

"Angst, angst, angst, angst…"

Jaden turned to find Kiran next to a column, lightly hitting his forehead against the stone as he growled that one word over and over again.

Keegan gestured to Kiran, trying to hide a smile that refused to go away. “As you can see, he’s clearly distraught. This game that he talks about seems to continue on.”

Arching an eyebrow, Jaden asked, “What game?”

With a shrug, Keegan leaned back in his chair. “Not sure. But I believe I’m winning.” He lifted a mug to his lips and sucked down a large gulp of his drink. “Ahhhh…” Lowering the mug, he asked, “Jaden, would you like a cup?”

Shaking her head, Jaden replied, “I don’t drink coffee.”

“I know. That’s why this is hot chocolate.”

Jaden blinked. He knew? “What does that mean?”

Keegan eyed her, looking a bit confused. “It’s milk and cocoa powder, plus…” He plucked a shaker off the table. “I’ve got cinnamon!”

That just irked her more. “That’s what I’m talking about!” she barked, “How in heck did you know that I like hot chocolate with cinnamon?”

Exhaling in a manner that mimicked Jessi’s huffs, Keegan fixed how he sat in his chair, his arms on his legs and continuing to hold his mug in between. Glancing up at her, he said, “You’ve been overloaded the past few days, haven’t you?” When she nodded, he cast his eyes at the chocolate liquid in his mug, swishing it around a little to create ripples. “Trust me, I know. I know everything that happened. All I needed to do was be near you, and I knew it all. You have a gift similar to that. The broad term is psychoscopy. I’ve strengthened mine over the years so I just need to be in close proximity to an individual, and I have access to their whole life thus far. Took time, but it’s worth the work. The reason I didn’t come when Lana first called was because I was locked inside your memories. Thanks to my many years of honing my talent, I could see days of memories in a matter of about ten minutes, taking in everything that had happened to make you so scared."

Straightening, Jaden argued, "I wasn't scared."

"Of course you were." She could feel a vein in her head throbbing. "You don't need to admit it, because I lived all of it through you within only a few minutes time. Trust me, there's nothing that's happened in the last two or three days that I don't already know."

"Really?" she snapped, "How about the demon haunting my dreams?" She vaguebooked it as much as she could, as she didn't want her deep fear of her nightmare becoming a reality to scare anyone else.

Brow furrowing, Keegan asked, "A demon? No, can't say I saw that. The last time you had that nightmare must've been further back than the three days I observed."

Face heating up, she snapped, "Try about an hour ago."

"What?" With slightly wide eyes, Keegan stood up and dashed out into the hallway.

As his hurried footsteps got further and further away, Jaden glanced between Jessi and Lukas. "Is he okay?"

Jessi shrugged in reply. "Master Keegan is extremely talented and bright, but he's always kept to himself and stayed out of trouble. He probably has knowledge and secrets that his enemies couldn't even imagine existing. But, he's a brave soul, and never runs away from a fight."

Keegan ran into the doorway, grabbing the edge to stop. "Get your things. We're moving locations."

Arching an eyebrow, Jaden asked, "Why?"

"They're almost here," he replied, "And I don't want to be here when they arrive." Then, he zipped back the way he came.

The hurried, slightly panicked tone to his words worried Jaden slightly. She ran through the doorway and stopped right there in the hall. "I'm sorry, what?"

Lukas snickered, "So much for not running from a fight."

As she walked by, Jessi patted Jaden's shoulder. "Trust me on this. It's better to go with it than argue. In an argument, Master Keegan always wins."

Jaden wandered back into the room they'd been in and spotted Lukas trying to coax Kiran away from the column he was using as a self-harming post. "C'mon, buddy, we've gotta go. Keegan says-"

"Keegan can eff himself!" Kiran snapped, "I don't trust a word he says. The immature, twisted sadist…" After a soft sigh, Lukas wrapped his arms around Kiran's torso and hefted the kid over his shoulder. Kiran cried out and started kicking a bit. "Let me down!"

Lukas aptly ignored him, instead meeting Jaden's eyes. "You got the pack?"

Spotting the backpack only a few feet away from her, she swung it onto her shoulders and curtly nodded. "We're good."

With a crooked smile, Lukas replied, "Alright then. Let's head out."

As they exited the temple, she spotted Keegan with a bag of his own, Jessi with her own pack she'd somehow miraculously acquired while Jaden slept, and a giant, dark orange wolf standing near more forest. How there was a space so thick of plant and animal life this high up, Jaden would never know. Glancing back at the village, she wished they'd been able to stay longer. The beauty around her beckoned for her to stay and admire the sights.

"Jay?" Her head snapped back to Lukas, whose comforting gaze made her relax again. "You good?"

Smile stretching across her face, she nodded. "Yeah, I'm good." A few minutes later, they reached the rest of their group, and, together, entered another forest, with only Keegan the Wise and Crazy knowing where it led to.

Jaden huffed quietly. *Great.*

Chapter 13

They trudged through the woods, mostly in silence. Kiran's constant mimicking of a child by groaning, "Are we there yet?," got old really quick. Jaden's expression brightened when Lukas silently fished out an mp3 player and earbuds from his lower cargo pants pocket. She stared at him with wide eyes and mouthed, *Does it work?* He held a finger to his lips to keep her quiet as he nodded. She'd giggled in her head and snatched it from him. Luckily, they were at the back of their traveling party, and only Jessi had been keeping an eye on them. When Jessi saw Jaden with the music player, Jaden mirrored Lukas' finger gesture, to which Jessi gave her a wide smile and two thumbs up.

Kiran, Keegan, and Lana – who apparently was Keegan's paladin, and currently walked as an orange wolf the size of the ones in *Game of Thrones* – remained oblivious until Jaden started dancing and mouthing the words as they trekked forward. More specifically, they didn't notice until she danced through them without noticing. She'd realized the reveal when Kiran ripped the earbuds from her ears and glared silently at her before walking again. She'd stood there until everyone but Lukas had passed. The two friends shared grins and silent laughter before following after the rest.

Finally, they reached a clearing, and Keegan dropped his bag. "We're camping here for the night."

Jaden had pulled out the buds when he'd stopped, and his statement caught her off guard. "Wait, here? We'll be sitting ducks if we stay out in the open."

Keegan had already started pulling out a blanket, firmly responding, "In case you didn't notice, my dear Princess, the sun is setting, and motion in the woods at night attracts creatures that will really give you nightmares. Now… Kiran, firewood. JV, fill the water jugs. Lukas, prowl around and make sure we weren't followed."

As the three nodded and headed by themselves into the forest, Jaden pointed at herself. "And what about me, Master Keegan?"

Walking over to a stump and plopping down onto it, he told her, "Come join me. There's something we need to discuss."

Jaden hesitated, glancing in the direction Lukas had gone. "I'd rather not. At least not without Lukas."

"No, trust me, this is not a topic you want overprotective pretty boy to hear, or else this whole mission of getting you home will be violently cut short."

That piqued her curiosity, so she gradually walked over to him and sat on a log across from him. "Oh-kay, so, what's up?"

"Well, I took a peek into your memories to better understand what you mentioned this morning…"

She arched an eyebrow. "*Yeaaaaah?*"

Keegan's expression darkened as he picked up a nearby stick and ran it through the dirt. "I want to talk about your nightmare you had last night."

Crossing her arms, she asked, "What about it?"

After heaving a deep sigh, he said, "What you saw… There's a decent chance that might come to fruition."

Jaden's heart pounded in her chest strong enough that she could feel it without a hand over it. "You mean with that demonic person killing me?"

Keegan shook his head. "No, I mean the demonic person being Kiran."

Her world screeched to a halt. Chuckling weakly, she waved a hand at him. "That demon wasn't Kiran! I could only see the red eyes and a blacked-out face."

"Eyes that mirrored Kiran's when he gets pissed. I tried to get him to reveal them to me this morning to confirm what you'd witnessed at the abandoned cabin, and I got a slight glimpse before you arrived."

Jaden took this in, processing it. "That's why you've been teasing and annoying him the whole time. You wanted to prove I wasn't crazy and making it up."

With a gentle nod, Keegan continued, "Kiran's lineage and past is a rough one to go into, and Kiran himself is not even aware of most of it. His family kept him in the dark of what his future could hold, because they feared it might spur that possible future to happen sooner. Kiran's bloodline has ties to demons, spanning as far back as a couple centuries. He is unaware of this. Jessica is of that bloodline as well, but history has only shown those..." He cleared his throat. "Tendencies in the males of the family. We still need to be wary, but her DNA is definitely more stable and steady."

Jaden couldn't help the snort she sounded. "I'm sorry, but Jessi seems the furthest thing from stable and steady."

"Her personality, yes. Not her abilities. Kiran believes his only talents are technopathy and electrokinesis, correct?" When she nodded, he said, "That is a lie. A complete and total lie, fed to him and everyone he interacted with to avoid an uproar and for him to live a normal Kinetic lifestyle."

Wow, now she felt empathy for the kid, because something similar had been forced on her as well. "Well, he's older and more mature now. Can't you trust he has more control and can handle the truth?"

Keegan glanced out of the corners of his eyes at her, the clearest "Bitch, please" look she'd ever seen. "Kiran Godric Theron, mature? Didn't you just see the same thing I did back at the temple? Trust me, he is more unstable today than he was even six years ago." He reached out and patted her leg to get her attention. He kept a firm hold on her gaze, and she couldn't look away. "There's a reason Kiran said they would save lives if they offered earlier than they would've been picked. It's because the only two that would safely get you home would be them. Fate and Destiny tied them to you for a reason, Jaden. Please stick by them, and the gaps in your knowledge will fill themselves. Trust me." He patted her leg a few more times and finished with, "Don't give up on him. Please."

Still caught off-guard by that information, she slowly nodded. "Uh, yeah, I can do that, Master Keegan."

"Please, Princess... For you, it's just Keegan."

A ghost of a smile cracked her face. "Of course... Keegan."

Now that she had confirmation of what had appeared in her nightmare, she couldn't help but feel uneasy. Yes, it took away the uncertainty and unneeded anxiety from not knowing the truth, but her stomach still churned, her head still spun, and her nerves still remained wired tight. She did mean what she'd said though. Kiran had helped her, in his own crazy way, so sticking by him felt like she'd build up some good karma to pay him back. He really was a sweet teenager, and she knew her nightmare actually becoming reality would be most regretted by present-day Kiran out of anybody else. And she'd never forgive herself if it happened either.

A hand touched her shoulder, the static shock making her jump. Twisting around, she saw Kiran standing there, one hand held up while his other arm clutched a bundle of sticks to his chest. "Sorry, Princess. Did I startle you?"

His nervous expression set Jaden's heart slightly at ease. "No, you're fine, Kiran. What's up?"

"Um, you've been zoned out for about an hour. We just wanted to make sure you're okay."

She nodded. "Yeah, I'm fine." Her eyes scanned the campground and picked out a human Lana, Keegan, and Jessi, before moving back to Kiran. "Where's Lukas?"

Kiran arched an eyebrow. "We thought you knew."

All color and heat vanished from her face. Bolting to her feet, she shouted, "Lukas!" When no one responded, her wide, terrified eyes zipped every which way before she took off into the woods, shouting for her best friend. As she ran deeper and deeper, the only thought on her mind, *God, Lukas, I hope this isn't another stunt. And, please, for goodness sake, don't be dead.*

Chapter 14

"Lukas!" Jaden called out for the hundredth time. Her throat grew sorer and burned more and more with each shout of her best friend's name. She slowed to a stop, catching her breath. At first, she'd heard the voices of the others chasing after her, but now she heard nothing but silence. With slow, measured inhales and exhales, she quickly regained breath in her lungs. Her mouth had dried as well, and no matter how many times she tried, she couldn't form enough saliva to soothe her aching windpipe.

"Missing something?"

Her head shot up to spot Skylar leaning against a nearby tree, arms crossed. She staggered back a few steps, hands held out defensively. "Stay there."

The small twitch of Skylar's smile always managed to annoy the crap out of Jaden. "I told you last time I won't touch you. Wouldn't want to damage the package, as it were."

She barked, "What do you want?"

"Well, what do *you* want?"

Rolling her eyes, she huffed, "I don't have time for guessing games. I've got someone to find."

As she went to turn away from him and continue her search, Skylar spoke up, "Master Kohei, correct?" Jaden stopped in her tracks, frozen. "Or, I guess you call him Lukas in human form, correct?"

Regaining her composure, she spun back to the spirit. "And why do you care?"

"Well…" He drawled, dropping his arms and pushing off the tree trunk, "Two reasons. For one, he is your paladin. Paladin's are magical companions born within the same range of time as their charges. The matching of paladins and Kinetics is an extremely old tradition, mainly to accompany each Kinetic as well as stabilize their charge's magic. It's extremely difficult to form a bond with a new one once your body has adjusted to your present one, so killing him, or alternatively, letting him die, goes against my morals and my goals. So, my side won't be killing him."

Jaden wished she could relax, but she'd need more than just his words to believe him. "And the second reason?"

His mouth twitched into the tiniest of smiles. "The second? Knowing you'd chase after him."

Jaden heard a series of clicks and looked around the small clearing to find those soldiers in black, identical to the ones storming the warehouse back in Nashville, pointing rifles and other assorted firearms right at her. Slowly, she raised her hands in the air, keeping an eye on as many of them as she could.

"Well, well, well."

She stiffened again before turning around to find Shalbriri stepping out of the trees. "Took a lot of talent to be able to draw you to me, Miss Jaden. You are quite the slippery eel, aren't you?" The young man couldn't have been much older than herself, upon closer inspection. He was decked out in a spandex shirt, skinny jeans not unlike her own, and a nice, lightweight trenchcoat. In his hand: a pistol that appeared to have jumped out of a sci-fi movie.

Knowing he was the bigger threat, she focused on him and ignored the other guns that could wipe her out. "Well, a girl can try, can't she?"

Shalbriri's shoulders rose and feel in silent laughter. "You've got quite the wit, now haven't you?"

With a shrug, she replied, "I try. Took years of practice."

The young man's smile appeared genuine, at least to Jaden. "Well, glad you've mastered a decent sense of humor. Not too many individuals have a funny bone anymore."

When Jaden met Bri's gaze, she found herself lost in them. Her muscles tensed as the blue irises started swirling. The color spread, covering her entire line of sight with a scene akin to being in a whirlpool without getting wet. Then, at the bottom of the funnel, a circle spread, revealing a scene of some kind. She took steps forward to get a closer look. As she walked, the blue spiral never rippled or broke, contradicting the whirlpool appearance.

Once close enough, she heard muffled voices. On the screen before her, someone, whose appearance sparked more déjà vu, sat in a heap on the ground. "Dad!" The teenager, around the twins' current age, had been shackled to a far wall and was yanking on his restraints. The image panned toward the direction the kid kept looking at to show two men fighting, and the fight's violence would have been rated R in theatres. She based that on the amount of blood, injuries, and cursing that Jaden heard from the teen.

When the red-headed man's face came into vision, Jaden instantly recognized Skylar. His appearance was carbon-copy of the Skylar she'd seen, like a single day hadn't gone by. The other man she did not recognize. His blond hair had been slicked back with gel, but over the course of this battle, hung down in messy, gooey strands around his skull and face, stained in dark blood.

"Rai, it's okay!" Skylar yelled as he deflected another parry from the blond's glowing sword. "It's okay, Rai. Breathe, alright?"

This Rai did not respond. Instead, Skylar's words infuriated him more, and he started putting more energy and strength behind his thrusts. Eventually, Skylar's sword flew out of reach, and the blond kicked him to the floor. As Rai hovered over him, Skylar held out his hands, almost as a plea to spare his life.

"Dad, no!" The teen cried out, tugging even more at his restraints.

Skylar locked gazes with Rai, begging, "Rai, it's me. It's Skylar. Snap out of it, or else I'll have to do something I don't want to do."

Rai cocked his head and pointed the sword at his chest, the tip just inches from Skylar's heart. When his muscles tensed, Jaden squeezed her eyes shut. She didn't want to watch this! Why did she have to watch this?

Then, the sound of ripping fabric gave Jaden pause. Slowly opening her eyes, she caught sight of Skylar holding a dagger in his hand, and a large gash on Rai's lower leg. Rai stared down at the wound, as if confused by what had occurred.

"It's laced, Rai..." Skylar breathed, "That blade is laced with poison… I was told to stop you before you were too far gone..." It was then that Jaden saw blood soaking Skylar's shirt. At first, its reason was unknown. Soon after, however, she spotted the sword Rai had been holding lying next to Skylar, the lower end of the blade coated in blood.

Rai staggered backward, falling to the ground a few moments later. Finally, Jaden could see the man's face. The features of his face looked sickeningly familiar, but she couldn't place from where. However, what stuck out above all else was the pair of blood red eyes, still narrowed into a dazed hatred.

Suddenly, she gasped for air as a vacuum sucked the air and blue that surrounded her into that screen. She fell to her knees, trying to breathe when she was a fish out of water. Her world went dark for a few moments before the vacuum vanished, leaving Jaden coughing and gasping for air. She felt solid ground beneath her. Her wrists had been tied behind her back. With rope based on the rough feel as she tugged and twisted her hands.

"Having fun?"

Her eyes shot open. Jaden gratefully recognized the darkness of night surrounding her. Any bit of strong light would only aggravate the headache or migraine that just started prickling in her temple. She jerked her head up to find Skylar sitting on a stump again. He now wore a red tee and jeans, and actually had a bottle of water in his hands. Gaze narrowing, she replied as bitterly as she could, "No one would have fun with that."

Nodding in agreement, he replied, "No, I suppose not. I should know, I lived it."

Her fight-or-flight reflex tugged on her restraints, scared at not being able to take action. Shoulders dropping when the ropes wouldn't budge, she forced a weak chuckle that fooled nobody. "Sorry, you've lost me."

"You think I'm powerless here in Limbo?" His chuckle, however, was genuine. "Please. I have talents and sources that you will never fully know. But, I do know what you saw, and I know it must've been terrifying to watch. It was terrifying to live, after all."

As much as she hated the humor Skylar found in all of aspects of her current, twisted adventure, he seemed to be the one with all the answers. Since she was tied up and stuck anyway, what was the harm in having a casual conversation about fleeing danger, demonic tendencies, and magic flying every which way? "What exactly did I just see, if you don't mind me asking?"

With a soft, almost nostalgic sigh, Skylar leaned back on the stump, hands supporting him on either side. His gaze aimed at the twinkling night sky, he responded, "There's a simple answer with little description, but also a story behind it. We can do it this way; you ask questions, I'll answer them. I'll try not to overload you, as you are exhausted from the last few days of chaos and new information. Simple answer?" He sighed deeply. "That was the day I died. Six years ago, to be exact."

That would explain why he looked exactly the same. "That man you were fighting? Who was he?"

"That, my sweet girl, is an excellent question." He rolled his shoulders and leaned forward, arms resting on his legs again. Geez, did he only have a handful of positions he used? "That man was once my best friend: Raiden. That morning, I awoke to find everyone running through the community. The two of us resided in a giant building, almost like an apartment complex, but with larger rooms, more intricate layouts, and more ornate décor and furnishings. Rai stayed at the far end with his family when visiting, while my family and I took up residence a floor below him on the opposite end. While my family's accommodations sat nearest to the exit, I couldn't leave with them. My son had been unaccounted for. I could feel something off and went to investigate.

"Eventually, my wandering landed me in the ballroom on the bottom floor, used mainly for celebrations and dinners or parties with royalty and other nobles. Everything had been destroyed. Paintings and wallpaper scorched from fire blasts. Chairs and other furniture scratched and ripped to pieces. Glasses and dishware shattered all over the tiled floors. When I noticed spattering of blood in random places, I felt both scared and determined. That's when I spotted Rai, choking my son, who'd found this horrific scene first. My fear and determination then spurred me to action. Rai sensed me before I got close enough, chained up my kid, and faced me in the duel that ended both our lives. The only part of that I don't regret was distracting Rai enough to spare my son." His eyes cast downward, staring sadly at the dirt.

"Wow..." Jaden found herself at a loss for words. "I... That's horrible. I... I'm not sure what I can say about that... aside from "I'm sorry," which mostly does more harm than good."

That got a weak chuckle out of Skylar. "Yes, I suppose that is true. No words can help. Not anymore."

After a few brief moments of still night air, Jaden broke the silence. "If you don't mind my asking, what happened to your son?"

Skylar's eyes lifted and looked past Jaden, nodding in that direction. "You can ask him yourself."

Jaden spun around as best as she could on her knees to find Shalbriri sitting on a stump behind her. He had to have been there the whole time, but he had some serious control of his breathing if she didn't hear him make a single sound. "That teenager was you?"

Shalbriri stared at the dirt, his hands clasped tight and slightly shaking. "Yes." The reply was curt and quick, easily revealing the pain he felt in reliving that memory through his father's words. "Yes, that was." Pulling from that memory she'd seen, she finally made the connection of the déjà vu she'd felt for the kid from what she'd seen. His hair, a dark auburn that looked black in the darkness of night, matched with the teenager, the bright, sky blue eyes mirror images as well. That solidified that answer.

Giving Bri her full attention, she took a deep breath. "So... can you see him too?"

He gave her a curt nod. "Yes, of course I can. I also have too many talents and sources to count." His stoic lip twitched, just enough to see the humor in repeating his father's words from earlier.

"So… another question…" She didn't know who to direct her question at, so she scooched to the side and sat between them. Now that she could give them equal attention, she asked, "How did I just see that?"

Skylar brightened a bit as the conversation gradually moved away from the depressing violence of their past. "Another simple answer. You're a talented Kinetic. You already know about the Channeling aspect, but most Kinetics possess two. Your second one is psychoscopy."

Wasn't that what Keegan has? She kept that thought quiet, as she didn't know if they knew he had joined their adventure party. "What does that entail, if you don't mind me asking?"

"It simply means you can learn anything you want to know about anyone," Shalbriri answered, "Usually, it's by touch. Shows how much raw talent you have. Only a handful of people could see memories that clearly, and pretty much all of them have been honing it for dozens of years. Even without formal training, your abilities are so strong that they are reflexive and sensitive, meaning any of your talents could trigger whenever you feel a rush of emotion. Be careful, or else you might unwillingly perform an act you might regret."

She cast her eyes at the dirt, taking it all in. When she remained in processing silence for a few minutes, Bri broke through her concentration: "You should get some sleep. We've got a long walk tomorrow."

Sighing, she tugged on the uncomfortable ropes again. She lifted her gaze to look at him. "Could my ropes be moved to lock in front of me? I'll be too achy to walk tomorrow if I sleep like this."

With another curt nod, Shalbriri stuck out his hand, twisting his wrist and bending his fingers every which way. As he did so, the ropes started untying themselves. Her arms yanked forward once freed, and the floating ropes wrapped and tied her up again. Once they stopped, Bri lowered his hand. "That good enough, Princess?"

As she stared in awe at her restrained hands, she nodded, again reverting to her shocked, "Uh huh," response.

"Then get some sleep. We start at sunrise."

Laying down sideways on the dirt, she shivered from the cold. Her mind floated in and out of consciousness, until finally, her mind blacked out and dragged her to restless sleep.

Chapter 15

Another tunnel stretched before her. Blood from dying fingers created wavy lines on the walls that ended at bodies collapsed on the floor. She wandered down it again, glad she'd found herself closer to the exit. This time, it was broad daylight, but the slight heat made the stench of death even stronger.

She thanked God when she broke out into the warm, fresh, spring air. Gazing around, a field of golden grain lay straight ahead, while woods stood proud to both her left and right. The stalks seemed more comforting, so she started weaving through those. As she made her way through the thick plants, the sounds of a struggle gradually increased in volume. She heard quick bursts of wind, the crackling of fire, and grunts and cries of other people. As much as she wanted to stay away from whatever chaos was happening, her feet continued forward. Gazing above the tall grain, she saw smoke drifting higher into the sky. She soon smelled that smoke and the scent of burning nature.

Finally, she broke through into a clearing and immediately felt fear grip her. That shadowy figure from her nightmare knelt next to a dead body, his glimmering, garnet blade shoved into his poor victim's chest. There were a few other people there with them, though no longer among the living. Blood spatter surrounded her, completely three-sixty, staining the golden grain and trampled stalks with crimson. She inhaled sharply again, and her hand clapped to her mouth in hopes this killer hadn't heard.

Of course, she wasn't that lucky.

The murderer lifted his head, his gaze snapping to meet hers. There were those cursed demonic red eyes again. However, this was a different killer than she'd seen before. The features had burned into her mind from her captor's memories as the Advisor's best friend, this Raiden.

Raiden yanked his blade from his most recent victim, the blood shining just a shade darker than the color of the metal itself. He eyed her hungrily, stalking her with gradual steps and a curiously intrigued look in his eyes. Yet again, she stood glued to the spot. He stood only inches away, cocking his head to the side. Then, in a surprising turn of events, his mouth opened, and he spoke in a rich, hypnotizing tone, "Save them from this. Please."

Not knowing what he meant, she nodded rapidly, hoping that her agreeing would spare her from the violence. However, seemed this scene didn't hear her hopes. Raiden pulled his sword arm back and thrust forward. This time, she didn't wake up before the attack hit. Pain radiated from her stomach, unbearable. She cried out as he yanked out the blade, falling to her knees. She clutched her gut, wet and sticky blood oozing between her fingers. Her vision blurred as she looked up at the killer standing over her. His stone-cold eyes flickered for a few seconds, now showing a bit of sadness or pity or maybe regret. Then, he spoke again:

"I'm sorry."

As darkness and lightheadedness consumed her, she heard a loud scream. It apparently echoed, and sounded really close. It took her a few moments to realize that she was the one screaming. Tears stung at her squeezed-tight eyes, leaking out of the corners. Her hands, still bound, pressed tightly to her stomach. It still felt sore, but more like a bruise than a stab wound.

A gentle hand touched her shoulder, and she pried her eyes open to see Shalbriri gazing at down at her, eyebrows drooped and face tense with what she could only interpret as worry and concern. And it appeared genuine. "Princess, are you alright?"

Her breathing came out in gasps, her throat burning even more, if possible. "I'm… I'm… I'm okay. I-I-I think…"

Bri reached a hand up, and a soldier standing near him passed him a canteen. He placed it to her lips and tilted it. The cold water that entered her throat instantly soothed the burning. She honestly didn't care that a bit of it dribbled down the side of her face and to the dirt. That was her captor's problem if there was a shortage of water, not hers.

After a few moments, Bri took the water container away and screwed the attached cap back on. Then, his eyes darted back to her as he blindly handed the canteen back to the soldier behind him. "Are you sure?"

Sitting up was no easy feat, thanks to the lingering ghost of a stomach wound that filled her whole torso with sharp pains. But, she eventually sat upright, sighing once she had. Then, she met Bri's gaze again from where the young man knelt on one knee next to her. She smiled slightly and nodded. "Yeah, I'm sure. I'll be okay. Nothing lasting." *I hope…*

Even though not appearing convinced, Shalbriri stood up, brushing dirt from his pants. "Pack up camp. We've got a decent walk, but we'll be there before nightfall."

As the soldiers with him went about packing things in the woods around them, Jaden looked up at him curiously. Something felt incredibly strange about this whole situation. They still hadn't told her what they needed her for, but Shalbriri seemed more protective of her than she would've expected from a hunter pursuing its quarry. "Um… Shalbriri?"

Eyebrows lifting in surprise, he turned his attention back to her. "Bri, please, Princess."

"Right, okay." Jaden cleared her throat. "So… Why do you need me exactly?"

He stared at her for a bit, looking a bit shocked at her asking. Then, he smiled, a warm smile that relaxed her muscles, if only a little bit. "I'd rather not discuss details at this time, but I was sent to locate you. Right now, the less you know, the better."

Jaden nodded, but wasn't satisfied. She kept her thoughts to herself though. She'd seen a sampling of what this young man in a trench coat was capable of, and she had a sickeningly scared feeling that example only rested at the tip of an iceberg. "Uh huh. Okay."

Getting to her feet was a challenge by itself. She succeeded on getting the soles of her shoes flat on the earth, but when she pushed up, found herself stumbling backwards. Before she hit the ground, Bri grabbed her arm and yanked her completely to her feet. Three seconds later, she had steady footing. She met his eyes, just as dull as they'd been before. "Be careful."

Somewhere underlying in that order lingered a slight sense of concern or care. Or, at least that's what Jaden felt it was. She wasn't certain, but a large piece of this million-piece puzzle remained missing. If she had anything to do with it, she'd find it.

And then, once that's done, she'll ask him again:

Why?

And why me?

Chapter 16

The sun stood high in the sky, signaling midday. Jaden squinted, gazing up at the tops of the trees in all their miraculously beautiful shades. While getting physically lost posed a danger to any individual, getting mentally lost in the beauty and majesty of the various colors of this forest felt euphoric.

"Princess Jaden."

Her head snapped back down and locked gazes briefly with Bri, who had stopped about fifteen feet away. "Yeah?"

Bri jerked his head in the direction of his soldiers. "Come on. You're lagging behind."

Nodding, she jogged to catch up. Why she was willingly going with them, she'd never fully understand. But, she couldn't help but sympathize with Shalbriri. He'd lost his dad, and being able to see him as a spirit all the time must be painful. That begged the ultimate question: why was Skylar stuck in Limbo? Clearly, he didn't want to pass on to the next world, because otherwise he would have shortly after death, or found one of those 'special people' to send him on his merry way. He'd mentioned those special people could also reverse death and bring spirits back to life. Maybe that's what he wanted.

Wait a sec here...

Her eyes widened slightly, and she stopped dead in her tracks. That giant piece of puzzle had just dropped down and landed on her hard, sending crippling shock through every part of her body. Mind racing, she finally connected the dots.

She was one of those certain people.

Shalbriri wanted her to resurrect his father.

"Princess?"

Her wide eyes lifted and met Bri's. His brow furrowed in concern and he quickly walked back to her. Once he reached her, he reached out a hand, probably to pat her shoulder. "Are you alright?"

She knocked his hand away, scowling at him. "You are stupid, you know that? Stupid and twisted!"

Slight confusion shone in his concerned gaze. "I'm not sure of what you mean, Princess."

One of the soldiers at the front of the line cried out, "My gun!"

Shalbriri spun around when a shot rang out a split second later. A voice shouted back, "Yeah, your gun, but my shot!"

Jaden grinned from ear to ear at Jessi's over-hyper voice. Man, she never thought she'd miss that wild ball of crazy! She searched through the tops of the trees and caught a glint of metal in one nearby. The figure waved at her like crazy, and her grin widened. Yep, that was Jessi.

As Shalbriri went to aim a gun where Jessi crouched in the treetops, a black and white blur jumped on him, tackling him to the dirt. The blur grabbed the gun with his mouth and flung it a few feet away. *Leave my girl alone.*

"Kohei!"

Kohei's head lifted to look at her, and she could swear the Husky smiled back. He ran up to her and tackled her as well. She went down softer, onto her knees, while Kohei licked the crap out of her face. Laughing loudly, she pet him fiercely, "Okay, okay, I know. I missed you too!"

Stiffening, Kohei moved off her and got between her and Bri, who was now standing. The gun in his hand aimed right at her head. While Kohei growled, the fur on his neck bristled threateningly. Her heart raced. Even though she knew he was bluffing, she couldn't help but fear for her life when a pistol was pointed right at her.

A figure appeared behind Shalbriri from the shadows and pressed the barrel of a rifle to his back. "Drop it. You're outnumbered, Bri."

Bri slowly lifted his hands, the pistol sliding out of his grip. When it hit the dirt, Jaden exhaled a held breath. As Bri got onto his knees and put his hands behind his head, like she'd seen in action movies and cop shows back home, the shadowy savior came into full sunlight. And, despite the nightmares, the relief she felt at seeing Kiran's face couldn't be measured.

As Kiran tied Shalbriri's hands behind his back, his eyes darted up to meet Jaden's. She picked up on a whole slew of emotions in his gaze. Fear. Worry. Concern. Panic. Fury. Among other things. Looks like she'd freaked everyone out. Great. Like she could have done anything about it.

Someone slammed into Jaden, holding her tightly. "Jay, we were so worried!" Jessi cried out.

"Jessi?" Jessi's head lifted off her shoulder, but the arms remained wrapped. "Don't I need to breathe?"

"Oh yeah, right!" Instantly, she released her, and the two of them exchanged smiles and relieved giggles. "You had all of us worried," she said, sawing at Jaden's bindings with a pocket knife.

"I wasn't." Jaden moved her gaze to Keegan, who gradually drifted down from the trees. Once he'd landed firm on the ground, he brushed off his sleeves. "She's a tough girl, and we already knew he wanted her alive and in peak condition. He wouldn't hurt her. The difficult part was tracking her down, but since our group included one with a fateful connection with her..." His eyes briefly darted to Kohei before directing it back to the sleeves of his jacket. No dirt or dust flew off, so that action must've been some sort of OCD quirk. "It was a lot easier than I hoped."

"Than you hoped?" Jessi shrieked, the rope finally snapping and freeing Jaden's wrists, "We freaking took out a squad of his men and caught him while you hovered in the stupid trees drinking your stupid cocoa!"

Okay, trouble in admiration paradise...

Keegan sighed, pressing two fingers to his temple. "Okay, note to self…" he muttered under his breath, "Accurate feelings, but wrong words to say aloud."

"Master Keegan. What a surprise."

With another heavy sigh, Keegan lifted his head again and locked eyes with Bri. "Shalbriri, you had such a brilliant mind, and topped most students twice your age. What made you succumb to hunting down and kidnapping a Princess of the Five Kingdoms?"

Bri rolled his head on his shoulders, the stoic expression usually found on his face twitching. Then, he met Keegan's gaze again. It was then that Jaden acknowledged Bri's twitch reflecting negative feelings for once and not humor-related. And, based on the firm fire burning in his eyes, she could tell.

He. Was. Pissed.

"These children you are helping…" He finally said. "Do you know what they've done? What they are in the process of doing? What they eventually will do? My father did. He knew all of it: past, present, and all possible futures… or so he claimed. We need him to stabilize the Five Kingdoms."

Kiran snorted in derision as he tied the final knot. "Skylar? Stable?" He circled Bri's body and brushed off his hands as he joined everyone else. "And everyone says you have no sense of humor."

Bri stiffened, glare in his eyes now evident and aimed directly at Kiran. The fire in them appeared ready to explode into a fiery inferno. "And the instability of the Five Kingdoms is thanks to your pathetic excuse for a father." Disdain filled those words, and Kiran instantly bristled.

"Uh, oh…" Jessi whispered, scooching a few inches behind Jaden. As if she could protect her. What was with these twins anyway?

Kiran took three large strides and moved his face just inches from Shalbriri's. "You listen here, traitor," Kiran growled, "My father was a nobleman who valued his kingdom more than his own life."

Shalbriri's face remained stoic, but Jaden caught a humored glint in his eye, reflecting a similar one she'd seen in Skylar's. "Then explain why my father had to kill him in the end? I'd love to hear the story your over-protective mother told you to hide the truth of his demise."

Kiran growled under his breath, though everyone could hear it. Luckily, before the kid could start pummeling the taunter, Keegan leapt forward and grabbed Kiran around the waist, yanking him a few feet back. "Kiran, no. He needs to be delivered in one piece for judgement."

Bri blinked at this new development, as did Jaden. "I'm sorry for asking a stupid question, but… what judgement?"

Keegan shoved Kiran over to the other three and turned to give Shalbriri his full attention. "Listen here, you twisted excuse for a soldier. I made you who you are now, and I could just as easily take you down. But, I will have to give that opportunity to the royal government, as it was their princess you kidnapped and took away from her assigned guardians and guides. I can't wait to see how King Cabrera will handle you."

Jaden swore she saw Bri swallow nervously at the veiled threat. "Well, I can see your point. But, don't underestimate me. Even you, Master Keegan, have not even begun to see what I'm capable of. I don't even think you would believe me if I told you."

"Yeah, yeah, story time is for the courts, not me." Keegan grabbed Bri's shoulder, spun him around, and shoved him forward. "C'mon, kids, I've solved Kalea's next puzzle."

Jessi's gaze narrowed, and her voice sharpened high-pitched again: "You got the next puzzle?"

"Isn't that what I said?" Keegan answered, shrugging and keeping the rifle pointed to Shalbriri's back as they walked. "It leads to Pride Falls. Only about two hours from here. If we hurry, we'll beat the cold evening breeze and won't freeze to death out here."

Kiran and Jessi followed after Keegan, but Jaden remained put. She stared at the ground, mind lost in the rambling of thoughts in her head.

Penny for your thoughts?

Her eyes darted to Kohei, who had taken a few steps around her to enter her line of sight. Ruffling the fur on his head, she replied, "Too many thoughts, so too many pennies." The sideways smile should've told her companion plenty. When Kohei nodded, she knew he understood.

He nuzzled his head against her leg. *C'mon, kiddo, we don't want to get left behind or lost again.*

Looking up, she noticed her travel party far off. Jessi, with her signature eager smile, waved at her to hurry up. A small, weak, but genuine smile cracked Jaden's face, and she ran for them, Kohei at her heels.

Man, what she wouldn't give for a track suit.

Chapter 17

With the trees and plants and wildlife she'd seen in this world so far, Jaden didn't think anything could top it.

Until they reached the waterfalls.

The falling water looked like glittering rainbows. The sunlight glinted on it, amplifying the bright beauty of the multiple colors reflecting off its surface. The pond at the base was more of that clear water she'd fawned over a few days ago.

"This is ridiculous!" Kiran shouted, starting up his short, quick line of pacing and muttering to himself again.

Jessi hung her head and walked over to Jaden, sighing, "He's a piece of work. But he's my piece of work."

A quick laugh jumped from Jaden, surprising even her. "Yeah, he is."

Keegan and Lana had been searching the tunnels nearby for a few hours, so it was just her, Jessi, Kiran, and Lukas, who was back in his human form.

"You're wasting your time."

Oh, and him. Mr. Stoically Stupid himself.

Kiran's head snapped up, glaring daggers at Shalbriri, who sat calmly on a stump and stared into the clear pond. "You stay out of this!"

Bri's lips twitched up into a temporary smirk. "Gladly. Gives me more time while you try to figure out where to go next. Not like I want or need to help you kids who are about to ruin my life." His eyes never left the water, staying incredibly focused as it rippled from swimming fish, and his smirk dropped, the unfeeling, blank expression returning.

"You think you know something I don't, jackel?" Kiran barked.

Bri's eyes darted to him, acknowledging the male twin for a second before focusing his line of sight on the water again. "It's not a thought, just pure knowledge and fact." After a brief pause, his gaze glanced at Kiran again, who had started turning a light shade of pink. "Okay, I'll say it so your tiny brain will understand. Yes, I know something you don't."

Face now almost beet red, Kiran exploded, throwing his fists up in the air, "I know what the bloody hell you meant, you twisted little SOB!"

Jessi sighed, "Great, now he broke my brother."

Patting Jessi on the back, Jaden told her, "We'll fix him again. He's been fixed before, but always seems to break again. Maybe he's defective."

With a snicker she covered with her hand, Jessi replied, "Too late to return him though."

Jaden patted her back a few more times before telling her, "Wait here." Then, she walked over to Kiran, who glared daggers at an unfazed Bri. Stepping into his line of sight, she placed a hand on each shoulder and stared in his eyes. The strange static shock stabbed her again, but not strong enough to warrant any worrisome thoughts. "Kiran, look at me." When he did, she almost jumped back at the blood red glare that now aimed at her. Almost. With Keegan's plea in her mind, she inhaled a deep breath and remained rooted. "Breathe, Kiran. That's just what he wants. He's toying with you."

Kiran's glare eventually faded the longer their gazes stayed locked. She watched as the red gradually faded, swirling with his natural blue-green color until that ocean shade was all that remained. Once all the red vanished, Kiran's muscles relaxed. "Thanks, Jay," he said, taking measured, shaky breaths.

With a genuine smile, she told him, "Why don't you and your sister go over there and see if you two can figure out what we're missing."

After a slow set of nods, Kiran hobbled over to Jessi at the far end of the pond, clearly dizzy. Jaden kept her eyes on him to ensure he made it without falling into the crystalline water. When she gave Lukas a quick look, he nodded, understanding, and went over to join the twins.

"You really think you can hide him from the truth?"

She spun around to face Shalbriri, who still remained focused on the ripples in the water. "What truth?" she asked, lying through her teeth.

A ghost of a smile appeared on Bri's face. "Drop the innocent act, Princess. You're not fooling anyone."

Brow furrowing, she took two steps to reach his stump and slapped him on the shoulder. Even though he winced, she had a feeling it was all for show. He clearly had better power and strength than appeared on the surface, so assuming he had a high pain tolerance was a decent hypothesis. "I could say the same for you," she snapped, circling his stump before stopping in front of him.

He blinked, the connection he'd had with the pond now blocked by her legs. Lifting his head, his gaze firmly on her, he frowned. "This is about more than just that stupid puzzle, isn't it?"

"Ya think?"

Sighing deeply, he rolled his shoulders. There sounded a crack from his back. He gasped quickly, but a calm swept over his expression a split second later. "That felt good." After rolling his shoulders a second time, he directed his attention on her. "What can I do for you, Princess?"

"The reason you need me is to bring your father back from the dead, isn't it?" When Bri bit his lip and looked away, she squatted in front of him to force him to look at her. "Start talking, Into Darkness Khan wannabe."

That made Shalbriri chuckle softly. "Glad I've seen enough Earth movies to know that reference. Is that's the vibe I give off? Benedict Cumberbatch in *Star Trek Into Darkness*?"

"Well, you've got the look down," Jaden replied, gesturing to his trench coat and other clothes with a wave of her hand.

His shoulders rose and fell with silent laughter. "Point taken. What look should I aspire towards then? Anyone in particular I should attempt to emulate?"

"Well, actually…" Jaden's brow furrowed, and she now understood the apple didn't fall far from the tree. Both father and son knew exactly how to best distract and annoy her. Pressing the side of her forehead to balance a growing headache, she hissed, "Off topic. Spill, jerk, before I turn into bad cop."

"Oh, this is still your good cop?" Bri asked, lip twitching in humor again, "I gotta say, more like anti-hero cop, or dark-depressed cop. You're missing the mark a bit, love."

Now Jaden felt heat rise to her cheeks, starting to get why Kiran got so riled up so easily. "I will ask one more time. Tell me what you want."

"Hmmmm…" Bri moved his gaze to open air, as if pondering her request. "Now, the short version would be a simple "Yes, that's what I need," but being in your company like I have been for the past day, I know that brief of an answer will not suffice." He glanced at her out of the corner of his eyes, clearly amused. "Or is that off-base?"

Jaden glared at him, fingers digging into her palms. She, unlike him, was clearly not amused. "Stop trying to piss me off."

"Yes, kiddo, stop toying with her."

Her narrowed gaze snapped up to find Skylar a little ways into the forest, sauntering over as if coming to a fancy party and not spying on the group that captured his SOB of a kid. "Stay out of this."

Skylar's mouth easily twitched into that annoying, "I-know-more-than-you" smirk. If she was grateful for one thing right now, it was that Shalbriri at least had a decent poker face. "Calm, Princess. I just wanted to check in on my son. If that's alright with you?"

"No," she barked, "That's not alright with me."

"And what exactly can you do about it, hm?" Jaden glared so narrow that she thought her eyes would burst out of their sockets. Her reaction seemed to humor Skylar, as apparently everything happening presently did, seen by the glimmer in his green eyes. "I thought so. I just want to make sure he's not injured is all."

"Well, you've seen him, he's fine, you can go now."

"Now hold on a moment." Skylar walking extremely close to her made her flinch. The memory of what started this little journey blared warnings in her mind. She knew the lasting damage of a spirit's touch, and she certainly didn't want to experience it in the present chaos. "Aw, sweetheart, is everything alright?" He had circled extremely close to her body, and she stayed still as a stone to avoid even passing contact.

"You know, Father," Shalbriri piped up, "If I had to fashion a guess, I'd say she's afraid you'll touch her. Or does that sound crazy?"

"No, kiddo, I think that's an accurate observation. Would you like to weigh in, Princess?" When her personal space bubble felt more invaded, she recoiled and staggered a few steps back, using her hands as a barricade. "Stay. Back," she breathed, taking slow steps backward.

Skylar advanced just as gradually, as if in an attempt to tease her. "You've gone quite pale, Jaden. Does one little touch really terrify you *that* much?"

She continued back until she felt the dirt turn soft. Looking down, she noticed mud underfoot rather than dirt and grass. Risking a glance back, she realized she'd stopped just inches from the pond, the rainbow waterfall splashing drops of water near her. Then, she directed her attention back onto Skylar, only a few feet away from her. However, he'd come to a stop as well. She rolled her eyes in her mind. What a gentleman.

"Now, I will request this only once," Skylar said, holding up a single finger, "And if you don't abide by it, I will not hesitate to make your life a living Hell on earth. You understand?"

Slowly, she nodded, wide eyes still fixated on him and any little movements he made. He'd just given her a valid threat. She debated grabbing the attention of the other three, currently at the other end, oblivious to what was occurring. Instantly, she decided against it. This was her fight, and she feared what Skylar might do to her if she didn't let him finish the threat.

"Alright, I will make this as simple as possible." He locked gazes with her, and the concern mixed with fire in his eyes told Jaden exactly how serious he was about what he was demanding. "My son does not die. You understand that? If any ruling, or revenge, or anything else ends his life, it will be on your head. Even if you had nothing to do with it. You make sure that the only day he'll die will be from old age. Is that understood?"

All Jaden could do was nod and give her standard answer when terrified out of her shoes: "Uh huh."

Satisfied, he turned around to face Shalbriri. As he walked by, he whispered something to his son, something that made Bri's eyes widen suddenly. "What?" he hissed, loud enough for Jaden to hear.

With the smallest of smiles, Skylar pressed a finger to his mouth and winked at his kid. "I'll see you around, kiddo." Then, that massive breeze slammed into him, and Jaden watched as his body blew away in multicolored specks like sand blowing in the wind.

Finally, the strength in her legs vanished, and they buckled. Luckily for her, she narrowly missed tumbling into the crystal-clear water. Her arms shook as if shivering to death in the tundra. Clutching them to her chest, she took deep breaths, calming herself before she lost it.

"So, guess that went well?" The lingering tone that made his statement sound like a question brought furious fire into her eyes. She aimed it at Bri, whose eyes laughed at her. He feigned surprise, and corrected, "Didn't go well. Got it."

Rolling her eyes, she focused on the ground and on her slow, steady breaths:

In.

Out.

In.

Out.

Chapter 18

About a half hour later, Keegan finally returned. And someone was with him.

The group turned around at his arrival. They had been sitting in a circle in the dirt next to the pond, resorting to stupid Guess Who type games to pass time and clear their mind. Jessi's eyes brightened. "Jakob!"

Jakob, the man who'd come back with Keegan, lifted his arms in the air. "The one and only. And cue the applause!" He dramatically bowed in the most conceded way Jaden could imagine. Knowing her group by now, Jaden looked to see Kiran's reaction. Yep, his face was beet red. He was pissed.

Kiran stood up and started twirling his hand. As Jaden watched, bolts of electricity surrounded the limb, occasionally striking up the arm. Then, he threw his hand in Jakob's direction, the bolts flying and hitting the newcomer. Jakob flew off his feet and backward. When he hit the ground with a deafening slam, Jaden winced. He'd only said two sentences, and Jaden already felt sorry for him. "What applause, jackrider? You led us on a wild goose chase for days!"

Weakly chuckling, Jakob got back to his feet, brushing the dirt off his dark blue tee and jeans. "Easy, kiddo. It was fun, wasn't it?"

Kiran's eyes flashed to blood red again, and a brief jolt of fear shot through Jaden. Taking a few deep breaths, she powered through it. "Does it look like I'm having fun?"

Jakob cocked his head, confused for a moment. "No. To be entirely honest, it doesn't appear that way. I'm not sure why, because Gar and I are having a blast watching you guys progress."

The wide, innocent smile on Jakob's face triggered something in Kiran again, and within seconds, the kid had zapped the man once more. Groaning as he got to his feet, Jakob said, "Okay, I know I deserved that."

"Yeah, you did, jackrabbit!" Kiran snapped, "Do you not care about the safety of the Princess?"

"Of course we did," Jakob replied, shoving his hands in his pockets and leaning against a tree, "That's why there were so few puzzles and so tame in difficulty. Plus, we were watching diligently, so if things went south, we'd intervene. Don't think we don't care about your precious mission to bring the Princess back home, even if it's partially for selfish purposes."

Kiran grinded his teeth and hissed at him, "Up shut, jerk." The kid's eyes darted back to Jaden briefly before focusing on Jakob again. "And, where was your intervention both times the Princess went AWOL?"

Averting his gaze, Jakob admitted, "We went to sleep."

The red in Kiran's face almost matched in shade with his furious glare. "You *went* to *sleep*?"

"Yes." The curt answer accompanied by a simple nod sent Jakob flying again, this time partially hitting a tree. Jaden winced again. That had to have hurt.

When Kiran went to march forward, Jessi grabbed him, holding him in place. "Kir, breathe."

Kiran's breathing slowed, and eventually he glanced at his sister. "You do know that request annoys people when they're angry?"

Jessi simply smiled and replied, "Yes, I do. And I don't care. It's good advice that helps me manage my anger and frustration. Why can't it help other people too?" While Jaden had yet to ever see the female twin even glare, she told herself that maybe a few days wasn't enough to know her whole story.

Rolling his eyes, Kiran murmured, "Quite the optimist, aren't we?"

"Yes. Yes I am. Someone needs to be."

A soft sigh directed Jaden's attention to Shalbriri, still sitting on the stump and staring into the infinite abyss of the clear pond. "Kiran, you're quite a pistol, but I'd listen to your sister."

Jakob, who'd stood up after some difficulty, had gone white as a sheet when Bri spoke. His gaze narrowed as he walked back over to Keegan. "You failed to say you took Shalbriri Meisyn into custody." Based on his sharp, quick tone, Jakob obviously didn't like this new knowledge.

Keegan shrugged and affectionately scratched Lana the orange wolf behind the ears. "Wasn't vital information."

"Wasn't vital..." Jakob sputtered, clearly shaken up, "Are you insane?"

Keegan closed his eyes and continued to pet Lana. "I think Kiran defined you as the insane one. If my summary of your spat is accurate."

Jakob's eyes darted over to Shalbriri. When Bri lifted his gaze to meet his, the man looked about ready to jump out of his shoes. *Well, guess that says a lot about Bri...* Jaden thought to herself as they had a frozen, locked stare-down. After a few moments, Bri smiled and moved his gaze back to the pond, staring into its depths once more. An audible sigh escaped Jakob's mouth, his shoulders relaxing slightly. Relief showed evident in his facial expression.

"Well, that explained a lot."

Keegan's comment apparently put Jakob on edge again, as his muscles tensed. "Are you insane?" he hissed again.

As a clear sign of his amusement, Keegan's mouth twitched. "I thought we established you were the insane one. How many more times are we going to repeat the same ridiculous Q and A?"

"What were you guys thinking? Dragging him into one of my puzzles?"

Heaving a heavy sigh, Keegan commented, "I don't know what the problem is. He's been on his best behavior, so no biggie."

From where he was still fixated on the ripples, Bri interjected, "I don't have a best behavior."

Other than a quick stiffening of muscles, Jakob ignored the captive. "No biggie? This is a big biggie, Keegan! A big biggie, you hear me? Like, a giant biggie!" As he shouted, he quickly walked in no particular pattern, throwing his hands about for emphasis. Jaden saw a bunch of similarities between Jakob and Kiran, and it made her giggle in her mind. Both couldn't apparently stand each other, but had so much in common it was laughable.

Keegan opened his eyes, raising an eyebrow. "Jessica, what do you tell people to do when they're stressed?"

Jessi brightened at being addressed and replied, "Breathe. He should breathe."

"Right." Keegan smiled and shoved Jakob playfully. "JV said it best. Just breathe."

The glare on Jakob's face caused Jaden to snicker aloud. Her hands shot to her mouth, but the smile remained. The similarities were uncanny. Jakob spun to her, and his glare softened. "I apologize, Princess, for any trouble I've caused you." He bowed again, without the joking bravado of the last one.

Again, she had no idea the mannerisms of royals, and part of her wished from the bottom of her heart that she never would. However, in light of recent events, chances of that ranked extremely slim. Taking a deep breath, she forced a kind smile. "It's alright, Mr. Kalea. It's been... interesting, to say the least."

When Jakob straightened up again, Kiran asked in a snide tone, "Where's our apology?"

Raising a confused eyebrow, Jakob asked in response, "What apology?"

Kiran's gaze narrowed again. Jessi sighed and murmured to Jaden, "And to think I just calmed him down."

Then, when she opened her mouth to address Kiran, her brother growled through a clenched jaw, "Do. Not. Say. It."

With a soft huff, Jessi responded, "Fine. I won't. Geez." She finally released him. "Just don't do-"

Kiran's hand shot out again, hitting Jakob at such an angle that he spun in midair before tumbling across the dirt.

Jessi slapped her forehead, eyes closed and head shaking. "-*That*," she finished, "Just don't do *that*." When she flashed him a stern look, he grinned sheepishly and shrugged.

"Sorry."

"You should be," Jakob coughed. After he got back to his feet, he got within inches of Kiran and pointed a finger in his face. "Lay off, pipsqueak. I should teach you a lesson, but out of respect for your father and mother, I will restrain my desires."

Uncontrollable cackling came from Shalbriri, as he doubled over in laughter. "Oh my God, this is hilarious!"

Jakob's eyebrow raised, the man stepping back two paces. "What's so funny, brat?"

Bri's laughter slowed as he glanced from one person to another until he'd met everyone's gaze. His laughs spread out more and more, eventually diminishing. "You're not joking? Respect for that pathetic excuse of a nobleman?"

Keegan's brow furrowed. The warning tone he used next verged on murderous intent: "Watch yourself, Shalbriri. If you haven't noticed, you are currently not able to defend yourself. I doubt you want to experience what will happen if you keep exposing your twisted, entitled attitude. Mind your manners."

Large question mark appeared in Jaden's mind. She partially raised her hand like preschoolers do, as she didn't know how else to insert herself in the conversation. "Excuse a Princess for interrupting, but that tone you addressed him with felt a bit threatening. I mean, I understand the insult is rude, but that seemed a bit overboard on the 'Danger' meter."

When no one responded or even looked at her, Bri spoke up, "You do know she'll find out eventually, right?" Still, nobody said a word. "Okay, fine. I'll take it upon myself to tell her." He met Jaden's eyes, and she recognized a mix of negative emotions, so strong they looked supercharged. "Raiden was their father. You remember Raiden, I take it?"

The red eyes of the savage killer caked in blood refocused that scene in her mind. The images flashed between the two murderous people in her dreams, and it finally made sense. Kiran's family had ties with demons. Of course his father must have too.

The memories consumed her, and she lost touch of reality. Scenes played tug-of-war with her, dragging her from her nightmare with Raiden, to the day of Skylar's murder, to Kiran falling into the same hellish being his father had. Pain shot through her skull like lightning, and next thing she knew, she hit the dirt.

"What did you do, jackrabbit?" Kiran's shrill tone spun her line of sight to her ragtag group, all of them focused on Bri, who was only partially visible on the edge of the frame.

"I did nothing. All I am guilty of is telling the truth."

Kiran's face darkened, both in color and emotion. "Fix her!"

"You demand the impossible, Kiran," Bri answered lazily, "She brought it on herself. She'll come to eventually. Besides, I'm a bit tied up at the moment."

Kiran marched up to him, standing only a foot away. Then, in the darkest tone Jaden had ever heard from him, he growled, "If you've done anything to her, I swear I will end you."

That seemed to amuse Shalbriri, triggering a soft chuckle, a quirk that now defined him. "Really? You'll end me? I'd like to see you try."

She guessed the teen's response would be something like, "You asked for it!" However, Kiran's reaction surprised her.

He backed off.

He took gradual steps back, keeping his eyes locked on Bri. Each step made Shalbriri's mouth twitch, a visible smile to say the least. "What's wrong, tough guy? Afraid to fight me? Or is something else wrong?"

"No!" Kiran spat, "Not that. Fighting you would be a waste of my energy. You barely deserve the breaths I'm using talking to you."

The twinkle in Bri's eyes reflected his father's so much, as apparently did their love of annoying people with it. "Once sixteen, always sixteen, right, Kiran?" The boy blanched, his eyes snapping to Jaden's still figure on the ground. "No worries, kiddo. She's still down for the count. You are quite lucky that paladin of hers is off scouring the perimeter for a way out of this mess Kalea put you in."

"Hey!" Jakob sounded offended, but no one even paid his outburst any bit of attention.

A sharp whistle directed everyone's attention back to Shalbriri.

He was standing upright.

His arm stuck up in the air.

Loose rope gripped in his hand.

The wicked smile on Bri's face said it all: they were in trouble. Dropping the rope, he brushed his hands off together, as if he'd just finished woodworking and was clapping off sawdust. "Now…" His dangerously confident gaze darted from the dirt to Kiran, who had somehow gotten even paler. Bri's mouth twitched, an external visual of his adrenaline pumping and excitement growing. "Let's play!" He lunged forward, swiping out a hand. Kiran stumbled back and fell onto his rear. Not before Bri's hand hit him.

Or maybe not.

Jaden's heart pounded in her chest as she slid partially upright.

Bri's hand swiped right through Kiran.

Right.

Through.

Him.

Her hand went to her mouth, eyes wide as her mind raced. Kiran's gaze landed on Jaden, wide eyed while breathing heavily. He was clearly terrified, but of what? Shalbriri attacking him?

Or the truth being revealed?

Chapter 19

Bri roughly grabbed Jaden's arm and catapulted the two of them into the pond. Seconds before they hit it, she noticed the bubbling and foaming of the now hazy water. Instead of plunging into water, she hit a soft lump of snow.

Wait, snow?

Before she could look up, Bri flipped her over and sat on her thighs, keeping her firmly stuck in the fluffy frozen rain. He grabbed her arms and wrapped rope around her wrists. Once secured, he hauled her to her feet. She yelped at the sudden jerk, snapping, "Watch if, jerkoff."

He didn't respond, but led her through the blizzard they were currently in. The blur of the last few minutes muddled in her brain, where she couldn't even comprehend how lush forest with crystal waterfall could instantly change to snowy winter wonderland. Or, more accurately, frozen Hell.

They soon reached a cave of sorts. Once sheltered from the cold, he pushed her forward. The shakiness of her limbs make her knees buckle, and she crashed to the stone floor. She grimaced at the slam, but immediately started tugging fiercely at her bound wrists.

"That will only give you rope burn, you know."

Refusing to look at him, she barked, "Shut it." As she continued to yank and pull, what he'd just said started coming to fruition. She honestly didn't care. She just wanted to run.

When she winced at the throbbing, stinging burns, her captor sighed loudly and told her, "I warned you."

"You – and your warnings – can go freeze to death for all I care!" The bitter tone spoke plenty by itself, even disregarding the hateful words.

"Be reasonable, Princess," he replied, "You have questions, I have answers. Take advantage of this situation."

Brow furrowing, Jaden rolled over on the stone toward the mouth of whatever cave they were in. Outside blinded her, as a brightening sun hit the white, snowy tundra. Once her eyes stopped spotting and came into focus, she met Shalbriri's bored gaze. He had plopped down on a decent-sized stone a few feet away. A tiny, knowing smirk twitched onto his face. "Oh, intrigued, I see?"

Jaden's eyes narrowed. "You're bluffing."

His eyes laughed at her as he replied, "Try me."

Challenge accepted, jerkwad. "Okay, you asked for it. What happened back there?"

Bri sighed and fixated on a spot on the stone walls surrounding them. "Would you prefer words? Or can you comprehend what you saw on your own?"

Glaring at him, she snapped, "What the heck do you mean by that?"

With a chuckle softer than the freezing wind outside, Bri's mouth curved into a playful smile. He glanced at her out of the corners of his twinkling eyes. "Did I make contact with him?"

Jaden's heart pounded, recalling Shalbriri's hand swiping right through Kiran's body. The look of terrified horror on the sixteen-year-old boy's face when he met her eyes. She squeezed her eyes shut tight, cheeks warming as she gripped her head. *No more... no more...*

"They're not real either..."

"Good, you do have a good head on your shoulders."

Oh, right, she wasn't alone.

Her eyes opened slowly and met Shalbriri's crystal blue. She realized she was still laying on the stone floor and rocked back and forth until she swung into a sitting position. Took a few times, but she finally got upright. Satisfied, she looked back at Bri again to find him staring out into the blizzard outside. "What's with your obsession of staring at nature?"

"I find it rather calming," he replied softly, "Compared to the rest of my life, nature's life is simple, and spelled out for each plant, chemical, and animal. I suppose at one point in time, the same applied for people. We've developed for thousands upon thousands of years to the point where nature's functions become overshadowed with human's flaws and developed mind. Wants matter more than needs. Needs are worth killing for. Innocent people get punished for crimes they didn't commit and get blacklisted for the rest of their lives." He heaved a heavy sigh, his shoulders rising and falling with it. "So, I find myself lost in nature's simplicity, wishing life as an evolved *homo sapien* hadn't become so complicated."

Jaden raised an eyebrow. "Okay, deep and confusing much?" There was that soft chuckle again, constantly a mocking gesture. "Why do you always laugh at me? You'd be confused too if you were in my shoes."

"You mistake my humor as degrading," he explained, "When, in fact, the chuckle is meant to be complimenting on your innocence, your new perspective of things, and your baby-like reactions."

She blinked a few times, staring at him. "Is that Bri-speak for saying I'm cute?" She didn't know whether to feel embarrassed or annoyed, so she settled on her mind's current favorite: questioning confusion.

The smile on Bri's face supported her assumption. "Bri-speak? That's a new one."

Rolling her eyes, Jaden scoffed, "Glad to add to the oral tradition. Explain to me what just saw." She opted for a blunt and straight approach, hoping she'll get answers quicker and avoid getting off-topic. Again.

Shalbriri aimed his gaze on the stone floor. His feet took turns rolling a small pebble under the thick rubber soles of his shoes. "I think you know what you saw," he answered softly.

"Yeah, I do, but it doesn't add up," she countered, "I mean, I touched them plenty of times and didn't get shocked. Explain that."

"You haven't touched Kiran, have you?"

She blinked, staring at him while his gaze remained on the pebble he fiddled with. After thinking about it for a second, she replied slowly, "Well… No, I don't think I have. Actually…" She bit her lip, thinking a bit more before continuing slowly, "I'm not sure, though, because everything that's happened blurs in my mind. But, I've touched Jessi plenty of times."

"The answer's staring you in the face, but you can't link the pieces, can you?" When Jaden furrowed her brow and stared into space, Bri continued, "My father can touch you because you are a Channeler. You can touch him, but get shocked. If you tried to touch Kiran, the results would replicate. Jessi, on the other hand, you can touch until kingdom come. The answer is so simple: emotions."

"Emotions?" Her voice went flat, as she doubted that feelings factored into ghostly shocks.

Bri nodded, all traces of his previous smile gone. "A bit unbelievable, right? But, that's what it boils down to. My father and Kiran resented someone when they died. Their hatred and frustration at losing the life they could've had charges them up, resulting in displacing the shock through a grounded object. Example, a Channeler. Their built-up charges jump from them, to you, and into the earth."

Jaden's gaze darted to the pebble Bri kicked around. Her mind raced, not comprehending everything. "But, what about Jessi? She doesn't send those 'charges' through me. Is she in Limbo too?"

When she looked up, Bri glanced up out of the tops of his eyes, a look that mixed disbelief with slight understanding. Yes, it contradicted itself, but that's what Jaden saw. "Hard to believe, but yes. You've spent a few days with her. Has she ever showed extremely negative emotions? Any at all?" Jaden looked away and bit her lip. "That's what I thought. Jessica Theron has never been furious a day in her life or her afterlife. It's just not in her nature. Her heart is warmer than most, and, as such, harbors no resentment. She's only in Limbo because she didn't want to abandon her brother's choice of fate."

It made sense. She didn't want to believe it, but the logic matched up with reality. They seemed so innocent and full of life. From their energy to their skills... *Wait.*

"Hold the phone," she blurted out, "They used magic, or Kinetic abilities, or whatever the heck those tricks are called. If they're dead, how can they still use them in the living world?"

"Easy enough to answer," he responded, "Limbo is almost on the same plane of being as reality, meaning they can still affect things in our world. The only thing they can't do is physically interact with the living world, namely people and animals. Also, to add onto that, have you ever seen their paladins? If they had been living, they would've been out and about just as much as your buddy Lukas."

Lukas! She'd spaced out and completely forgotten him. The image of him frantically searching for her made her eyes sting. Swallowing past a lump that had grown in her throat, she answered, "No, I guess they don't have their paladins… Wait, what about you? I have yet to see your paladin." Her eyes narrowed, her way of challenging his knowledge and smarts.

Bri sighed deeply and slowly got to his feet. "I locked him up. Took a lot of training to master that, believe me." When she stared blankly at him, he sighed, "You want a show? I'll give you a show." He held his arms straight out to each side of his body, closing his eyes. As he inhaled, a light golden glow shone around the outline of his body. When he exhaled, it shrunk to nothing again. After a few more seconds, a red, swirling wisp twisted around his body, growing with each turn. Finally, the red strand had increased in thickness and length enough to swirl next to him. A slight pull of wind almost knocked Jaden over as the thick threads blew like a mini tornado. Then, the garnet color shot down, vanishing into the floor.

In its place stood a young man with long black hair in a ponytail. His arms tensed at his side, with his wrists tilted and palms stiffly facing the ground. He rolled his neck, first clockwise, then counterclockwise. When his eyes opened, his dark purple eyes gazed at her and didn't move. Jaden felt locked into a staring match with this guy, but for some reason, couldn't look away.

"Quit it, Kaelan," Bri spoke, breaking the silence, "She's frightened enough already."

Kaelan twisted his torso to look next to him, just now noticing Bri. "Oh, hi."

"Yeah, hi." With a roll of his eyes, Shalbriri sat back on his rock. Gesturing to each of them with a hand, he said, "Kae, meet Princess Jaden. Princess, meet Kaelan."

When he grinned at her, she took note of the sharper canines his mouth sported. "It's a pleasure, Princess." He bowed to her, almost lazily, and quickly got back upright.

"Pleasure's mine, I'm sure. So, you're Bri's paladin?"

Shalbriri stiffened at that question, but his gaze had returned to the pebble, and he resumed messing with it. That tensing didn't go unnoticed by Kaelan, who chuckled a bit. "*Bri*? Well, now, look at that. You've gotten all buddy-buddy with the Princess, haven't we?"

Jaden could swear Bri's cheeks reddened slightly. "She may call me whatever she wants, Kaelan. She is royalty and can do whatever her little, innocent heart desires."

"That is quite true." Kaelan's eyes landed on Jaden again. The paladin sauntered over to her and plopped on the ground next to her. "Now, I'm usually a good listener, if you'd like to rant to me? I only offer because you appear to have gone through the ringer."

A good listener, huh? She needed one of those right now. Taking a deep breath, she started, "Well, I was at a conference for business majors…"

Chapter 20

About 30 minutes of shivering and ranting storytelling later, Jaden finished recounting the past few days' events. Sometime in the middle, she relaxed a bit. Kaelan remained silent almost the whole time, aside from some "uh huh"s and a lot of acknowledging nods. He listened to every word, and Jaden mentally thanked him for that. Because of that, her rant lifted a huge weight off her shoulders.

She exhaled, shoulders dropping. "So, yeah, that all happened."

Kaelan nodded. "I see. However, I think there's a gap in your story."

Cocking her head slightly, she asked, "Really? What gap?"

"The gap that tells how you ended up here."

Biting her lip, she replied slowly, "I… I'm not sure."

Kaelan's eyes narrowed, and he twisted where he sat to look behind him at Shalbriri. As he stared at a pebble under his foot, Bri sighed, "I know you're looking at me, Kae."

"You didn't tell her?"

Bri shrugged, responding simply with, "She didn't ask."

Groaning, Kaelan looked back at Jaden and asked, "Do you want to know?"

Jaden glanced between Bri and Kaelan. "Only if he wants to," she said as cautiously as she could. Since she hadn't been around Shalbriri that much, she had no idea what might set him off. Care and caution were her best friends right now.

Bri continued to kick around the rock and added, “And he doesn’t.”

Rolling his eyes, Kaelan looked at Bri again. “Tell her, Shalbriri.”

Bri’s brow furrowed as he lifted his gaze to meet his paladin’s. Kaelan flinched at the cold glare. “Excuse me?” Bri slowly growled, “Are you demanding something from me, Kaelan? Keep in mind you exist because of me. You have no power over me.”

Sighing in clear annoyance, Kaelan told him, “I don’t, but she does. Are you going to deny the Princess what she wants to know?”

Eyes narrowing more dangerously, Shalbriri snapped, “She said I didn’t have to.”

With a loud, long, dramatic groan, his paladin drawled, “Alright, let me rephrase that: Are you going to deny her what she *deserves* to know?”

Shoulders rising and falling in a silent sigh, Bri snapped back, “Fine. I’ll tell her.” He stood up. His gaze fixated on the small rock he’d been fiddling with. With a quick swing of his foot, he propelled the pebble into the stone wall of the cave. *Into it.* It actually shot *into* the wall, now surrounded by cracked ripples as a result.

Shalbriri then walked closer to them and proceeded to sit on another decent-sized boulder. “Okay, what would you like to know first?”

Trying to pick a single question out of the tornado that was currently her brain, she finally asked, “How did we go from bright, warm forest to a blizzard-ravaged tundra?”

Bri reached behind him to a pouch on his waistline. From that pouch, he produced three colored objects that looked like golf ball sized bath bombs. “These.”

Arching an eyebrow, Jaden drawled, “And what be these? They look like bath bombs.” After a brief pause, she asked hesitantly, “Do they have those here?”

The tiniest flicker of a smile twitched at the corner of his lips. “Yes, we do. This dimension is an alternate reality to your Earth, so most of what you grew up with is also here. Aside from magical items, like these.” He twirled his fingers to roll the chalky balls around the palm of his hand. “These are called portal summoners. Toss one into water, jump through the now swirling portal, and reach a destination in a new location, completely dry. However, if you haven’t noticed, there’s a lack of water here. We have to wait until the blizzard dies down so I can locate more water and get us out of here.”

“Sooooo… A bath bomb that teleports?”

Bri hung his head. “Yes, I suppose that describes it fine as well.”

Keeping the giggle at his exasperation in her head, Jaden asked a supplementary question: “Why a tundra?”

With a soft sigh, Shalbriri gazed at the ground again. “I picked the wrong summoner.”

A loud groan and slap directed Jaden’s attention back to Kaelan, who had a hand to his skull. His head shook with disbelief. However, his expression contradicted the movements, as he also had a small smile and weak chuckle. So, partially disappointed and partially humored.

Damn, why couldn’t she read this guy?

“Seriously, Bri?” Kaelan chuckled, “You chose the wrong one?”

Face blushing red, Bri barked, “Quit the laughing! I was in a hurry, alright?”

“I’d say!”

Glare turning murderous, he growled, “Kalea and Kelly were there too, Kaelan.”

Kaelan's laughter abruptly stopped. His eyes widened. "Jacob Kalea and Keegan Kelly?"

Crossing his arms and leaning back against the rock wall, Bri answered, "The very same. I'm lucky I got away."

"Lucky you got away?" Kaelan yelled, his voice sharper and cracking, "Based on your track record with those two, you're lucky to be alive! Are you crazy? If they are on the twins' side, you could've been killed!"

As the two continued to bicker, Jaden moved her gaze to the rocky floor, mulling everything over. If Keegan and Jacob were so strong and powerful, why didn't they kill Shalbriri the second they saw him? That would have eliminated the problem. If Bri was a threat to their goals, surely they could end his life lickety-split.

Then… How was he still alive?

To herself, she muttered her conclusion, "They didn't want to…"

"They didn't want to what?"

Her head shot up to find Shalbriri and Kaelan staring at her. When she silently glanced between the two for a few more seconds, Bri repeated, "They didn't want to *what*, Princess?"

"They…" She inhaled slowly and blew out a heavy sigh, her muscles relaxing again. "They didn't want to kill you. If they are as strong as you are implying, then they had an opportunity – actually, multiple opportunities – to end you. Why wouldn't they, if they saw you as a threat?"

Kaelan held his hand sideways against his lips, lost in thought for a moment. "Hm… Princess makes a valid point."

Frowning at the ground beneath his feet, Bri replied softly, "I was already aware of that, thank you."

Kaelan's expression crossed confused with a rage strong enough to probably hit his charge. "How in blazes were you aware of that?" he shrieked, his hands stiff claws with bent, rigid fingers. Jaden pictured him as a cartoon character, with steam coming out of his ears. Or, rather, an anime character whose wide eyes and hyperactive movements visualized them freaking out. Jaden grinned at those images. When she realized the humored smile existed, she covered her mouth with both hands. Luckily, both males in the cave with her were otherwise occupied.

"Kaelan, cease and desist, alright?" Bri groaned, pressing two fingers firmly to his right temple, "You've been locked up for a while, so I'll use confined insanity as the stress behind this 'episode'."

The paladin's face puffed up in frustration, his cheeks reddening. "Your confinement, your insanity! If you thought you were in the slightest chance of danger, you should have called me out! Locking me inside is for ease of travel and convenience, not just for life or death, action-packed battle sequences!"

Bri waved that away. "Relax, Kaelan. I can handle myself, alright?"

Kaelan's breathing quickly slowed, the blush of anger draining from his face. Finally, he breathed, "You're right, *Bri*. My outburst was uncalled for."

Again, Shalbriri dismissed his paladin's words with a wave of his hand. "Don't worry about it. No broken bones, no injuries. At least this time."

Jaden blinked, lowering her tied hands back into her lap. "This time?"

Both boys' heads snapped to her, giving her their undivided attention. It seemed they'd forgotten her for a moment or two. A secretive, cunning smirk tugged up on Kaelan's lips. "Let's just say things get smoky when I crack."

Cocking her head, she asked, "Crack? Like rage, depression, overloading emotions?"

"All of the above, Princess." His smirk grew into a wicked grin that reminded her of the Cheshire Cat. "I'm certain you'll see soon enough." He clapped his hands once and said, "Okay, enough about me and my burning alter ego. I'm pretty certain the young Princess has more questions, no?"

Jaden shifted her gaze to meet Shalbriri's. After a few seconds of them staring at each other, Bri averted his gaze to the ground, cheek flushing a light pink. Clearing his throat, he asked, "What else would you like to know, Princess?"

Jaden's first question would've been to ask him why he'd looked away, but she decided against it. If he was even the slightest bit of an introvert, like he seemed, she might upset him. Instead, she focused her questions on the missing blanks in this fantasy book she now found herself within. "Now that I know the truth about Jessi and Kiran, could you tell me…" She faded off, uncertain if she truly wanted to know that answer.

"Tell you what, Princess?"

Taking a deep breath, she finished, "How they died?"

Shalbriri's face instantly fell, pain seen clearly on his face. Jaden glanced at Kaelan, who had paled and grimaced as well. When she looked back at Bri, he cringed. "It's… It's a rough memory, Princess, so it might take a while to…" He swallowed, and Jaden recognized a lump in his throat. "… To recount it all."

Shaking her head, she replied hurriedly, "No! If it's that painful for you, I don't need to know." *Yet.*

With a sigh of relief, Bri smiled weakly and nodded. "If that is your desire, Princess, I will gladly – and thankfully – oblige." He lifted his gaze to meet hers. She found herself lost in his milky sky blue irises. His relieved, quirky, honest smile made her heart flutter. *Wait… Do I actually like this crazy?* She squeezed her eyes shut and shook her head, an attempt to snap her out of whatever crazy hypnosis he tried on her.

A hand gently touched her shoulder, and her eyes shot open again. Bri knelt on one knee next to her, gazing at her with a furrowed brow and concerned eyes. "Are you alright, Princess?"

Nodding with a semi-stunned expression, Jaden replied, "Uh huh."

What the heck is wrong with you?, she screamed inside her head, *Snap out of it! He freaking kidnapped you, idiot!*

His concerned expression remained as he pressed, "Are you sure?"

Trying to hide her thoughts and rapid heartbeat, she scowled. "Yeah, I'm fine." Her curt answer must've been a bullet, based on Bri flinching and stiffening. Guess he hadn't expected her response to be so caustic. Either the young man was caught off-guard, or… *Maybe I hurt his feelings?*

No, from what she'd observed, Shalbriri controlled his emotions so well that he seemed to only have a few weak-hearted ones. However, his rare expressions could probably make an elderly woman swoon. The usual passive, uncaring stoicism tended to be his go-to, and he excelled at it. Surely it wasn't that easy to hurt his feelings, right?

Just as sudden as that concern appeared, his poker face returned in a flash. With a shrug, he said, "Alright, I get it."

As he stood back up and walked away, she asked, "What's that supposed to mean?"

Sitting back on his rocky pedestal, he sighed deeply. "I'm a stranger. Why should you talk to me, let alone trust me?"

Jaden's eyes looked down, resting their gaze on her bound wrists. Arching an eyebrow, she drawled, "You know, it'd be much easier to trust you if you trusted me first."

The blank expression stared back at her, blinking in what she surmised as confusion. "I'm not sure I understand, princess. Why do you think I don't trust you?"

Rolling her eyes and scoffing, she lifted up her restrained hands. "Does this answer your question?"

Shalbriri hesitated. She could see it in his eyes. With a huff, she groaned lightly, "Really? Where am I gonna go, huh?" She jerked her head toward the entrance of the cave. The outside blinded her with a white wall as the snow poured down with sun shining on it.

When she gave him a sideways glance, his face finally cracked a rare smile. "Alright, Princess. If that's what it'll take to earn your trust..."

As he stood up and unsheathed a dagger from his waist, she smiled back. "Thank you. I'm a Princess, not a POW."

With a soft chuckle, he replied, "There's nothing saying you're not both." He knelt in front of her and held out his hand. "May I?"

Scowling, she lifted her hands and placed them into his. As he gently sawed at the ropes, like a gentleman, she asked sharply, "What do you mean 'both'? I'm supposed to be a Prisoner of War?" Obviously, he tuned her out, as he didn't make a single noise in acknowledgement, much less an answer. He just continued to silently cut off her bindings. To get his attention, she yanked her arms back. In that instant, his head jerked up. He met her eyes again, and she easily read the concern within those blue pools. "Answer my question."

His eyes glanced at her bindings again, only partially cut. "I thought you wanted those off."

Eyes narrowing, she replied curtly, "Answer first, ropes second."

His body dropped instantly. Jaden stared down at him as he clutched his chest, grunting in pain. "Um, you okay?"

Kaelan dropped to his charge's side, snapping, "Does he look like he's okay?" The fire and concern in those pain-filled words spoke volumes as to the pair's unlikely match.

Shalbriri pushed Kaelan back, struggling to sit up. "No..." he gasped through convulsions of pain, "She deserves to know." After Bri closed his eyes and took measured breaths, Kaelan's figure shone blood red again. The human shape became fuzzy, twirling like a tornado and becoming thinner and thinner strands. Finally, the strings flew around Shalbriri's body and vanished inside him. With a bitter smile, he commented, "Quite the light show, isn't it? But, I didn't need his harassment anymore. I can show you this myself." He yanked his shirt up, a challenge in itself as his body still jerked from whatever pain he felt. Finally, the shirt got over his head, and he dropped it into his lap.

Jaden stared at his chest. While he maintained quite the muscular physique, that wasn't what struck her hard. It was the jagged purple lines radiating from his heart across half his chest. It reminded her of *Iron Man 2*, when Tony Stark was dying from his Arc Reactor. And, she had a funny feeling this situation just went Hollywood.

Through grunts and spasms, Bri said, "Those lines... Are from that day... six years ago. Raiden... cursed me with demonic blood... The blood didn't mix well... with my abilities and lineage... And caused this. A slow, painful, poisonous death."

Cue the second superhero end credits scene.

And this one didn't include shawarma.

Chapter 21

Jaden felt at a loss for words. "Okay, wow…"

"Cat got your tongue?" A ghost of a smile spread across his face. "I don't blame you. Shocks a lot of people."

She ripped her gaze away from his chest and the jagged pulsing lines, instead focusing on the face of their victim. "Is there a cure?"

Averting his gaze, he replied softly, close to a whisper, "That why we need you. I need my father's blood to reverse the curse and fix all the damage it's caused. Obviously, can't manage that if he's six feet under."

Oh. That explained a lot. Except one little detail. "If you just need your dad brought back to life for medical reasons, why do Jessi and Kiran not want me to? I mean, it almost seems like they hate you, because they call you insulting names and say you're a traitor."

Sighing, Bri ran his fingers through his hair. "They hate my dad, and me by association, because he killed their father. My dad was in the right, putting others before himself, and was killed as a result. They don't see it that way. They feel that Raiden was killed unjustly, and that their lives being resurrected take priority to atone for that injustice."

"Um… selfish much?" The kids were sweet and caring, but it still seemed a bit drastic to say the least.

That brought a smile back to Shalbriri's face, at least slightly. "Yeah," he said in response, "I suppose it is. It's even more twisted when you know the whole story of that day…" When he shivered, he pulled his shirt back over his head. Then, giving her a sideways glance, he added firmly, "You know what? Painful memories be damned. You want to know how they died? They died at their father's hand. They were wandering town with him when he went berserk, and he cut them down. As he ran into the complex of nobles, I chased after him to avenge them. After he wiped out everyone in that ballroom, he attacked me. Obviously, you know what happened after that…"

Sighing, he stood up and stretched his torso. "Biggest massacre in the capital city in a millennium. The sad thing is, neither Kiran nor Jessica know I tried to atone for their deaths by hunting their father down."

After sliding his trenchcoat back on, he sat on the nearest boulder again. "That's why I can see them. If anyone witnesses a death, and that soul remains in Limbo, they can see the victim. There were at least a hundred souls or more who witnessed their deaths at the hands of their guardian. It was a brutally public killing, right in the main square."

Jaden's eyes stung as she listened to his memory. It wasn't just the story that influenced her sadness. It was the way he told it that hit her hardest. She heard the pain in his voice, the slow-paced tone, the slight crack in his words, the painfilled, laborious emphasis on certain words. It all spoke volumes about not only his past, but who he was as a person. Sniffling quietly, she asked, "So… You guys used to be close?"

A nostalgic expression rose to his features, both with bloodshot eyes and a soft, gentle smile. "More than close. We were practically family. That is, until the day they died so horribly and didn't know who or what to blame. So, they fixated on the son of their murderer's killer. Ironic, isn't it?"

Jaden grimaced as the stinging worsened, squeezing her eyes shut tight and cringing. She felt a small drop of salty water roll halfway down her cheek. A gentle finger wiped it away, and she opened her eyes to find Shalbriri right at her side. "No tears, alright? Life is meant for the present, not to dwell on the past. What's done is done, and there's nothing anyone can do to fix it. Why waste brain space?"

As she nodded, she rubbed her eyes to rid herself of the horrid stinging sensation of rising tears. "Yeah, you're right." With a sniffle, she asked, "Was your dad a philosopher or something?"

While she'd said it in jest, it received a quick hiccup of a chuckle from Bri. "King's advisor. So, close guess."

Jaden slammed back to reality, the crazy confusion her life had become crashing onto her again. "The King. So… my dad? My real dad?"

"Yes." Shalbriri nodded to accompany his answer. "His Highness Seth Cabrera. The previous King, your grandfather, died when he was ten, so he inherited the throne at a young age. One of the many reasons he sent you away was to avoid a repeat of that with you."

Now her curiosity piqued. "Why would that be a motivating factor? History rarely repeats itself, statistically speaking."

"Ah, but, dear Princess…" He lifted a single finger for a second or two before lowering it again. "It would've been. See, your grandfather was assassinated by someone who hasn't been identified still to this day. His Highness also has many enemies and feared they'd use you to their ends. He wanted you protected. Oh, and King Cabrera will like how analytical your mind is. Wouldn't doubt that your minds will have very intellectual debates. Wouldn't doubt it for a second." After he winked, he held out a hand again. "Now, back on track. Would you like me to finish?"

She didn't understand what he meant at first until his eyes flickered from her face to her hands. Oh, right, she was still tied up. Funny how he distracted her so easily. She lifted her hands and set them in his gentle grasp again. They sat in silence as he sawed through the ropes. The quiet unnerved Jaden a bit. While it normally relaxed people, silence in her present situation put her on edge. A calm-before-the-storm feeling.

She felt a bout of prickling chest pain before Shalbriri could finish. The pain and prickles grew stronger, but with Bri still cutting her hands free, she couldn't use her normal reflexes to apply pressure. Right when she squeezed her eyes shut in an attempt to block out the pain, it vanished. Slowly, she opened her eyes. *What the-*

She suddenly flew backwards and slammed into the wall that was behind her. She felt warm liquid dribbling down her fingers and looked down. The ropes only hung by a few strands, but the sudden movement sliced Bri's blade across her hand. Man, was it deep! And stung like crazy! Twisting her hands in an escape attempt failed miserably, and only made the gash sting and burn more.

"You stay away from my girl, got it?"

The familiar voice temporarily blocked the pain and directed her attention elsewhere. Shalbriri lay on the floor, a glowing blue blade at his throat. The wielder of this energy sword?

"Lukas!" Jaden called out, not caring how excited, relieved, and desperate she sounded.

Her best friend turned to look at her, which gave Bri an opening. In the split-second Lukas was distracted, Bri kicked his feet out from under him. Lukas slammed to the rocky floor and visibly winced. His glare sharpened, shooting daggers at the now upright Shalbriri. The latter drawled, "Well, it's about time, puppy. Get a bit lost along the way?"

The taunting resulted in an almost dog-like growl from deep in Lukas' chest. "You traveled quite far, and I can only teleport to my charge within a certain distance of her. You of all people should know that extremely well."

The confident, cocky smile dropped off Shalbriri's face like a hot rock, a slight rage burning in his gaze. "Watch yourself, pup. You are standing on thin ice."

"Oho," Lukas chuckled, eyes narrowed determinedly, "I'm just getting started!" He swung his legs around. As Bri jumped back to avoid another repeat of a few minutes ago, Lukas used his momentum to spin to his feet. Once standing upright and still, he brushed the dirt off his hands. "Ready when you are, jackel."

The fire burned stronger in Bri's eyes now. He walked the few steps to reach his opponent and threw the first punch toward his head. As Lukas dodged, Bri got a solid blow to his enemy's gut. Lukas staggered back a few steps, glare turning murderous.

Bri's mouth twitched in a micro expression of brief happiness. "You haven't fought in a decade, Kohei. Do you honestly believe you have a chance?"

Lukas stared at him for a few more moments before cracking a small, cocky grin. "Yes. Yes, I believe I do."

From nowhere, a large stone slammed into the back of Shalbriri's head, knocking him to the ground. As Jaden stared at the dazed, groaning Bri, a hyper, high-pitched squeal echoed through the cave: "JAY!"

Before she could look, someone slammed into her and grabbed her in a tight hug. With a heavy sigh, she nudged the hugger with her head. "Jessi, I need to breathe, you know."

Jessi instantly released her, sitting back on her heels next to Jaden. Rubbing the back of her neck, she replied sheepishly, "Sorry 'bout that. I got worried we would never find you. It scared me, so seeing you safe and sound makes me relieved and optimistic and crazy and…" As she sucked in a dramatic breath, her eyes darted to Jaden's hands, widening at their condition. "Jay, you're bleeding!"

A sharp pain shot through the injured hand, making Jaden wince. "It's okay," she insisted, "I can barely feel it."

Arching an eyebrow, Jessi's condescending, motherly scowl said the girl wasn't convinced. "Uh huh, right, I can see that through your flinches of pain."

On cue, another stinging shock shot through her hand again, and this time, even up her lower arm. Grinding her teeth to balance the pain, she grunted, "I'm fine. I promise."

Brow furrowing, Jessi grabbed the frayed, almost cut ropes with both hands. Snapping her hands apart, the ropes broke off. With a proud grin, she drawled, "You are so welcome." Jaden muffled a snicker, and Jessi's giggling and brightening expression as a reaction cheered her up.

A loud grunt brought the girls' attention back to the boys and their brawl. With a scowl, Jaden got to her feet. She had to flinch and bite through pain in her hands as she pushed herself up, but the sharp shocks disappeared soon enough. After she got close enough, she grabbed Lukas' collar with her good hand and yanked him back. In that same motion, she stepped in front of him, becoming a barricade between them that neither side wanted to hurt. "Okay, quit it!"

Bri's finger snapped up to point at Lukas. "Princess, he initiated battle. I was simply defending myself."

Lukas crossed his arms and scowled. "Are you seriously tattling on me like a two-year-old?"

Face blushing, Shalbriri barked, "Up shut, you pathetic excuse for a paladin! Can't even do your job right."

A loud, rough bark left Lukas' mouth. Right after, he grinded his teeth, his sharp, large canines glinting in the low light. A soft growl continued to hum in his throat as the two had a stare-off.

Rolling her eyes, Jaden turned to her best friend and placed a hand on each shoulder. "Calm down and look at me, Wolfe. You don't want to go and get us into trouble again."

Lukas closed his eyes and took a dozen deep breaths. When his eyes opened, the burning rage that had consumed him no longer existed. "Yeah," he sighed, "Don't need any more trouble. Can't afford any more required community service."

Jaden couldn't help the snort that shot out of her. When she looked at him again, his expression of humor and taunting confidence made her nostalgic. Now this… This guy was the Lukas she'd been friends with. *I'm glad he can still act like he used to*. Then, she spun around to face Shalbriri, to find that he'd sat back down on another boulder. He gulped down water from his canteen. Once satisfied, he lowered the container, wiped his mouth with his trenchcoat sleeve, and started messing with a pebble on the ground. Again.

"I suppose you are going to lecture me too, Princess?"

Eyes narrowing, Jaden snapped, "Of course I am, idiot!" She walked up to him and slapped him hard on the shoulder.

Bri clutched where she'd hit him and yelped, "Ow!"

With a roll of her eyes, Jaden told him, "You're fine. That was barely a slap. Get over yourself."

Sighing, he rubbed his shoulder, glancing up at her. "Guess I deserved that."

"You deserve a lot worse!" Jessi barked, startling Jaden. She'd forgotten the girl was there with them.

Looking past Jaden at Jessi, Bri's mouth twitched. Jaden wondered if it was an uncontrollable tic, or if he just liked doing it to taunt people. "Nice to see you again, Jess. Where's your brother?"

The hesitation filling with silence urged Jaden to turn to her. Crossing her arms, she drawled, "Yeah, Jessi. Where is Kiran, exactly?"

"He fell behind." Jessi's short answer said plenty about the truth they'd hidden from her. Looks like Shalbriri's memories and stories spoke the truth.

"Uh huh, and how exactly did you get here? That blizzard outside is impossible to see through, much less travel through."

Jessi's eyes darted rapidly around the cave, briefly landing on each of them before darting to another rocky surface. Her bit lip showed just how nervous she felt. "Um..."

Rolling her eyes - a tic of her own - Jaden groaned, "Look, Jessi, I know the truth."

"The truth of what, exactly?" Jessi's attempt at acting innocent fooled nobody.

Taking a deep breath, she finished, "That you and Kiran are in Limbo like Skylar."

Jessi's face fell instantly, her gaze now firmly fixated on the rocky ground. "Oh. That."

"Yeah, that." Scowling, Jaden continued, "Why didn't you guys just tell me? Don't you trust me? Or did you not learn before you died that lying to people is mean, hurtful, and selfish?"

Her sharp, blunt tone made Jessi flinch, as if Jaden fired shocks of lightning through her body. "I'm sorry, Jaden..." Jessi mumbled, loud enough for everyone to hear, "We didn't know how you would react, and we're desperate to come back more than anything else in our lives."

"Come back? You mean tricking me into tagging along with you just so I can bring you back to life?"

Jessi's eyes remained focused on the floor, but her lips started quivering a sign of holding back tears. "Not tricking," she muttered, shaking her head, "Never tricking."

Fingers digging into her palms, Jaden barked, "Then what word would you use to describe the truths you hid from me? Lying? Secretive? Betrayal? Traitorous?" Heat burned in her cheeks as she yelled at the female twin.

Each accentuated term cause more jolts of Jessi's body, almost as if Jaden was physically hitting her. "I… I'm sorry, Jay. We thought it would be best to wait until-"

"Yeah?" Jaden yelled aloud, face burning terribly. "Well, you thought wrong!" She spun around to face a wall and walked toward it. When she was only a foot away, she dropped to the ground and crisscrossed her legs. As she stared into her lap, hands twiddling there, she took deep inhales, held each breath for a few seconds, then released it. She did this to cool off, and giving the others any bit of attention would only escalate the rage and worry. It was a relaxation method Lukas taught her a good number of years ago, very early in their friendship. Well, their human friendship anyway.

If only life could've remained that simple.

Chapter 22

Time passed by in a blur. Jaden kept her eyes glued on her hands, still fiddling in her lap. Her fingers kept running over the gash on the side of her hand, how it healed being a top question in her head. Thoughts raced like a NASCAR speedway in her head, and trying to organize them easily became an impossible task.

A loud sigh breathed directly behind her. "Are you done pouting yet?"

Jaden twisted around and looked up to where Lukas stood over her, hands shoved deep into the back pockets of his jeans. Scowling, she spun back around, continuing her brooding, simmering silence.

"Guess not." Lukas sighed again and then plopped down next to her, his legs stretched out instead of crossed like hers. "Jay, I know this is a bit much to take in-"

"No, *really*?" Jaden interrupted, over-exaggerated tone obviously mocking him, "I never would have guessed that."

Frowning at her, Lukas replied, "Quit the sarcasm, Jay. I'm trying to help you right now."

Looking away from his hurt expression, she spat, "I didn't ask for your help."

"No, you didn't. But I don't need your permission to do what's right. So, I'm helping anyway. I actually have some free will, believe it or not." A snorting, single laugh shot from Jaden's mouth, her hands instantly shooting up to cover her face. As she peeked through her fingers, she spotted a soft, gentle, caring smile on her best friend's face. If anything, at least that relaxed her a bit, despite the situations they were now wrapped in. "That's the Jaden Walker I remember."

After collecting herself, she rolled her shoulders and stretched her limbs to return a sense of feeling to them. "So, what now?"

"You mean about getting out of here? Well, the ginger says he might have an idea, but I really don't-"

"Great!" Jaden practically leapt to her feet, scrambling to brush the dirt off her butt and pants. She asked, "What's the plan?" When she noticed he didn't stand or respond, she looked down at his annoyed expression. "What?"

"Do you have to do that? Not let me finish a single, full sentence?" When she cocked her head, slightly concerned as to the current teenage crisis he seemed to be in, he scoffed, "Never mind. Forget it." He stood up, clapping the particles from the stones off his hands. Then, he looked at her out of the corners of his eyes. "What?" he asked, repeating Jaden from moments ago, but his with more bite.

The caustic tone of that snapping bark shocked Jaden. It was a rare event for Lukas to be mad at her. They stayed thick as thieves for their whole lives, and *now*, when she needed his support most, he finally broke down? "What's wrong with you?"

"Me?" His voice cracked as he pointed a finger to his chest. "Me? What about you? What's wrong with you?"

Brow furrowing, Jaden responded with a slightly sharp tone, "Nothing's wrong with me. Why would you assume-"

"I'm assuming nothing," Lukas interrupted. When she aimed an annoyed glare at him, he said, "See? It's not fun getting cut off, is it?"

Jaden huffed a sigh. "Lukas, why are you upset? Your high-strung anxiety meter has just broke through its highest limit, and I don't like seeing you like this."

"Why am I upset?" Lukas grimaced, but eventually replied softly, "You didn't let me finish him."

Blinking in slight confusion, she asked with the most cautious tone she could, "You mean finish off Bri?"

With a loud, exaggerated scoff, Lukas drawled, obviously annoyed, "Look who's so familiar with the enemy!"

Jaden snapped back instantly, "I can call him that if I want to. And he's not the problem, nor the enemy anymore. You are starting to become the problem."

"Brainwashing you, I see."

Jaden felt her fingers clenching in frustration, but a thought occurred to her. It would explain everything weird going on with her best friend, and his intonation and motions only proved it more. Her muscles relaxed as she grinned from ear to ear. "You're jealous!"

Light blush rose to Lukas' cheeks. With narrowed eyes, he insisted, "No, I am not!"

"Don't worry." She patted his shoulder. "It's kind of adorable, to be honest." The twitching in his faltering expression said more than words ever could. With a taunting grin, she added, "It's kind of an eye opener that you would feel threatened." She left him standing stock still, lost in his thoughts with bright red cheeks. Walking over to the opposite wall, she approached Shalbriri, who was currently whittling a stick to a point with his dagger. Where he found a stick would forever be a mystery. "Bri?"

"Nice to see you mobile, Princess." He lifted his gaze to meet hers. A small, warm smile appeared faintly on his regularly stoic face. His attractiveness appealed to her more when he smiled. *Okay, push that thought away...* "What can I do for you?"

"Lukas said you have an idea?"

That kind smile grew just a tiny amount, and a humored gleam shone in his light blue eyes. "He did, did he? Wow, shocker."

The sarcasm helped her crack a smile. If he could joke around in this situation, she failed to understand why he'd gotten pinned as the bad guy in their journey. With a soft giggle, she responded, "Yeah, he can be a bit of a hard head at times."

"At times?" Bri laughed, "He's been a pain in the posterior the *entire* time. Relentless, I tell you. *Re-Lent-Less*." Jaden covered her mouth to hide a snicker. "But, I hate to admit, he's a perfect paladin for you."

A compliment? For Lukas? Seemed a bit out of character. "What makes you say that? He definitely doesn't like you very much."

Bri's eyes glinted more before he resumed whittling his stick into a spear. "I honestly don't care much for him either. But, you can't deny the chemistry. Paladins are matched and groomed to be the perfect guardian for their charges when each Kinetic is born. They foil each other, challenging each other's limits while covering each other's weaknesses."

Arching an eyebrow, Jaden asked, "What about you and Kaelan? Your relationship seems... dysfunctional, at best."

His chuckling revealed the humor he found at her expense and naïveté. "Kaelan may be a little over the top at times-"

Jaden exaggerated a gasp, repeating Bri's own words from moments ago: "At times?"

The soft smile on his face twitched bigger. "Funny. But, in case you haven't noticed, I don't usually open up. Kaelan is my match because he's hyped up and my total opposite. He may be hardheaded and stubborn, but he keeps me in check, as I do him. That's what it means to be partners."

"But, Lukas and I aren't opposites like you two. How do we match up then?"

Continuing to whittle, he replied, "Believe it or not, you two are very different. Not total opposites, but pretty close. He takes risks, protects others he cares about no matter what it means for him, and isn't afraid to be himself."

Jaden crossed her arms, bristling slightly at his words. "You barely know me. How do you know I'm not all those things?"

"Please. I know plenty. For a fact, I know you've never taken a life-altering risk ever, at least until the twins showed up and pulled you into this insane journey you didn't want anyway. Also, you've been snappish and hurtful to your little rag-tag group, not kind or overprotective. Add on your low self-esteem and hiding your personality behind suits and calculators, and you two couldn't be more different."

Her fists shook as she stared at her feet. She didn't want to admit it, but his logic was sound and spoke the truth. Was she really as pathetic as he made her sound? Apparently, at least she was when you compared her to her best friend.

Bri's hand waved in her line of sight, snapping her back to reality. When she looked back up, he pulled his hand back. "Are you okay, Princess?"

She nodded. "Mhm, I'm good." Since he didn't look convinced, she added, "I swear I'm fine."

Shrugging, he picked up his dagger off the rock next to him. He must've set it down while she was lost in thought. "If you insist, Princess."

"Where's Jessi?"

The slightly amused expression dropped in an instant. Without a single word, he pointed toward the entrance of the cave. When she looked over there, she saw Jessi sitting against the wall right in front of the blizzard. The girl hugged her legs to her chest as she stared out into the snowy storm.

Sighing, Jaden approached her. She came to a stop a few feet away from her. As she opened her mouth to speak, Jessi cut her off: "You don't need to say anything. I already know what you'd say, and I don't need your pity."

"I'm not going to pity you," Jaden replied, crossing her arms, "You don't need it. You're already doing that enough yourself."

Eyes firm on the falling wall of snow, Jessi replied dully, "Good. What do you need then?"

"I'm gonna help you."

That got the girl's attention. Jessi twisted to her, her legs stretching out, slightly bent. "Help me how?"

Mouth twitching into a tiny, comforting smile, Jaden sat down next to her and told her, "Well, I've given it some thought, and though it might take time to learn how to do it…"

When she paused, Jessi urged, "*Yeaaaaah*?"

After taking a deep breath, Jaden finished, "I'll try to bring you and Kiran back."

Jessi's eyes widened. "Really?" Her tone revealed the teenager slowly returning to her normal, hyper, optimistic self.

Jaden nodded, mentally happy at Jessi's reaction. "Yup, I will. Based on what I've heard, you two didn't deserve what happened to you. I'll give you your lives back."

A wide smile, filled with excited wonder, spread across Jessi's face. Practically tackling Jaden in a tight hug, she squealed repeatedly, "Thank you, thank you, thank you, thank you!"

Wrapping arms around the shaking girl, Jaden whispered back, "No problem, girlie. We've gotta stick together, right?"

Jessi sniffled and released her. Wiping tears from her eyes, she said, "Yeah, we do. Thank you, Jaden. I can't wait to tell Kiran."

"Yeah, where is he anyway?"

Rubbing the back of her neck again, she answered, "He's waiting for us to bring you back, hanging out with Master Keegan and Jake. To be honest, he's probably worried sick."

"Right, right, the attachment complex."

"Yeah, that." She sniffled again, but seemed fully recovered. "So, I heard Shalbriri has a plan to get us out of here." Her tone sounded bitter and annoyed, but for what reason?

Jaden asked, "That's a good thing, right? I mean, we'll get out of here."

Scowling, Jessi looked elsewhere. "He has a condition."

"Like what?"

With a heavy sigh, she told her, "He wants to come with us without being tied up."

Well, that was a huge relief. "Oh, just that? The way you said it made me think it would be something a lot worse!"

"It could end up worse, Jay," Jessi responded, tucking a strand of hair behind her ear. "If he's freely walking with us, he'll have any opportunity for a repeat of yesterday when he snatched you right in front of us. Now that he knows how he messed up, he won't make the same mistake again. He's brilliant and conniving, which you wouldn't know about, and a traitor to us. We can't let him kidnap you again, understand?"

Patting Jessi's leg, Jaden told her, "And he won't. I've been a bit shaken up with all this stuff blasting me so suddenly. But, I'm not anymore. I'm grasping this reality a lot better, and I'll be more aware from now on. Trust me on this, Jess; I can take care of myself."

"Yeah, and I'm not letting her out of my sight again." Jaden leaned her head back and looked up at Lukas, standing over her. "I've learned too. And she'll be stuck to my side like glue."

Jaden threw out a hand into his lower leg. Crying out, Lukas stumbled back. "Careful! These boots are authentic."

Giggling, Jessi said, "As is your stuck-up ego."

Jaden snorted in laughter at the tone and dramatization of that final exclamation. Her hands shot to her mouth, glancing between the humored grins on both Lukas and Jessi's faces. She scowled and lowered her hands. "Not funny."

"Actually," Jessi replied, trying desperately not to grin like a lunatic, "I have to say that was pretty funny."

Lukas added, "I concur, and contribute my opinion of, Damn, I'm starting to like this chick!" He punched out a clenched fist, to which Jessi happily fist-bumped.

With a roll of her eyes, Jaden stood up, "Okay, fine, keep laughing. I'm going to tell Bri we have a deal, so we can get out of this horrid winter wonderland."

After only two steps, Jessi sang, "*Walkinnnn'...*"

"Don't you dare!"

This time, a loud slap sounded from them, and Jaden knew they'd hi-fived. Sighing, she resumed walking over to Shalbriri. "Hey, Bri?"

He had resumed kicking around a rock since she'd left, the stick and knife sitting at his feet. As he lifted his gaze to meet hers, his feet continued to fiddle with the small rock. "How can I be of assistance, Princess?"

"We have a deal."

The glimmer of amusement shone in Bri's eyes. That annoyed Jaden, as she'd seen the same knowing, confident, cocky glint in Skylar's eyes. Like father, like son. She found it hard to believe that it'd only been a week since that final test that yanked her into this insanity. Seemed so much longer than that.

"We do, now?" He asked. "Was it unanimous, or are you just gonna take a bullet for me later?"

Crossing her arms, Jaden replied, "They want out of here just as bad as I do. But, I've got a counter-condition."

His mouth twitched, but for once she couldn't figure out whether it reflected humor or annoyance. "Shoot."

"I bring Jessi and Kiran back first."

All signs of humor vanished from visible view. "Princess, I'm not so sure that would be wise..." When she glared at him silently, he huffed a sigh. "Alright, I will agree to your terms."

Smiling boastfully, she said, "Good. Now, what's this plan of yours?"

"There's no *natural* water source..." Mouth spreading into a clever smirk, Bri reached behind him and brought around his canteen. As he shook it, the sound of water sloshing reached Jaden's ears. He looked from the container to her.

"Let's make our own water source."

Chapter 23

Jaden hit the ground hard as she came through the portal. It felt like her butt bruised. As she rubbed, a high-pitched squeal of excitement cut through the air, and someone landed behind her.

"Let's do that again!" Jessi exclaimed.

Jaden couldn't help the exasperated sigh at Jessi's childish excitement. "If I have a say in the matter, we will never 'do that again', capiche?" She struggled to get to her feet, her body feeling much heavier than usual. Another shout, this time a yelp, and a slam banged to earth behind them. Turning around, she told Lukas, "Nice of you to make it."

With a sharp glare, Lukas stood up, rolling his shoulders. "Cut the sarcasm. It's not becoming of you."

Sticking out her tongue, she replied, "I'll decide what's becoming of me, thank you very much."

One more slam from behind her again, but no shouts accompanied it. When she turned around, she found Shalbriri standing upright. It didn't appear he'd landed on his southside while travelling. Guess he may have had some prior experience with those magic bath bombs. "Alright, Jess, where are the rest of your lot?"

Jessi scowled, "I'm not telling you. Zip lip and follow me like a lost puppy if you really want to stay unbound and free walkin'."

Bri blinked, but Jaden knew it was mocking confusion. "Like it or not, I'm a part of your party now. I've got resources and abilities that will shorten our search mission."

"Pish of your fancy schmancy abilities," Jessi responded, almost bitterly, "You are travelling with us, but you are not one of us. You go with us, and keep your stupid mouth shut. Understand?"

Sighing, Bri agreed with, "Yes, I understand. I promise I will follow, but I can't guarantee my mouth."

When Jessi turned to Jaden's right, she told them, "Alright, this way. I can sense Kiran in this direction."

As they all started walking, their formation had Jessi at the front, Shalbriri in the middle, and Lukas and Jaden bringing up the rear. The first ten minutes or so, the group walked in silence. A little bit after that, Lukas's hand slowly slid into hers, gripping it comfortingly. She looked at him to find a caring smile on his face. "You hanging in there, Princess?"

"Stop calling me Princess."

"Why?"

"Because it sounds weird coming from my best friend."

"I've called you Princess before."

Jaden nodded. "True, but usually you say it mockingly. The whole overprotective, paladin companion role of yours, that is now common knowledge, makes it sound strange and awkward otherwise."

His smile turned softer, almost lovingly. "Yeah, I suppose it does. I'll stop if you want me to."

"Yes, please."

"Okay, as you wish, Miss Jaden." Coming to a stop, he over-exaggerated a bow and caused Jaden to stifle an inappropriate snicker. When he straightened back up, they continued walking again, grinning at each other like crazy lunatics. More silence filled the air for another fifteen minutes, aside from Lukas and Jaden glancing at each other and dissolving into muffled laughter.

Then, a soft click reached Jaden's ears. She screeched to a halt. As she heard more, she definitely recognized it.

The cocking and priming of guns.

Lukas stopped a few feet away, looking at her worriedly. "Jay, everything okay?"

Shalbriri and Jessi came to a stop too. Jaden watched Jessi's eyes gloss over before returning to their rich shade of blue. "We've got company."

Lukas suddenly shoved Jaden to the side right as a shot went off. Jaden watched a bullet streak right where she'd been. She fell on her rear again. Shaking her head helped eliminate both the ringing in her ears and the spotting in her vision. Once recollected, she focused on Lukas, lying on the ground a few feet away. "Lukas?"

Her friend only replied with a grunt of pain. Jaden skimmed his body, trying to figure out what had happened. That's when she spotted thick, red liquid oozing out from in between the fingers that grasped his side.

Frantically, she crawled over to him, eyes stinging. Upon reaching him, she rolled him onto his back. "Lukas, you're going to be okay, okay?"

Flashing her a weak smile, he replied gently, "If you say so, Jay. What a Princess says, goes. Right?"

Water welling up in her eyes, she gasped, "Yeah. That's right." She swallowed back tears, but it hurt to do so due to the large lump that had instantly developed in her throat.

Another shot sounded, making Jaden flinch. This time, however, it was followed by a plastic echo. Jaden looked up and saw a translucent blue wall towering high a few feet away. The one who created it?

Shalbriri.

Scowling, said protector barked, "Cease and desist, you idiots! It's me and the Princess!"

No more shots rang out. Tense silence filled the forest. As the four scanned their surroundings, nothing moved or made a sound. That is, until the sound of crunching leaves sounded nearby, drawing everyone's attention.

"Hey, JV," Keegan greeted, "You hanging in there, sport?"

Jessi's face lit up. "Master Keegan!" She ran up and slammed full force into him.

Keegan hugged the hyperactive teenager back, muttering, "You had me worried, kiddo."

Jessi's shoulders rose and fell in silent laughter. "You know me better than that. I always come through."

A warm smile appeared on the mentor's face. "You're right. I shouldn't have doubted you, Miss Theron. You never cease to impress." When his gaze landed on Bri, all signs of happy reunion vanished instantly. Gently prying Jessi away, he snarled, "Why is he here and not tied up?"

Shalbriri groaned, lowering the blue shield wall to nothingness. As he knelt down next to Jaden and Lukas, he replied lightly, "I think we have bigger problems than your unwarranted hatred of me, Master Keegan." He proceeded to take off his trench coat. With a quick yank, it ripped. A few tears later, he had a few scraps of fabric lying in his lap. He pressed a few squares against the grazed bullet wound, and then wrapped a longer strip around Lukas' waist. After a tight knot, he wiped his bloodied hands on what remained of his coat. "There. That should last until we reach the capitol."

Keegan appeared incredulous, lifting an eyebrow. "You're being helpful." The dull tone sounded like a statement, but underneath, the words relayed it as a question.

Getting to his feet, Bri replied simply, "Yes."

After a brief disbelieving pause, Keegan asked, "Okay… Why?"

"Believe it or not, Master Keegan," Bri drawled, brushing dirt off his pants, "I do actually have a heart." Then, he held out a hand toward Lukas. "Fancy a bit of help, Kohei?"

Lukas stared at the offered hand for a few seconds. When he glanced at Jaden, almost looking for permission, she nodded. Grabbing Bri's hand tight, he finally got to his feet. The second he was upright, he stumbled to the side and slammed his shoulder into the thick base of a tree. "God, friggers, that hurts!" He cursed, using the trunk to remain standing. "This is pathetic!"

Jaden hopped up instantly by her friend's side. "Take it easy, Wolfe. I don't want to bring you home in a body bag."

Lukas' face cracked a smile. "Looks like you're returning to your normal mocking, annoying, condescending self."

"Yep, I'm a regular crack-shot again. Feeling a lot better."

Lies…

The voice hissed in her ear, and she definitely recognized it. Her gaze snapped to various points of her surroundings, trying to pinpoint that wicked tease that was Shalbriri's father. When she couldn't locate him, she scowled. *Damn…*

"Jay?" Her eyes darted to Lukas, whose worried expression calmed her slightly. "Is everything okay?"

Okay, so, no one else could hear him except her? Great. Just bloody friggen great.

Sighing, she forced a small smile and replied, "Yeah, everything's good. So, I've got a question." She turned to Keegan and glared murderously. "Who. Shot. Lukas."

She swore Keegan paled just a bit, but why, she didn't know. And, honestly, nor did she care. "Well, turns out, the twins weren't the only ones searching for you…" As he said that, black clad soldiers stepped out of the shadows and into the light, all brandishing either swords or guns.

"No, they weren't," Bri snapped, "I was. These are my men. Why are they helping you?"

Crossing his arms, Keegan countered "You know, I would like to pose the same question to you. These are Five Kingdoms soldiers."

With a firm glare, Shalbriri replied dangerously slow, "Yes. They are. Because His Majesty sent me to bring his daughter home."

"That's a lie!"

Kiran materialized behind Jaden from out of nowhere. The sudden shout and entrance shocked her heart as she practically jumped out of her shoes. Gasping for air, she turned to look at Jessi's brother with a deadly glare. "Don't. Do. That. Ever. Again."

A sheepish, slightly embarrassed smile appeared on Kiran's face. "Sorry, Jay. Didn't mean to startle you."

"Just… Give a warning or something before you just poof your spirit self into existence, okay?"

Kiran arched an eyebrow. "What do you mean by that?"

When heat warmed Jaden's cheeks, Jessi stepped between them. "Kir, she knows."

The boy's face fell. "Oh."

"But…" Jessi added, grinning from ear to ear, "She said she'd help us, Kir. She said she'll bring us back!"

"What?" Kiran's expression brightening touched Jaden's heart. In the short time she'd been around him, she couldn't remember ever looking as happy as he did right then. "Seriously?"

Jaden nodded, allowing a small smile to spread across her lips. "Yup. I did say that. And I will follow through, I promise."

Jessi grabbed Kiran and hugged him tightly. Her brother, on the other hand, remained in motionless shock. "Can you believe it, Kir?"

Kiran nodded. "Mhm, yeah, that I can believe. What I can't believe…" He pushed his sister away and turned a focused, firm glare on Bri. "… Is that this idjit was sent by King Cabrera. We were sent to get her back!"

Bri matched the twin's glare, but his seemed more confident and gloating. "Yes, His Majesty did send you. *Two years ago*. When Queen DD went into a coma five weeks ago, he sent me. Thought you two had moved on."

That seemed to shock most of them, as the number of astonished looks outnumbered Jaden's confused one four to one. Jessi held up a finger. "Hold up. You mean to tell me that DD is in danger?"

Bri nodded. "Until we return the Princess to her side, yes. Very much in danger. In case you didn't noticed the still, stoic muscle surrounding us." He gestured to the soldiers in their perimeter. "He couldn't afford to waste time on a pair of twins that chose poor allies and planned last minute for everything."

The acid could be heard by everyone, certainly by Kiran, whose face burned bright amber. "You talk big, Shalbriri, but want to prove your toughness? Take action instead."

Shrugging, Bri replied, "Alright." Then, without another word, he walked up to Lukas, draped the paladin's arm around his own shoulders, and started leading the disabled young adult into the forest.

"What the heck are you doing?" Kiran exclaimed, tone obviously confused and exasperated.

Shalbriri came to a stop, glanced back at the group, and told him calmly, "You said take action. He needs medical attention. That required precedence on my list of actions. Trust me, you're on there too. However, very, very low priority."

Kiran shook, obviously furious. "You'll regret underestimating me, Meisyn."

The tiniest of smirks tugged onto Bri's face. "What are you going to do? Hit me?"

When Bri started walking again with Lukas in tow, Kiran's growl came from deep down. "I'm gonna kill him someday…"

Jaden glanced at Jessi. "Should I be concerned with what he just said?"

Jessi shook her head. "No, he won't actually kill him." After a brief pause, she added, "I think."

A hand patted Jaden's shoulder, and she looked to her right side to find Keegan smiling warmly at her. "You're almost home, Princess."

Her lungs instantly knotted, breath knocked out of her. Home. Where she'd come from. The life she never got to experience. Just thinking about it made her stomach churn. Did part of her miss her old life? Well, yeah, obviously. A life where she wasn't shot at, or where she couldn't see into people's horrifying memories; of course that would have been preferred. However, her analytical brain acknowledged that was no longer her life. It acknowledged that fact, but that didn't equate to complete, comprehensive acceptance. Swallowing past a lump in her throat, she nodded. "Yeah… Almost home."

They walked for about twenty minutes. Jaden's scared thoughts of going back home to this new life quickly became thoughts of relief, as when they reached this so-called home, she wouldn't have to walk constantly like they had been the last couple of days.

Then, giant bushes towered in front of them, stretching so high nothing peeked over the top. Shalbriri stepped to the side with Lukas, both smiling at her. Jerking his head toward a break in the foliage, Bri told her, "See you on the other side, Princess."

As he and Lukas stepped through, her muscles tensed. Something important must lie beyond the massive plants for them to look so expectant and brimming with joy. She looked to her other side, where Keegan, Jessi, and Kiran stood. The instructor nodded toward the bushes, while Jessi told her, "Go on. We're right behind you."

Jaden sucked in a deep breath, held it, and exhaled. Then, she pushed through the crack. It turned out harder than it looked, as twigs and tiny leaves kept hitting her and scratching up exposed skin. After a few more seconds, she broke back out into sunlight and screeched to a halt.

Massive, towering structures stretched into the sky, ornate in their carvings and crisp in their edges. A gate stood before her, blocking her view of beyond those initial buildings. The walls shone a bright off-white in the sunlight. She heard the laugher and screeching of children and smelled fresh pastries right out of the oven. She gradually approached the gate before her, both from caution and frozen shock. She reached out and ran her fingers across the stones, taking in the texture and warmth.

"So, Princess?"

She spun around to see everyone else on her side of the bushes. Her smile widened. Nodding, she told them, "It's beautiful."

"And," Keegan replied, walking over to her, "One day…" He pushed in a slightly protruding stone, and the stone gates rumbled open. Jaden's eyes widened upon seeing the giant city on a hill, filled with bustling cobblestone streets, kids playing soccer on them, parents conversing while watching, vendors with all sorts of things to sell on their booths. Keegan clapped a hand on her shoulder again, smiling down at her. "One day, this will all be yours."

"Really?" Jaden's voice cracked, and she partially felt embarrassed by her shock.

"You there!"

About five soldiers dashed down the main drag down to them. When they got within a few feet, they stopped. One of them announced, "The battalion informed us of your coming." Jaden realized they meant the black clad soldiers from earlier. They hadn't followed after their group, but she felt out of the loop at how they had told others about their arrival. Didn't seem like cell phones were used around here much. At least, based on her limited, week-long experience. Bri had mentioned the alternate Earth factoid, but the differences would only be determined as time wore on.

The soldiers then dropped to one knee and bowed their heads. "It will be an honor to escort you home, Princess."

"Actually," Bri said, stepping forward, "That would be my honor, Captain."

The one that had spoken looked up from the ground, eyes widening. "Prince Shalbriri! Of course, that is your right."

Jaden's mind shut down for a moment before she closed her eyes and shook her head. "I'm sorry, but what?"

Bri's mouth twitched again, but ignored her outburst. "It is. Now, Kohei needs medical attention. Can I trust he will be taken care of?"

The captain's eyes darted to Lukas, who now used Keegan for support. "Yes, your Highness, you can rely on us." All five then stood up and jogged over to Lukas.

Jaden only took one step in Lukas' direction when her best friend called out, "Go, Jay." When she opened her mouth to protest, he pushed, "I'll be fine. They'll have me fixed up in no time. Go meet your parents."

A weak smile quivered on Jaden's face. "Okay. I'll hold you to that promise."

With a soft breath of a chuckle, Lukas replied, "Wouldn't want it any other way."

"Princess?" She turned back around to find Shalbriri bent over with a hand out. His head angled up and met her eyes. "Will you do me the honor of being your escort?"

Nodding, Jaden placed her hand lightly on top of his. "Yeah, that sounds like a plan."

After Bri stood upright again, he led her down the stony streets. She finally comprehended a large castle looming over the city off in the distance. That had to be where she was going. To the castle. To the royal family. To home.

Chapter 24

"The inside is even more beautiful!" Jaden exclaimed, spinning slowly as they walked down a wide hallway. Rich reds and golds colored the walls in crisp floral and swooshing patterns. Large ornate chandeliers hung from the ceiling, lighting their way.

"I am glad this all is to your liking, Princess."

She pushed against the floor, firmly stopping her twirling and giving Shalbriri her undivided attention. "Yeah, pertaining to royal titles…"

Bri sighed, but the small smile on his face showed the humor he seemed to always secretly feel. "I suppose you are referring to mine?"

"Um, yeah!" She snapped. All the secrecy during this journey grated on her last nerve. "Didn't you think that information might be just a *little* too important not to mention?"

Shaking his head, he replied, "It would neither help nor hinder my mission, so I saw that knowledge as a minor, unimportant detail."

"Unimpor- Are you bonkers?"

With his usual clueless, stoic expression, Bri replied cautiously, "I believe to be as sane as anyone else in my position, as many others can attest t…" He paused for a moment, brow furrowing. "That was pointless rhetoric, wasn't it?"

Dramatically sweeping an arm and mockingly bowing, Jaden drawled, "You have great wisdom in your mind, your Highness."

Bri sighed deeply, shoulders dropping as he pressed two fingers to his right temple. "The sarcasm was not called for, Princess."

With a smug smile, she told him, "No, entirely called for. And well-deserved."

Hanging his head, he walked silently away from her, continuing ahead toward their destination. Jaden jogged to catch up. When she reached him, she matched his pace and stride. "What's wrong? Can the spoiled royal not succeed in a battle of wits?"

His stoic looked remained focused ahead as he responded softly, "I do not fight with an enemy that is unarmed."

She halted, staring at the floor. When those words had sunk in, she shrieked, "Did you just call me stupid?" When she looked back up with fire in her eyes, she saw he'd just kept walking, and now was a good distance from her.

"No, I did not. I will not argue that it could have been implied though."

Her fingers curled into tight fists. "Ugh, you are a jerk!"

As he continued to walk forward, he twisted his neck and flashed her a sideway grin. "Guilty as charged, I suppose."

As much as he annoyed her, that smile of his always seemed to calm her and occasionally stirred a mixture of emotions she could never process before they vanished. Shalbriri continued to remain a huge question mark in her book. First, he's the bad guy, then he's the supportive leader, then turns out to be royalty? Nothing added up with him, did it?

A sharp whistle brought her back to earth. She spotted Bri standing at the corner of a connecting hallway. Waving his hand at her, he shouted, "C'mon, slowpoke. You don't want to keep them waiting, do you?"

Those lingering questions about him pushed to the back of her mind. *Later. I'll deal with those later.* She dashed to catch up, screeching to a halt right next to him. With a proud smirk, Bri commented, "Good agility and control on that stop, Princess."

"Well," Jaden replied, puffing out her chest smugly, "I did play basketball for a few years. Suicide drills across the gym's court eventually pay off, I guess."

Bri gently shoved her with his shoulder, causing Jaden to crack a smile. "Okay, enough boasting. We all know you're special, alright?"

Jaden giggled for a few seconds before stopping. She met his gaze and asked, "You're joking around."

His smile fell, almost worried. "Is that a bad thing, Princess?"

Shaking her head, she told him, "No, of course not! It's just... You said you don't really open up to people."

"Yes, I did," he responded slowly, "What of it?"

"You're opening up to me."

Shalbriri blinked a few times, brow furrowing as he became lost in thought. "I... I suppose I am." Looking at her again, he added, "Guess I just feel comfortable around you. Can't say that about many people."

"Yeah, I can see that."

A twinkle of humor gleamed in his sky-blue eyes. "Can you now? Is it that obvious?"

Jaden smirked. "Very obvious."

"Well now, didn't realize that. Thank you for informing me."

Returning the shoulder slam, Jaden commented, "Look who's sarcastic now."

"Yeah," Bri chuckled, "Guess I'm a bit more uncivilized than I thought. Remind me to tell people next time. Now, I think we have a King to greet."

Her stomach twisted into knots again. Swallowing, she nodded meekly. "Yeah, we do."

They walked down that connecting hallway. Every step felt weighed down by heavy chunks of lead. Jaden worried like crazy about what awaited her at the end of their trek. Would her real parents accept her? Her appearance screamed punk rocker, but her personality espressed sarcasm, annoyance, and introversion. She'd learned to get to know someone before trusting them with anything, and if the King and Queen had similar tactics, how would they feel about her?

Bri came to a slow stop outside of a set of grand, carved double doors. He knocked three times on them and took a step back. In the few moments left, her heart threatened to pound out of her chest. When the door started opening inward, she debated running. As if knowing how she felt, Bri slipped his hand into hers and squeezed comfortingly. "Relax, Princess. You'll be okay."

The doors completely opened to reveal a crazed man dashing all over the place, grabbing and throwing papers off tables. His frantic behavior confused Jaden, as she and Shalbriri continued to stand in unexpected shock in the doorway.

Clearing his throat, Bri called out, "Your Majesty?"

The man's head snapped up, all motion halting like a deer in headlights. The three papers he'd bit with his teeth fluttered to the carpet when he opened his mouth. His glasses sat crooked on the bridge of his nose. Shutting his jaw rigidly, he cleared his own throat and brushed wrinkles off each sleeve. Once satisfied, the man straightened his glasses and grinned wide, finally acknowledging their arrival. Throwing out his arms, he greeted, "Prince Shalbriri, aren't you a sight for sore eyes! I'm so happy you've returned safely!"

Bri nodded once. "Yes, and I've brought you something." He nudged Jaden with his shoulder, urging her forward. She stared at him with wide, 'you're-kidding-me' eyes. When he jerked his head in the man's direction, she sighed deeply. She took small, careful steps into the room, Bri at her heels. The man gracefully rounded the desk he'd been behind. Once on the other side, he leaned his rear against the edge of the piece of office furniture, hands behind him supporting his body. Bri grabbed her arms when she was six feet away, effectively stopping her. "Your Majesty, I'd like to reintroduce you to your daughter. Jaden, this is His Majesty, King Seth Cabrera."

As the King analyzed her in silence, she averted her gaze. For some reason, the examination of her made her feel slightly naked somehow. She just had this feeling he was gazing into her soul. Finally, a soft chuckling breath compelled her to look up. The caring, loving smile on his face even dwarfed her adoptive parents'. This time, it really meant something special. "My sweet baby girl is all grown up."

Jaden felt tears stinging her eyes. In the back of her mind, her hidden memories sparked a relieved, relaxed, overjoyed feeling. She may have not lived with her real parents for a majority of her life, but the four-year-old inside her still remembered, still yearned, still believed in them. Now, putting a face to a name and idea, the happiness flowed through her system. Sniffling, she wiped her eyes with the back of her hand. "Sorry, your Majesty. I just… It seems…"

"Too good to be true? Or a huge relief?"

"Honestly? Both."

The King's smile quivered as he gazed lovingly down at her. "Same for me, sweetheart. Come here." He held his arms out, inviting Jaden for a hug. She paused for a moment until impulse propelled her into her father's arms. His firm grip on her implied he was afraid she was a mirage, as if she would disappear at any moment. He muttered in her ear, "Welcome home, Jaden."

The dam broke, and tears streamed down her cheeks. Short hiccups of sobs shot out every couple of seconds, which she had tried to hold back but couldn't. The King rubbed her on the back, nuzzling his head against hers. "It's okay, sweetheart. I'm not going anywhere, and you won't again. That I promise."

Jaden nodded, trying to swallow past the giant lump in her throat. The plugged nose that resulted from the crying changed her voice into a more pathetic tone: "I'm glad. I'm so glad." A few more seconds of hugging later, they broke apart. Their eyes locked, and Jaden's quivering mouth twitched into a weak smile.

"Your Majesty?"

Both of them directed their attention back to Shalbriri. Jaden had temporarily forgotten he was there with them. As Jaden wiped her eyes, Seth asked, "Yes, Bri?"

Bri replied, "I believe you two have somewhere to be." When both royals stared at him with confused looks, he groaned, "Queen Dove, your Majesty. Have you forgotten her through your crazed, crippling happiness?"

The King's eyes widened. "No, no, haven't forgotten!" He ran back around the desk, searching for something again. "I needed to find a few things first. Bear with me for a moment."

As the supposed leader of the Five Kingdoms ran around like a crazy toddler tearing the room apart, Jaden walked back over to Bri. "Is he for real?"

With a small, quirky smile, he responded, "King Cabrera has always been… strange, to say the least. His methods in his personal life tend to be unorganized, frantic, and unhinged. Those methods flip when it's politics or other important government duties. Both personalities are polar opposites. It's a wonder the Queen has put up with it for so long without stepping into that treacherous territory. Trust me, his paladin has a monstrous burden set upon him. And that's putting it gently."

Jaden turned her attention back to Seth, who still continued to rip apart the room in his hurried search. Finally, he stopped, breathing heavily as he scratched the top of his head. "Where the heck is that medallion?"

Shalbriri chuckled softly. "Unbelievable."

The King frowned. "What, might I ask, is so funny, Shabriri?"

Taking a deep breath, Bri pointed at him. "It's around your neck, your Majesty."

Seth's head snapped down. He tucked his hand down his collar and pulled a necklace out from under. Swinging it a few times, he commented, "Well, would you look at that? Never would've guessed."

Jaden resisted the urge to facepalm. Looking at Bri, she asked, "Is he *seriously* for real?"

Mouth tugging into a playful smirk, Shalbriri replied, "Yep, he is. Welcome to my Hell. And now, yours too."

Frowning, she looked at her father again as he studied the giant, multicolored opal in the center of the necklace. He had the same midnight locks that she did, cut in a crisp, layered bob that shortened toward the back. The tips stuck out to her most, as they appeared to have been dipped in pearly white, similar to her bleached tips. That style and coloring preferences could have proved their relations alone, at least in Jaden's mind. He also was of a slight build, but you couldn't tell based on the muscles in all the right places. He wore a black dress shirt and slacks, the picturesque appearance of a depressed anime character standing before her. Color added to that solid darkness in the form of a red tie and a garnet cape, which locked in place by a carved, golden brooch at his neck.

When she met his gaze again, he asked, "Everything alright, sweetheart?"

With a nod, she told him, "Uh huh. Perfect."

His expression flipped from worried to determined, his fingers tightly wrapping around the stone. "Follow me, you two."

As he walked past them at a brisk pace, Jaden gave Bri a sideways glance. "What's going on?"

Nudging her forward with his shoulder, he urged, "Just follow. I'm right here with you, alright?"

Raising an eyebrow, she replied, "Follow the king that's two Froot Loops short of a Rice Krispie treat? Alright, guess I don't have a choice."

"Hey, you're now responsible for 'the crazy', so I'd get over that annoying feeling toward him quickly. Unless you'd like to be scrubbing the pots in the kitchen for five hours."

"Seriously?"

He shrugged. "I've learned from experience. Titles don't give immunity when it comes to him. His word is God." He took two steps and stopped. Reaching back, he grabbed her hand and yanked her forward. She didn't resist, but didn't go easy either. He practically dragged her through the halls, having her tripping over her own two feet. Finally, she willingly followed, using her own willpower to walk rather than the willpower of the jerk that had no respect for her wishes of avoiding the spring-loaded King who was her lineage's current patriarch.

Seth entered a room, Bri and Jaden walking in soon after. The two young adults stopped just inside the doorway, while the King hurried to the bed. A woman lay in the bed, covered in crisp, purple sheets. Her blonde hair sparked déjà vu in her mind, but not from locked memories. In fact, it wasn't just the hair. It was the facial structure. The slight body build. The soft breathing and chest movements that accompanied it.

This was Dove.

This was her sister.

Wait... No, this has to be the Queen. My mother.

She thought over the things she'd heard about her sister and the Queen, trying to figure out how this Queen DD – her birth mother – looked like a slightly more matured version of her annoying, adoptive older sister. It didn't make sense logically, so her brain felt fried.

Seth knelt at the Queen's side. "Hello, love." He pulled the necklace over his head and pressed it into the palm of her hand. After closing her fingers around it, he moved her hand to lay on top of her chest. Without turning to them, he called out gently, "Jaden, sweetheart? Come meet your mother."

Jaden glanced at Bri before asking, "She's not dead, is she?"

Shalbriri shook his head. "No. Not yet."

She breathed a sigh of relief. "Good. Because three resurrection requests are enough at one time."

The King twisted to look at them, his expression clearly annoyed. "Jaden, please come here."

Swallowing back unwanted bile, Jaden stepped forward. Once she reached the bed, Seth patted a spot on the mattress. "Sit next to her." She did so. "Take her hand." She did that as well. His gaze darted to the Queen's peacefully sleeping face, staring at it for a few minutes.

Finally, the lingering silence turned awkward, prompting Jaden to ask, "Is something supposed to be happening?"

"Well, I thought so," Seth responded, scratching his head again, "I did everything she said: brooch, daughter, holding of hands... She mentioned a reminder..."

Bri spoke up by asking, "What reminder?"

Seth groaned, "I don't know, something about reminding her of the last chunk of years, why she did all this precautionary stuff, the protecting of our family and child, I don't know." His tone clearly spoke for his exasperation.

Jaden's gaze darted over her lap, lost in thought. A reminder of the last chunk of years? If this really was her sister, she'd spent most of Jaden's life back on Earth. It would be a long shot, but…

Almost on instinct, her hand snapped out and hit the Queen's shoulder with a soft slap.

The King looked absolutely appalled. "Jaden!"

She ignored him and barked, "Dove, I swear if you take my laptop again, I will kill you!"

"Oh, don't make me laugh, pipsqueak!" The Queen yelled back, bolting up where she lay in the bed. Instant stunned silence filled the room as Jaden and the Queen stared at each other. The snarling expression quickly flipped, smiling warmly at her. "JJ?"

Jaden smiled back. "The one and only."

Dove asked, "Didn't think you could get rid of me so easy, did you?"

"I might have been hoping."

Catching onto her sarcasm instantly, the Queen laughed, "Same old Jaden." She got onto her knees, albeit a little shaky, and hugged Jaden tight. In the girl's ear, she muttered, "Welcome home, pipsqueak."

Stifling a laugh, Jaden squeezed her back. "Good to be home, gym rat."

Chapter 25

Steam hissed from the curling iron. Jaden meticulously pulled small chunks of hair, consecutively wrapping each around the heated, metal cylinder and pressing the clasp closed. Once satisfied, she released the hair to dangle down in flawless curls.

No, not her hair. She'd pixie cut hers for a reason: low maintenance.

"Are we finished yet?"

Guess her 'sister's' impatience reflected the older Queen perfectly. Rolling her eyes, Jaden replied, "Hold your horses. Almost done."

Dove sighed, slumping in her seat. "Well, hurry up."

"Don't you have servants to do this for you? Ladies-maids? Anything like that?"

With a shrug, she replied, "We really don't have many, to be honest. Your father prefers us to live as much like our citizens as possible. Empathy and all that. It has brought us closer to them, and closer to peace with other kingdoms. Now, make this snappy. We still have to get you ready too."

"Okay, I'll ask again for the ten-millionth time," Jaden sighed, "*For what?*"

"Dinner."

The short, simple answer told Jaden absolutely nothing. "Um, elaborate, please?"

Dove picked at her nails, a habit sister Dove had possessed. The reality that her annoying older sister had actually given birth to her became more and more obvious.

And more and more unsettling.

"Your father has a grand welcome dinner for your safe return home. He invited nobles and royals from everywhere. It would be rude not to attend a dinner in your honor, doncha think?"

Jaden felt a quick throb around her left temple as her old annoyance at her fake sister continued to grow. "Yes, that would be rude. But, you fail to notice something kind of important." She untwirled the last set of curls and flicked off the curler's power switch.

As Jaden gently placed the heater on the vanity, Dove turned to her. "And what's that?"

Moving her face just inches from the Queen's, Jaden snarled, "I don't want one!"

After Jaden pulled back and walked across the bedroom, Dove countered, "Pfft, doesn't matter. What Seth says, goes. You're in his territory now. Get over yourself, pipsqueak."

Screeching to a halt, Jaden clenched her fists, face burning hot. As her eyes squeezed shut, she tried to regulate her breathing as calm as she could. "Why are you still mocking me?" she snapped, "You're my freaking mother. Act like one!"

Dove's chair made a slight squeak, signaling the Queen had turned around. "I apologize, Jaden. You must understand that after that day last week, when your life changed, mine did too. Melding two fully-formed personalities, the one that was your sister and the one that has been Queen for almost two decades, is no easy task. The more hyper one usually comes out on instinct, I've found thus far. In case you can't read into that, the Sister role usually overrules."

At the same time, that both made sense and didn't make sense. Jaden continued to calm her breathing, at least to try and understand where Dove was coming from.

"Cat got your tongue, sneakers?"

That does it!

Jaden spun back around, eyes narrowed in annoyed, pissed fury. "Look here, buff brat. I'm done with only getting parts of the whole truth. If anyone knows how much I hate being out of the loop, it would be my sister. So, stop being such a jerk!"

"Jaden!"

The roar of fury and disappointment drew Jaden's attention to the door, where the King, her father, stood shell-shocked and red-faced. "You do not talk to your mother like that, young lady!"

Rolling her eyes, she walked over to the bed, on which, as Dove always had, the sheets had been balled in a messy heap. Was this really how a Queen kept her bed? While her sister slash mother couldn't have cared less, Jaden's instincts urged her to fix the glaringly annoying problem. "To the best of my knowledge, she is my sister, not my mother. So, as such, I will address her as I always have. That okay with you, health nut?"

After pulling the last corner of the fitted sheet around the mattress, she grabbed the ball that contained both the Queen's sheets and comforter and started separating the two. When she realized the awkward silence hanging in the air, she lifted her gaze to her parents. Seth stared at her, his face a cross between shock and worry. "What?" Jaden asked, raising an eyebrow.

Seth blinked in confusion. For what reason? "You're making a bed."

Shaking out the flat sheet, she replied curtly, "Yup. Is there a problem?"

A brief pause filled the air until he replied, "You're a Princess."

"Sooooo? My arms and legs aren't broken."

She heard both a heavy sigh from her father and laughter from her old sister. The latter commented, "Still the same JJ. Stubborn as an ox with the obsessions of a perfectionist."

Jaden snapped back, "Who asked your opinion, Peanut Gallery?" Dove blowing a raspberry at her boiled her blood. Eyes narrowing, she glared daggers at Dove. "Stop testing me," she growled.

Waving a hand at her dismissively, Dove drawled, "That look didn't work before, and it doesn't work now. You don't intimidate me, pipsqueak. Now, I believe you were making my bed like a common maid?"

Growling quietly to herself, she continued her impulsive bed fixing. Her movements became rigid, almost jerking, perfectly portraying her frustration and bubbling rage.

"Look, I understand the reality of this is hard to understand-"

Jaden cut her father off, saying, "Really? I thought understanding all this was easy as riding a bike."

"You… You understand all this?"

Forcing an obviously fake smile, she replied, "Yeah, of course I do." Her eyes darted away from the sheet to see her father with the most confused and torn expression she'd ever seen on an adult. And she'd seen her ninth-grade history teacher watch Lukas gallop across a stage in a toga, skinny jeans, and hi-tops.

The look on his face didn't change until Dove told him, "Seth, dear? Sarcasm."

Realization mixed with a relieved sigh finally altered his stone-stiff look of perplexity. "Ah, that makes sense." Then, his brow furrowed, flipping emotions like a light switch. "Jaden, don't hide behind sarcasm."

"Oh no, I don't hide *behind* sarcasm," Jaden responded flippantly, laying the edge of the sheet toward the headboard, "I stand by its side and flick hats off of baseball players. They don't like that, but believe me, it's a blast." Her eyes darted back up again to see the confused expression gracing his Majesty's face again. Sighing, she added, "Can't you take a joke?"

Dove also sighed, standing up. "Seth, trust me, she's always been this difficult. You'll get used to her brand of crazy eventually."

As his wife sauntered across the room like a fashion model – *Yep, definitely my sister* – Seth replied with a furrowed brow, "To be entirely honest, I really don't understand what is happening here either. You two are acting close. Too close for being separated since Jaden's toddler years."

Jaden scoffed, "Why don't you ask Miss Legally Blonde over there, because I'm just as confused."

After two minutes of Jaden and the King boring their eyes into her, Dove groaned, "Alright, alright, I'll explain. Seth, you are already aware that my magic system is messed up. Always has been."

Seth nodded. "Yep. Keep going."

With another deep inhale, Dove continued, "I learned shortly after Jaden was born that I had a gift for duplication. Didn't you wonder how I could be a full-time mother and help run a kingdom?" When the King looked at a loss for words, Dove's lip twitched. "I thought so. When we made the decision to send Jay away for her safety, I couldn't just hand her over without some kind of fail-safe. So, I duplicated myself, and inserted the doppleganger into her new life as her sister. I had a contact that turned that doppleganger into a young child, so being an older sibling closer in age would be more believable."

"So…" Jaden had been slightly shocked at this revelation, but not as paralyzed as her father, who currently stood in the doorway, white as a sheet and stiff as a board. "How is it that you remember everything from all those years?"

"I started pulling bits of that clone back over six weeks ago. By recalling parts of that dupe's life, she started glitching, as it were."

Jaden thought back, instantly knowing what her mother was talking about. "Yeah, your memory started going downhill. First it was short-term, but then you started getting bitter and even more unbearable than the rest of our time together."

With a soft hiccup of a weak laugh, Dove added, "You'd be bitter too if you couldn't remember milestones in your life, while also dealing with a sister that kept bringing them up." Jaden averted her eyes, blushing and feeling horrible about herself. If she'd known at the time what had been happening, she'd have gone easier. However, she figured the Queen wouldn't have known the consequences when she'd made up her mind years ago to go through with this.

After a few more brief moments of silence, Dove continued, "The overload of emotions, relationships, and memories became too much, and my regular body overloaded, sending me into that coma. I left your father a note just in case that happened, explaining how to bring me back. I knew he couldn't do it himself, because it required someone from the coma-inducing memories to know what to remind me of: the mission I'd given myself to keep you safe. To remind me of watching my baby grow up." Her eyes swam with tears. Softly groaning, she wiped them away with the back of her hand. "Damn, I'm glad we haven't done makeup yet."

Jaden snickered, bringing Dove's attention back to her. "And yet, it doesn't feel like anything's changed. Are you planning on still acting like my bratty, workout junkie of a sister, or are you going to somehow turn into a frantic, overprotective parent like Sir Clueless over there?" She nodded in Seth's direction to find the King leaning against the door frame with his head aimed toward the ground, muttering to himself, "She hid this…She hid this… from me…She… She hid…"

As Jaden cocked a knowing eye back to her, Dove sighed, "Look, kiddo, I'm not going to mince words. I may have given birth to you, but I didn't raise you as a parent. I lived alongside you as an equal. I'm not going to be overbearing like a mother should. But, that doesn't mean I won't protect you. In my eyes – and probably yours as well – I've been your sister. And, if anything threatens you or anyone you care about, then Big Sissy's gonna whoop some serious ass. You feel me?"

Jaden's mouth tugged into a grateful smile. "Yeah, I do, Sis. Or do I have to call you Queen DD from now on?"

"Sis is fine from you. But, if Kohei tries to call me that, all bets are off."

Jaden's face fell. "Wait… Did Lukas know?"

Dove nodded. "Yeah, he knew the whole time. How else did he manage to flawless change from furry companion to human bestie that easily?"

The world stopped for Jaden. She'd known about his paladin status for a week now. Did it never occur to him at any point to tell her that her older sister was actually her mother? "Some bestie…" She muttered, sitting on the partially-made bed. Her fingers started fiddling again as she processed everything.

Taking a seat next to her, Dove wrapped her arms around her comfortingly. "But, that shouldn't matter. He was just doing his job."

As she bit back stinging tears, Jaden murmured, "He could have told me after the fact… He could have been honest with me…"

"Maybe he didn't want to accept it either."

That got Jaden's attention. Lifting her gaze, she pried, "What do you mean by that?"

"Well, I think he became content with the normal life. Keep in mind he grew up alongside you. While he knew the truth, he couldn't help but wish things could have stayed the way they had been. He dreaded the day when you'd get pulled back here, because it meant changing the only life you – and he – ever knew. In that aspect, he's in more pain and disbelief than you, because while he knew reality would set in, he didn't know when or how it would happen. This whole ordeal probably shook him up too. He wouldn't have told you, because he's supposed to protect you, and not the other way around. He probably held back information because he didn't want you to be hurt that he'd hidden all this from you."

The dam broke, and tears poured down Jaden's cheeks. Dove pulled her in tighter, clutching her daughter's head to her chest. "It's okay, Jay. At least you still have the two of us. Imagine if you had to get roped back in to all this without knowing anybody."

Jaden chuckled weakly and sniffled. "Yeah. That'd be horrible."

Dove rubbed Jaden's back. "You know, just because I'm difficult on you doesn't mean I don't care."

Nodding, Jaden replied, "Yeah, I know."

"In fact, you're the reason I was so annoying and difficult." When Jaden lifted her head to look at her, Dove's face had cracked a smile. "How else could I realistically be called a sister if I didn't push all your buttons?"

Jaden shoved her lightly, grinning. "You're unbelievable, gym rat."

"And you're unbearable, sneakers," Dove countered, mirroring her grin.

"And both of you are in big trouble!"

The two females directed their gaze to the doorway to find King Seth glaring at them. Dove asked, "What's wrong, dear?"

Swiping his hand rigidly through the air, Seth replied, "Don't 'dear' me! How could you have hidden this from me? For so many years, no less?"

Dove tucked a chunk of curls back behind her ear. "Well, it honestly wasn't that hard. Your mind is always running a million miles a minute, so hiding the exhaustion from the clone's activities is a lot easier than you might think."

The King's clenched fists shook slightly. "Were you ever going to tell me?"

Picking at her nails again, Dove told him bluntly, "Nope, not really. Knew the truth would come out eventually."

"What happened to you, Dee?" He asked, obviously angry and frustrated. "This isn't you!"

Rubbing her rough nails on her oversized graphic tee, Dove snapped, "Well, excuse me for having to combine two entirely different personalities inside my brain at once. Am I not adjusting fast enough for you, your Majesty?" Acid laced in her bitter words, more obvious than a railroad crossing and twice as red.

Her words visibly hit home to the King, seen by the red in his cheeks instantly paling. "Dove, sweetheart, I didn't mean to upset you-"

"You didn't, did you?" Dove countered bitterly, "What about planning a spontaneous party for a Princess that doesn't want one?"

Jaden stood up, hands up in the universal 'STOP' signal. "Whoa, hold up. Don't drag me into this."

Seth's hardened gaze softened as it moved to her. "Is that true, Jaden?"

Sighing, Jaden crossed her arms. "I will admit I wasn't prepared for one, but it might be f-"

"JAY!"

Hearing Jessi's voice for the first time in over twenty-four hours felt like a relieving breath of fresh air. Her expression perked up as the teen girl ran past Seth and barreled toward her. "Jess!" Hugging the girl felt so comfortable, so nostalgic, even if the last time they'd hugged had only been a day or two ago. "Oh, I missed you, girlie."

Jessi giggled, "I know. Me too." They broke apart, grinning like madmen.

"Hey, what about me?"

Kiran's voice came from the other side of the bed. Turning to him, Jaden asked, "Mister Tough Guy wants a girly hug?"

Rolling his eyes, he opened his mouth, pointed a finger toward it, and mockingly gagged. "Blech, please, of course not. I wouldn't mind hearing that I was missed though."

"Alright, I missed you too, Kiran."

Puffing out his chest, Kiran replied, "I know. People just can't get enough of me, can they?"

Jessi smiled, obviously holding back laughter at her ridiculous brother. "Okay, drama king, you can stop being overly dramatic now."

His hands on his hips, Kiran stuck up his nose. "But my audience demands it."

"Please, your audience is begging you for a swift death."

Jaden snorted again at Jessi's burn, hands instantly clapping over her face. The other three – Dove included – howled with laughter, obviously amused. When she glanced at her father, a curiously new emotion rested on his facial features and body language. Relaxed muscles. Kind, calm eyes. Sincere smile. Slow, measured breathing.

That was the look of a proud, content father.

And it made Jaden finally start to feel she was home.

After he turned and left the room, Jaden's attention moved back to the others. Jessi twirled around, the bottom of her dress flying outwards. Red and green cherries spotted all over the white fabric of the girl's sundress. Dove smiled warmly, commenting, "That's a really pretty dress,

Jessica. Guess being a spirit has its perks. I'd give my left arm to be able to snap my fingers and instantly change my clothes to my desires."

"No, you wouldn't," Jessi countered, "You need both arms to use an elliptical, right?"

Dove stared into space, tapping her chin with a finger. "That is quite a problem, isn't it? A choice between ultimate fashionista and fit as a bodybuilder… Hm, toughie…"

Jaden swallowed back a snicker, and then added into the conversation, "You, fit as a bodybuilder? Do you think buff chicks like that stuff their faces with cheesecake after a workout?"

Both Kiran and Jessi went ashen.

Dove smirked and countered with, "Do star business students still like riding the merry-go-round at amusement parks?"

Kiran and Jessi's mouths dropped open.

Crossing her arms, Jaden replied, "You don't see me insulting your love for Disney movies."

Fingers curling into fists, Dove snapped, "Hey, those movies have very adult themes!"

"What about when you cried when Flynn almost died in *Tangled*?"

"He finally loved another person! She was gonna lose him!"

As a single tear rolled down the Queen's face, Jaden closed her eyes and smiled smugly. "I rest my case."

Silence filled the air for a few moments before Jaden realized it existed. Opening her eyes, she instantly recognized expressions of mixed shock on the twins' faces. Cocking an eyebrow, she asked slowly, "Is there a problem?"

Jessi blinked a few times, then shook her head so hard her bob cut hair flew around. "Let me get this straight. You're allowed to speak to your mother like that?"

Kiran added, “A mother that is queen of the Five Kingdoms?”

Jaden and Dove exchanged looks, both of them cracking smiles. Dove wrapped an arm around Jaden’s waist and pulled her hard to her side. “More than a mother, more than a queen.” Looking up at Jaden, she finished, “We’re sisters.”

“Yeah,” Jaden said, “Sisters for life. Stuck with each other no matter what.”

Linking pinkies with her, Dove chuckled softly, “Forever and always.”

Chapter 26

A soft string of knocks echoed from Jaden's new bedroom door. She lifted her head, looking away from the mirror at it. Her hands remained near her ear, fiddling with a dangle earring. "Be right there!" she called out, focusing on her reflection and the annoyance that was pierced ears. Why she'd pierced them in the first place, she'd probably never know. From her personality to her fashion sense, she screamed low maintenance. But, she'd been so young at the time, she convinced herself it involved her sister, some duct tape, and a torturous romcom blaring through their home theatre system. Seven-year-old Jaden wouldn't have stood a chance.

Her pixie cut black and bleached hair had been slicked back with hair gel, making her almost unrecognizable. Dresses never impressed her, but the dark sapphire color of the one she currently wore surprisingly looked good. Mainly because it appeared black in low light.

Luckily, Dove knew her well enough to select shoes that would both complement the dress and feel comfortable. Enter black knee-high boots, laces only for decoration and flat soles solely to keep her upright. Just Jaden's style.

The knocking reached her ears again, just as she got the earring in. Sliding the plastic cap around the metal hook, she called out again, "Give me a sec!" Sighing, she took two steps back. The reflection staring back felt both like her and not like her at the same time. Not just because of the clothes either. No amount of makeup covered the dark shadows and wrinkles under her eyes. No amount of antiseptic healed the cuts on her arms, nor could an equal amount of base liquid disguise the bruising and rope burns on various spots of her body.

And nothing could repair the damaged, stressed, and overwhelmed emotions visible in the weathered gaze that reflected back at her. The week-long journey home had been rough enough. Now she had to sit at an extravagant table with fancy-schmancy food, probably talking to old nobility and getting multiple suitors hanging on her every word.

Great. Haven't I suffered enough?

For a third time, those knocks rang out again. A quick throb stabbed her head as she barked, "I'm coming!" As she walked to the door, she muttered to herself, "Can't catch a break, can I?" When she opened the door, a welcome guest surprised her, her eyes instantly lighting up.

"Good evening, Princess," Lukas greeted, bowing more dramatically than was required. "I am to be your escort this evening."

She easily caught the humor in his words and motions, her smile growing. "Why, I am honored, good sir." She curtsied with an eyeroll, which had Lukas snickering.

"The honor is all mine, I'm sure." He straightened, grinning from ear to ear. "Same old Jay."

She countered, "Same old Wolfe."

"Touché."

Jaden bridged the small gap and hugged him tightly. "I missed you, Lukas."

Rubbing her back, Lukas responded softly, "Of course you did. Everyone misses me when I disappear. The mystery is a part of my attractiveness and universal appeal."

Shoving him back with a smile, Jaden scoffed with a slight teasing tone, "Attractiveness? Please. Spare me the torture of having to lie."

"C'mon, Jay!" Lukas begged, "Just a small, white lie?" He lifted a hand and kept only a small gap between his bent pointer finger and thumb, symbolizing something miniscule.

Mouth twitching, she replied, "Fine. All ladies want you, and every guy wants to be you."

Grinning, he laughed. "Okay, I know that's bigger than a white lie." A few moments later, the grin softened, but didn't vanish. "You look beautiful, Princess."

Her breath caught in her throat as she took in his appearance. The sweet, caring look in his eyes only just iced the cake. He looked handsome in his tux. A red corsage had been pinned to his jacket, right over his heart. His shaggy hair now possessed some refinement, slicked back like a businessman. Or Draco Malfoy. Or Leo DiCaprio in *The Great Gatsby* remake. "You…" She forced a smile, albeit a bit twitchy. "You look handsome as well, Lukas."

Her smile wasn't forced because she was lying.

She definitely wasn't lying.

It was forced for one glaring reason.

She had feelings for him.

Her mind tried to deny the meaning behind her words, but couldn't hide the truth from herself. Yes, he was handsome. Her heart pounded in her chest, cheeks burning something terrible. *No, this has to be wrong. I'm just… overwhelmed. There's just no way.*

Lukas' brow furrowed. "You okay, Jaden?" Jaden nodded, but her friend obviously didn't look convinced. "You wanna lie down for a minute?"

She shook her head. "Dinner's already started, and I don't want to make my father mad." When Lukas cocked a knowing eyebrow, she huffed.

"Fine, I'll correct that. Dinner's already started, and the sooner we get out of that snooze-fest, the better."

Lukas smiled. "*That's* the Jaden Walker I remember. Now, if you are denying the lie-down, you'll probably regret it later. This dinner might wear you out."

Titling her head slightly, she asked, "Why would I regret it? It's just fancy food at a long dinner table, talking to old people and trying not to puke up anchovies or caviar."

Lukas crossed his arms and gave her a curiously condescending look. "What kind of dinner parties do you think they throw here? Sixteenth century royal balls with suitors and social graces?" While Jaden pondered her assumption – which seemed like she'd stereotyped her current situation – Lukas shook his head, small, humored smile evident on his face. "Setting your assumptions aside, this isn't an ordinary welcome home dinner anyway. His Majesty made it one you would enjoy."

"Please," Jaden scoffed. She pushed past Lukas and headed in the direction of the ballroom, one of the few rooms that she actually seen since arriving. Out of a thousand. Most of the others were a mystery behind their intricately carved doors, but she knew she'd be here long enough to find out what lay on the other side. "I doubt King Clueless could figure out what an Earthly, American young adult likes to do to celebrate good news."

The small, restrained smile on Lukas' face twitched. "You'll see, Princess."

As they got closer to their destination, the sound of pumping bass reached Jaden's ears. She stopped in her tracks, listening more intently. "Music? There's music? That isn't classical 'BS'?"

Lukas nodded, looped his arm around hers, and yanked her forward. "More than music, Jay." When they reached the massive double doors, the music became more discernible. And WAY more recognizable.

"Is that..." She stared at the doors as if she had X-Ray vision. "Is that what I think it is?" Her tone reflected both her excited shock and happy regret of her first assumption.

Lukas released her arm and placed a hand flat against each door. Turning his head to her, he replied, "You don't know the half of it." When he shoved the giant doors open with a loud grunt, the muffled hum of "*Hey Mama*" by The Black Eyed Peas blasted her full-force. The inside of the ballroom shocked her, but in a good way. The giant, long, dining table vanished, instead with small, circular tables clustered on both far sides. In place of the missing centrally-placed table were tons of people of all ages, dancing and singing and laughing and shouting. A disco ball and neon lights replaced the five chandeliers that had lit the room just that morning. The thrones still sat on the far side of the room with a sea of dancing, partying citizens to wade through.

"You like it?"

She ripped her gaze away from the party to look at Lukas. With a thin, partially-hidden smile, she punched him hard on the shoulder. She hit him a bit harder than she intended, making the playful meaning behind the gesture lost on most everyone else. Luckily, Lukas wasn't like everyone else, as seen by the soft, almost silent laughter. As he rubbed the spot of impact, she answered, "More than that. I love it."

"Good."

"But, I have one question..." she continued, "How did this music end up here? Obviously, we're not in our old... area." She still needed clarification on how her old world was in relation to this new one, this Five Kingdoms world. She hadn't had much time to breathe since she'd arrived, much less ask weird questions whose answers probably would make her head explode.

Lukas nodded, acknowledging her confusion and, to Jaden's delight, ignored it entirely. *Thank God. I've got enough to juggle right now.* "We had a method of transferring old mp4 files and converting them to the format that works with the tech here."

Cocking her head, she asked, "Where'd you get the mp4-" He lifted his right hand, the fingers pinching her iPod. "-files." Giving him a slightly condescending glare, she snapped teasingly, "You went through my stuff."

"Not technically," he answered, lifting a single finger in opposition. "Technically, I had it the whole time, remember?" He uncurled his fingers and held out his hand, palm and iPod on top. To Jaden's amazement, the music player floated just a few inches above his hand. Then, Lukas snapped the fingers on his free hand, and the device fizzled out in a cluster of twitching lines. After a few moments, she realized a stupid, amazed look graced her face.

Shaking her head, she scowled. "Yeah, yeah, tell it to the judge."

He smiled warmly at her, bringing those butterflies back. Was her body trying to tell her something? She didn't want a confirmation, but knew the truth behind her queasy stomach. And she'd already realized it earlier.

She *definitely* had feelings for Lukas.

But that couldn't be! They had been friends her whole life. These feelings would only complicate things and might even ruin their friendship. He had been like a brother to her since grade school. So, what happened in the last week that changed that feeling? When she gazed into his sapphire eyes, she felt lightheaded. Any worries melted away.

Lukas held out a hand. "Shall we crash this party?"

Snapping out of his hypnotic hold on her, Jaden recognized a song change. The Queen of Pop, Britney Spears, replaced the Zumba-esque, pop rhythms, the song "*Perfect Lover*" blasting through the giant speakers scattered around the perimeter of the ballroom. Smiling, she took his hand. "You bet."

They only took two steps inside when the throngs of partiers noticed them. Instantaneous cheering blared through the room, mixing with the pop song's bass to create a loud roar echoing through the room.

Smiling down at her, Lukas told her, "That's all for you, Princess."

Even as the cheers died down, warm blush dusted her cheeks. "Okay. Wow." That was all she could muster, but better than her usual shocked, "Uh huh."

As they walked for the throne side of the crowd, people cleared the way. The partiers smiled and waved as they passed by, the words they greeted her with muffled from the blasting music. She nodded and smiled, occasionally waving at some individuals that freaked out afterward. When they finally reached the other side, before them stood four thrones. Her father sat in one, while Dove occupied the one to his right. Dove slouched in her throne, fidgeting with the silver and amethyst ring that adorned her finger. Guess having a wedding ring on that finger felt slightly foreign, based on the curiously blank expression on the Queen's face. Or, at least felt foreign to the sister half of her.

There sat two empty thrones to the King's left. Jaden had a weird feeling one was for her. Seth patted the edge of the one to his immediate left. "C'mon, Princess. Take a seat."

Yep, knew it.

Sighing, she reluctantly let go of her friend's hand and approached the throne. When she sat down, it surprised her that it actually felt comfortable. Didn't expect that. She glanced at the last empty one. "Who's that one for?"

"For Shalbriri."

Oh. Great. "Really? Why?"

Sighing, her father answered, "Well, he is a Prince of the Five Kingdoms."

Muffling a snort of derision, she commented, "Prince of the Five Kingdoms? More like Prince of annoying stoicism."

"Okay, I get it. Because I've been informed you have mixed feelings about him."

Jaden turned to him, cocking an eyebrow. "And who exactly told you that?"

Seth smiled crookedly. "He did. And, just so you know, that upsets him greatly."

"At least I'm giving him a chance, unlike..." She stopped, scanning the throngs of dancing celebrators. "Where's the twins?"

Britney faded out. At first, the new song was so soft, Jaden couldn't guess. After about fifteen seconds, a yelp rang out, and not just from the intro to Michael Jackson's "*Smooth Criminal*".

"Watch and learn, gentlemen!"

Kiran's confident voice redirected Jaden's attention. He had his arms stretched out, clearing other people out of his way. A few moments later, he started performing perfect MJ dancing moves. She had to admit, his moonwalk was impressive.

"Does that answer your question?"

"Yeah..." Jaden replied, lost in thought. Then, she looked at her father again, asking, "How can everyone see them? I thought only Channelers and people witnessing their deaths could see spirits in Limbo."

After a heavy sigh, the King responded, "Everyone can't. Look around at how many people his audience consists of."

As Kiran continued his almost flawless MJ impersonation, Jaden gazed around the ballroom. Sure, a good number of people watched the teen spirit bust a move, but that number sat in the small minority. "That's still a lot of people…" she muttered, slightly unnerved and horrified.

"Their deaths had a large enough audience, unfortunately," Seth replied, "Even I witnessed it from my balcony. Brutal, undeserved murders."

Jaden glanced at Kiran again to find Jessi dancing near him, nowhere near as flawless as her twin brother. Despite dancing like nobody was watching, the two were smiling and laughing the whole time. Jaden smiled at their fun, but also felt a lump in her throat. After a few seconds, the smile faded as a rather important, unanswered question pushed into her train of thought. She was lucky that train hadn't derailed yet. "How did they die, exactly? I know it was their father delivering the blows, but how did he deal those blows, and did he have any particular reasons?"

"Someone probably already explained the demonic ties of the Theron bloodline, correct?" When she nodded, he continued, "He lost control. His hold on his demon shattered, and the vicious beast took him over, sending him on a rampage. He couldn't differentiate between ally or enemy, friend or rival, stranger or family." Jaden easily heard the King choking up. "He had no reasons, but he wasn't at fault in the slightest. He adored his kids. The raging bloodlust of his demon eliminated any regrets or guilt, and completely took him over. When he lost control of it, he also lost all of his morals, values, and sense of humanity."

"That's horrible!" Jaden looked back at the two teens, choking up as well. "How did they end up in Limbo anyway?" Bri had already told her, but she still wasn't sure she could trust him yet. A second opinion couldn't hurt.

Seth shrugged. "Guess God wanted to give them another chance."

She knew that wasn't true, but believed it was just lack of information on the King's part. While she wouldn't argue for or against a higher power, she'd been told first-hand knowledge from someone who'd been living it. Skylar explained staying in Limbo was a choice on the part of the deceased after death. Shalbriri had given more details on the twins in particular. Jessi stayed for her brother's sake, wanting to watch out for him. Kiran stayed out of regret, rage, and chance at retribution after his untimely death. There lied a big question in that explanation.

Why the rage?

And… toward whom?

The song ended, and loud cheers echoed from those watching Kiran. The yelling and merriment shocked Jaden back to reality. Kiran beamed with pride. Jessi walked over to him, hugged him, and then whispered something in his ear. It must've had something to do with her, because he then looked in her direction. After he nodded a few times, they broke apart and approached her. A few feet away, both stopped and bowed to her, Jessi's a curtsy in that same cherry-spotted dress. Kiran cleaned up nice, sporting a crisp, wrinkle-less red dress shirt, black slacks, and… sneakers? Really? She mentally rolled her eyes. Then again, a majority of the people there couldn't see him or his choice of footwear, so no risk of embarrassment or regret. Plus, this was Kiran. After only knowing him for a week, she should have guessed as much would happen from him.

"Good evening, Princess," they greeted in unison.

Jaden cracked a smile. "You too, guys." When they stood upright again, beaming smiles appeared on their faces.

"We got you home, Jay," Jessi said.

With a nod, Jaden replied, "Yeah, you did. Congrats."

"We should be thanking you, Jaden," Kiran added, "Your promise means the world to us."

Seth stiffened, abruptly halting whatever he was talking to his wife about and spinning to the three of them. "Wait, what promise?"

Jessi paled slightly, one foot stepping backward in a fight-or-flight instinct. Obviously, Jessi knew the King's words were not friendly. Kiran, on the other hand, remained oblivious to both his sister's fear and his King's worry and fury. "Princess Jaden said she'd bring me and JV back."

Seth's expression hardened, teetering on the ledge of frustration and fury. "She. Said. What?" His eyes darted between Kiran and Jaden as if unsure who to ask.

The King's tone finally broke through Kiran's naïve bubble, his face turning ashen as his sister's had moments before. His eyes darted to his sneakers, fiddling with his hands nervously. "Um… I…" He bit his lip, obviously not wanting to repeat something that enraged the King.

"She cannot do that. You understand, right? It would take years of non-stop training to even get close to achieving that skill set. A Channeler hasn't resurrected a spirit in centuries!"

After a brief pause of hesitation, Kiran muttered, "Mama said she'd be able to…"

When Seth's face burned red, Jaden pushed herself out of her comfy chair and stepped between the two. "Years or not, I promised to resurrect them. Is there a problem with that?"

A loud bang rang out, scattering a screaming crowd to opposite walls. Something hit Seth's throne with a metallic clang just inches from his head. His eyes widened to extreme shock, staring past Jaden. Jaden, however, focused on the projectile, now rolling on the floor next to the royal chair.

A bullet.

"Yeah, your Majesty…"

She froze. She knew that voice. Spinning to focus on what everyone else was, she instantly recognized the man.

"Is there a problem with that?" With a slightly cocked head, Jakob Kalea, one of the pair that had made the trip home seem like an escape room, held a small gun at arm's length, staring at the group near the throne almost hungrily.

Clearing his throat, the King asked, "Why are you scaring my guests, Jakob?"

Rolling his shoulders, he took a few more steps forward and stopped. "See, your Majesty, I have been given a special mission by my true royal ruler to ensure that Kiran and Jessica Theron get back the life that was wrongly taken from them."

Brow furrowing, Seth replied, "I recall giving you no such mission."

A soft, teasing smile twitched onto Jakob's face. "You didn't. King Raiden did."

Jessi drew in a sharp breath, hands slowly lifting to cover her mouth. Her body shook slightly as she stared at Jakob with wide, stressed eyes. "What?" she squealed, tone obviously more shocked and scared than excited and happy. That tone confused Jaden. Wouldn't Jessi be happy that her father still existed and cared enough to ensure their return to life?

Oh.

That was why.

He was the one that killed them.

Damn, almost forgot that detail.

Kiran's eyes narrowed. "Lies! My father died that day. At the hands of Skylar Meisyn."

With a soft breath of a chuckle, Jakob shook his head. "He's in Limbo, Kiran. I've seen him myself. He requested this of me. 'Bring my kids back'…" His gaze moved from Kiran to Jaden, and the confidently hungry look in it sent a sharp chill down her spine. "… 'Whatever it takes'. It would be disrespectful of me to not obey my King's wishes."

Jaden glanced first at Kiran, then shaking Jessi, finally her father and mother. "My King? I thought you were King?"

Seth waved her off dismissively, "I'll explain that later, sweetheart. In case you haven't noticed, he's threatening our lives." Then, he directed his attention back to the party crasher. "You're outnumbered, Jakob."

Jakob's smile twitched. "Am I? You fail to notice what's already been done." He gestured to both sides of the ballroom, where partiers stood in clumps in fear and terror. Jaden caught a slight, red rippling effect, almost like a wall.

"Damn…" Seth muttered, "He's barricaded us off."

Jaden looked back at the ballroom, and noticed soldiers flying back as they threw blows at the psychic barriers. Then, a handful of blue camo soldiers dashed into the ballroom, all sporting weapons of all kinds.

Jakob shrugged, his smile transforming into a wicked grin. "Your move, your Majesty."

Seth's skin burned red with rage. "Interrupt my daughter's party, you better damn well believe I'll make a move."

Dove's hand shot out, stopping the King mid-standing. "She's got this, love."

His head snapped to his wife. "She who?"

Jaden smiled, almost as confident and wicked as Jakob. She dug her fingers into the Velcro at the side of her sparkling dress and ripped it free. The dress fell to the floor, revealing the spandex shirt and leggings that had been hiding underneath. She ripped free two sticks from each thigh, twirling them in her hands. She looked back at her father, who sat in his throne dumbstruck. Shrugging, she told him, "I come prepared." She glanced at Jessi and Kiran, both who stared at her with wide, excited eyes. "I'll bring you back, but on my terms, not his."

After hopping down the stairs, she firmly planted her feet on the tiled floor. Gazing deep into Jakob's eyes, she called out, "Wolfe, '*Do It Well*'!"

Lukas shouted back from somewhere, "You got it, Princess!"

After a few seconds, Jennifer Lopez's "*Do It Well*" started, blaring through all the speakers in the room. As the intro played, she cracked her neck, confidence and adrenaline rising inside her. "Shall we?"

Right as J. Lo. started singing the first verse, she charged at the nearest soldier. Feigning a punch to the head, she dropped down and knocked his feet out from under him with a leg swipe. As he fell, another enemy reached her. As she spun back to an upright posture, she lifted a leg up mid-spin and clocked him hard in the skull. As he dropped his weapon, she swiped it up with one stick during her final twirl. Immediately after getting a firm grip, she shot a bullet from the weapon into that stunned man's foot. He crumbled.

Smile twitching confidently, she chuckled to herself, "This is cake."

A blur sped toward her in her peripheral vision. Without looking first, she twisted and threw out the rifle. It slammed into the man's skull with a sickening crack. As he fell in a heap, she lifted her gaze and met Jakob's. "Three down, one to go."

Jakob rolled his shoulders, but tossed his pistol to the side. "Mano y mano, Princess?"

Grinning at the adrenaline rush, she dropped the rifle and responded firmly, "Fine by me."

Jessi's voice reached her as she faced off with Jakob, "Woo! Go get 'em, Jay! Beat his hiney!"

Jaden's smile twitched at her friend's excited shout. When neither moved, she taunted, "What's the matter? Afraid to make the first move?"

Jakob's gaze narrowed dangerously. "I thought I would graciously allow you that honor, Princess."

"You think I'm that foolish? I'm not your ordinary Princess, dipwad."

His face reddened as he finally ran for her. They exchanged blow for blow, dodge for dodge, swipe for swipe. Only difference was Jaden landed a lot more than him. He obviously had at least been trained for combat, but his style and momentum lacked compared to her. When she shoved her knee into his private region, he yelped, grabbed at the impact location, and staggered back. He growled, "Resorting to that is low, Princess."

Shrugging, she replied, "I do what's necessary to ensure I don't die. Call it woman's instinct."

Jakob opened his mouth to counter, when loud electrical shocks sounded through the hall. Jakob convulsed, foaming at the mouth, and fell in a heap to the floor. The music went silent. Jaden's sight watched him as he fell, and she recognized pads with wires stuck to his back. She followed the wiring to the double doors to find a partially-friendly face.

"Not in this house, jackel," Shalbriri stated, pressing a button that yanked the wires and pads back into the Taser he held. His gaze lifted from the unconscious, twitching enemy to her, and she felt heat rising to her cheeks. And she had an unsettling thought it wasn't just the adrenaline. The smallest of proud smiles appeared on his lips. "Impressive, Princess."

Jaden crossed her arms. "I told all of you I wasn't helpless. Guess magical journeys to unknown lands with superpowered people can shock the want to fight out of a girl."

He chuckled softly. "I knew there was something about you I liked."

"Um, JJ?"

Dove's voice redirected her attention back to the throne area. Her adoptive sister jerked a head toward the throne next to her, where her father sat hunched over, elbows on his legs, hands fiddling, mouth muttering unintelligible things to himself. Jaden raised an eyebrow at Dove, who simply shrugged and said, "Don't think he was expecting that performance, Sneakers."

With a heavy sigh, Jaden walked back up the center aisle and up to the thrones again. Once there, she placed a hand on the King's shoulder. "You okay there, Daddio?"

A few stuttered syllables later, his head snapped up, wide, almost crazed grin stretched across his face. "That was freaking amazing!" he shouted loudly, voice echoing throughout the ballroom. Thunderous cheers almost turned Jaden deaf as the entire group of partiers applauded her battle. Music played again, the cheers dying down and the regular hum of chatting amongst themselves hovered through the air again.

"We definitely didn't expect that."

Jaden looked to her right at Kiran, who gazed at her with wide-eyed wonder. The look mirrored itself in his twin sister's eyes as well. She shrugged again. "I told you all. I'm not a helpless damsel-in-distress. I studied various fighting styles since elementary school and used it to fight off bullies of weaker, more scared schoolmates. Trust me, I'm the furthest thing from vulnerable and defenseless."

After that, silence filled the air, aside from the background music of Fall Out Boy. A voice asked from behind Jaden, "So, what now?"

Jaden instantly spun around to find Lukas with a grim look on his face. When she turned back to her father, his expression crossed concern and worry with fear and anger. "I think we have to pay the Second Kingdom a visit."

Kiran and Jessi snapped to each other, wide, excited grins decorating both of their faces. Jessi squealed and hugged her brother. "We get to go home!"

Jaden felt a twinge of happiness for the twins, but she had an empty feeling in the pit of her stomach that worried her. Also, something else in the room unsettled her.

The looks on Seth and Lukas' faces hinted this might not be a cordial visit.

Chapter 27

The Second Kingdom actually was the closest of all the kingdoms. Jaden had been wrong about technology here as well, because they flew by woodsy highways in the Five Kingdoms' equivalent to a Porsche. Weirdly enough, the royal protection detail followed them instead of sitting in either of the two vehicles their group travelled in. Another weird part of this protection detail?

"Oh, good Lord, that breeze feels amazing!" Seth shouted, sticking his head halfway out of the driver's side window.

They allowed the King of Chaotic Overreacting to drive his own vehicle.

Jaden rolled her eyes from where she sat in the back seat. Dove had taken the front passenger's seat, after a loud shout of "Shotgun!," and shoving Jaden to the side. Seriously, was this really a full-grown woman? Royal or not, she remained the immature sister she'd grown up with. Did she really order an entire kingdom around? Definitely wouldn't have been Jaden's first pick.

The first leg of the trip consisted of her parents explaining the government structure to her. There were five individual kingdoms, with their own flags, exports, drinks, and even indigenous languages and celebrations. All of these five kingdoms operated both separately and united under the Five Kingdoms monarchy, which was where Jaden's family came in. Her father and mother, as the Majora monarchy, oversaw all of the individual kingdoms, protected each one, sent aid or assistance when needed, and essentially had more power over those citizens than the governments' themselves. The name explained so much already, but the clarification was appreciated.

"Um..." As she spoke, she saw the King eyeing her through the rearview mirror. "I fail to see how you feel safe doing that."

Seth arched an eyebrow. "How so?"

"I mean, a sniper could shoot you from the trees or something."

The confused look continued to glance at her from the mirror while also watching the road. "At this speed?"

Jaden groaned loudly, throwing herself against the back seat. "Forget it. Get shot. See if I care."

After a brief moment of silence, her partner in the back bench-style seating leaned forward. "Your Majesty," Shalbriri said, "I believe she is confused over why you feel safe doing that because of threats to your life from political and governmental arguments or differences in opinion."

"Why?" Seth's simple question made Jaden's blood boil.

"Why?" she snapped, annoyance clear in her tone, "Because maybe I don't feel like you getting sniped and killing all of us in this car!"

After she huffed and fell back into her seat, Bri looked at her with that same stoic expression for a few seconds before clarifying, "I believe she is just as concerned about your life as she is about the rest of ours. And, I believe the misunderstanding is due to assassinations that happened back where she was from."

"Ah." The King refocused on the road again. "Jaden, sweetheart, trust me, nobody would think about killing me while I'm driving."

Jaden scoffed, "Really? With the whole royal family in one vehicle that they could kill with one bullet to your head? I've seen enough cops shows and action-thriller movies to know this is a really bad situation you've put us in."

With a soft chuckle, he replied, "We're only about two miles away from the gates, and the castle of the Second Kingdom is the closest compound. Trust me, I think your irrational fear of a sniper won't happen. Besides, there isn't any dissonance within the Five Kingdoms. Outside of them, you might have something to worry about. But, the Five Kingdoms has been at peace for a good few years now. Nothing to worry about."

Sure enough, a few silent moments later, they arched over a hill, and her first glimpse of the Second Kingdom appeared in Jaden's sight. The walls shone a pitch dark, glimmering black, almost as if painted with metallic charcoal. The castle stood front and center, just as her father had said, towering high into the sky. The highest tower made the Seattle Space Needle look like a popsicle stick.

They came to a stop at the gates, and a soldier approached the driver's side. When he saw Seth in the driver's seat, he looked like he'd just peed his pants in shock. "Your Majesty!" he gasped.

Seth patted the rolled-down window. "Easy there, sport. Breathe a bit."

The young man nodded. "Yes, Sire, I'm sorry. We weren't expecting you until next week for the Detail ceremony."

"I wasn't expecting to either," he replied, "Look, kiddo. I need to speak with Stell. Is there any way I could see her?"

Stell? Jaden cast a sideways glance at Shalbriri, but his eyes were fixated on the towers looming above them.

"Yes, yes, of course, your Majesty!" the young soldier replied, "I will send you through, and let her know you are coming."

Seth smiled thankfully. “Appreciate it, kiddo. Keep that aim sharp.”

The man nodded. “Yes, I will, Sire.”

As the young soldier walked back to the guard’s station, Seth twisted to look at the two kids in the back. “Charisma. You two will need that eventually.”

The gates opened, and their parade of three cars pulled through. Jaden glanced at the car behind her to see how the others were doing. Lukas had taken it upon himself to drive, while Jessi and Kiran sat in the back. She saw the excited wonder in their eyes, and could only guess what they were currently feeling. Before falling asleep, Dove had explained to her that Jessica and Kiran Theron were the two oldest children of the Second Kingdom’s royals. Their father had actually been King before losing control that day six years ago. Since then, their mother had single-handedly presided over her late husband’s domain, quietly obeying the Majora’s orders, while at the same time holding his virtues firmly in her heart and actions.

It had been mentioned not too long ago that the twins had only taken on the mission to find Jaden about two years ago. What happened in the other four years as spirits? Based on the multiple stories she’d heard, their murders had occurred in the Majora’s capital, where they’d just come from. That meant that probably a huge percentage of their own people couldn’t see them, and thought that they’d lost most of their kindgom’s future in a single take. But, being sixteen and brutally murdered, and then not be able to tell their family, friends, and citizens that they were still with them… Jaden couldn’t even imagine what that felt like to them. She could now also understand why they’d volunteered to retrieve her. Not just for promise of resurrection, but they’d be able to escape the silent, never-ending, incommunicable hell they’d ended up in.

They pulled off in a secluded parking lot right before a grand set of midnight double doors. The carvings on them seems a bit more flowing than the ones back where they'd been before. In fact, they almost felt like hieroglyphics, as if telling stories. They all got out of the car and shut their doors.

Well, almost all of them.

Jaden rolled her eyes and moved her head just inches from the passenger's window, which, luckily, was rolled up. "RAH!" she shouted, jolting Dove awake. The Queen shrieked as she was awoken suddenly, eyes narrowing instantly into daggers upon seeing her surprise. Jaden held her stomach as pain from intense, hysterical laughter crippled her. "Oh my gracious God, that was priceless!" she cackled, wiping tears from her eyes as they leaked out.

Dove slammed her arm into the window, shocking Jaden enough to jump back, but not to stop the laughter. Her voice was only slightly muffled as she snapped, "Drop dead, you insufferable twit!"

"I'm sorry if you almost had a heart attack," Jaden laughed, "But that was more of a reaction than I expected!"

"Bite me, pipsqueak!"

Jaden countered, "You wish, gym rat."

Both of them realized the silence from everyone else and turned their attention to behind the car. Lukas had apparently parked the second car, and him, Jessi, and Kiran stood there just as dumbstruck and disbelieving as the King and Shalbriri. Both females narrowed their gazes and snapped in unison, "What?"

All of the others immediately averted their gazes to various other locations with mutters like, "Nope," "Nothing," "Didn't see anything," along with shaking heads.

Dove and Jaden looked at each other, the former with a sly smirk. She rolled the window a crack, enough so Jaden could hear her fully, "It pays to be royal, doesn't it? It has its perks. Getting pissed and then getting your way is only one. And it's kinda fun to watch the reactions you get."

"Nice." Grinning, Jaden pressed a fist to the window, to which Dove pushed hers against, mirroring the grin. "Now, you comin' or not?"

Dove scoffed. "Please. Watching your father pester poor Stella about a worry that shouldn't exist would be a snooze fest, and I don't care to be counted in the company of royals harassing her." She reclined her chair and laid back. "I'll be here if ya'll need me." Then, she pulled a baseball cap out of the glove box and rested it over her face. "Have fun, loser."

"Sleep well, has-been." Jaden walked around the car to the others. When she continued to get weird looks, she snapped, "Guys, I've explained this already! She's been my sister for over a decade, and my mother for *three days*. Both of us need time before we can adjust to reality."

She caught a humored twitch in Lukas' lips. "And how much time will that take?"

Her mouth twitched as well, instantly picking up on his joke. "A million, bajillion years."

Jessi's laughter shot saliva as spraying projectiles. Her hand instantly clapped over her mouth. She wiped dribbling spit from her lips. "Sorry… Just really wasn't expecting that answer." She sheepishly rubbed the back of her neck, a nervous, apologetic smile on her face.

"It's okay, Jess," Kiran replied, patting her on the back of her shoulders, "Remember, you need to be able to talk, because I can't do it for us."

Jaden arched an eyebrow. "Wait, what does that mean?" Everyone's attention snapped to her and then averted again. "Guys," she growled softly, "No more secrets. I thought we were all in agreement on that."

"My baby girl!"

Everyone, including Jaden, looked at the double doors. Now ajar, a thin brunette woman dashed out of them toward the group. She screeched to a stop a few feet from Jessi, tears in her eyes. "My sweet, darling Jessica Ann." Jaden thought it was odd at first that the woman, as excited as she was, didn't go to hug Jessi. Then, she remembered. *She can't. Jessi's not alive.*

Jessi grinned, tears welling up in her eyes too. "Hey, Mom."

"Wait, what?" Jaden stared at them, dumbstruck. Don't tell me this is…

Seth held out his arms for an embrace. "Stell, darling, you look amazing."

Damn it…

The woman her father wanted to interrogate turned out to be the twins' mother.

And the late King Raiden's wife.

Greaaaaat.

After the two royals separated, Seth wrapped an arm around the woman's shoulders. "Stell, this is my pride and joy. Jaden, this is Queen Estelle Theron, ruler of the Second Kingdom."

Jaden, still slightly numb, lifted a weak hand. "Hi."

Estelle looked to Seth. "Is she okay?"

Jaden's father rubbed the back of his neck. "Complicated."

"Ah, of course," Estelle replied, nodding her head in understanding, "Now, I have been told your visit wasn't just an in-the-neighborhood drive-by?"

"Yes. It's actually about your husband."

Estelle's face lost all color as she broke free of Seth's arm. "Raiden? I'm not sure exactly what this is about. He's been dead for over six years, as have my kids."

"Yes, well…" Seth sighed, shoulders slumping, "That's what I thought too, until Jakob Kalea crashed my daughter's party and said he'd received orders from him recently."

The Queen of the Second Kingdom had gone stiff and tense. "Yes, well…" She tucked a strand of her long, brown hair behind her ears, visibly shaking. "Would you mind us discussing inside? Rather the journalists poking around here would have a field day with this, if they learned you all are here."

Seth nodded. "Of course."

As they all walked toward the castle entrance, Estelle took the lead with Jessi and Kiran, followed by Seth and Shalbriri, with Jaden and Lukas bringing up the rear. There was something unsettling about the Queen. One of the few? She kept talking to Jessi.

But only Jessi.

Kiran was ignored.

Chapter 28

They reached the throne room, with five thrones instead of the four Jaden's family had back at Majora. Instead of gold and gemstones decorating them, the fancy chairs reflected the black she'd seen everywhere, with dark red accents.

Kiran ran for one of the thrones. Once there, he ran his fingers along one of the red accent lines. "Man, I missed this chair."

Estelle didn't blink, didn't watch him, didn't acknowledge her own son's excitement. Granted, he was excited about a chair, but a mother should still notice her child no matter what the enthusiasm was about. Instead, she turned to Jessica and asked, "You two are alright? Nothing happened to either of you?"

Jessi shook her head, mop of blonde and brown hair flinging about. "Nope. Well, aside from Kir getting a bruised ego."

"Hey!" Kiran snapped, looking at them.

Estelle yet again ignored her son, not even looking in his direction. "Well, if that's the only injury you two ended up with, I couldn't be happier."

Jaden felt about to burst. This woman showed no attention or compassion to her son. She may be a Queen, single-handedly ruling over an entire Kingdom, but, Queen or not, family should be a priority. After a few more moments, she barked, "Hey, lady! Why won't you even look at him?"

Estelle lifted her gaze to meet hers. "What are you talking about?" she asked. Her soft-spoken tone relaxed Jaden slightly, as it was easy enough to discern her worried confusion, a trait a mother should have. Maybe she wasn't as neglectful as she first appeared to Jaden.

"Kiran," Jaden replied, still keeping slight steel in her tone. Hopefully that tone would convey how serious and firm she was. "He's been talking and running all over the place, and you don't even look at him!"

Tears welled up in the Queen's eyes. She squeezed them shut, a few droplets rolling down her cheeks. Then, with a forced, fake, quivering smile, she opened her now bloodshot eyes and looked at Seth. "You didn't tell her?"

Seth averted his gaze to his shiny dress shoes. "Didn't come up."

After heaving a heavy sigh, she asked, "She's got psychoscopic abilities, right?"

The King nodded. "Yes, she does. But, do you want to live through that memory again?"

Estelle bit her lip, then gave a small nod. "It's better for her to see it herself." She approached Jaden, stopping a few feet away. "Go ahead, dearie. See what I've had to go through, and your question will get the answer it wants."

Jaden cast Lukas a wary glance. When he gave her a single, curt nod, she sighed deeply. "Okay then. Here goes nothing." She met Estelle's eyes, and after a few moments of concentrating, that swirling tunnel stretched around her, the throne room disappearing behind its walls. Again, a scene played at the end of the funneling tunnel. She walked up to it, and quickly recognized the Majora's town square. Except, instead of laughing children, conversing parents, and merchants selling their wares with smiles, the scene greeted her with crying kids, crumbling storefronts, and injured citizens in heaps on the ground.

Something compelled her to keep walking, so she did. She vaguely realized she'd stepped out of the portal and into the Hell that stood behind her, but it definitely wasn't on the forefront of her mind. She approached a huge crowd, circled around something that had to be important.

"Outta my way!" A woman ran past Jaden, easily recognized as Estelle, and started pushing through the crowds. Jaden saw an opportunity and followed closely behind her. Once they both reached the hollow center, they stopped, staring at two teenagers in bloodied, mutilated heaps. Jaden had to swallow back bile at the vicious injuries. Then, Estelle fell down, kneeling in between them. She grabbed one victim's ankle and shook it. "Jessi, baby girl, say something!"

It only took a split second later for Jaden's hands to fly to her mouth.

These two were Jessi and Kiran.

Jaden's eyes darted to the other body and finally recognized the messy hair. One thing she didn't see? His chest wasn't moving. He wasn't breathing. That was why Estelle didn't acknowledge him earlier.

He was already dead before she arrived.

"Jessica, say something, baby!" Jaden looked back to Estelle and Jessi, eyes stinging at the carnage and upsetting reality.

Jessi's body stirred, and her head turned over slightly, weak, fading eyes meeting her mother's. "Mama..."

Estelle scooched closer, tucking a bloody strand of hair behind her daughter's ear. "Shh, don't talk, sweetie. You've got to save your energy. The medics are coming, so just hang in there, okay?"

Jessi's gaze moved to empty space behind her mother. "Kiran... Kiran's already..." The girl cringed, tears falling like a waterfall. Sucking in a shaky breath, she told Estelle, "Kir's behind you, Mama. I don't want him alone there..."

The Queen cupped her daughter's face. "He won't have to be, because you can still see him." Her weak smile quivered as tears broke and flowed down her cheeks as well. "Stay with me, baby girl. Just stay here, with me, with your father, with your Kingdom. You are my whole world. I can't lose you, baby."

Jessi smiled crookedly and touched the hand that cupped her face. "Trust me, Mama. You won't lose me yet. I'll always be there. I promise." Then, her eyes dulled and stared into space, her hand falling to the cobblestones.

She was dead.

Estelle's eyes widened as she started shaking Jessi's shoulder. "Baby girl? Jessica, don't you... don't you give up on me. Please, baby girl. Please..." She cringed, and the sobs that came out of her would've turned even a suicide bomber to tears. Jaden had started crying minutes before, and the finality of what had occurred finally sank in. These two sixteen-year-olds brutally murdered by their own father, surrounded by a crowd of citizens who had mourned for six years.

Sniffling, Jaden closed her eyes and let her shaky, numb knees give way. She cringed, the stinging tears making it harder to choke out the words. Finally, after swallowing past a huge lump in her throat, she shouted with her voice cracking, "Enough! I've..." She choked up slightly, "I've seen enough!"

The background noise of the town square vanished instantly, and silence surrounded her. Opening her eyes, she found herself in a pitch-dark room. She could vaguely make out two tables with some stuff on them.

Groaning softly, Jaden muttered, "Great. Another unconscious setting change." Louder, she called out, "You know, this is getting really old really quickly!"

Two spotlights cracked on, centered over the two cloth-covered tables. The lumps were covered with black fabric, but she had a feeling it wasn't china or dishware underneath. Sure enough, when she stood up, she recoiled back two steps.

It was Kiran and Jessi.

While only their faces remained exposed, the skin shone milky white, the paleness of death evident. The bodies look perfectly preserved, identical to their appearances as spirits. Jaden thanked God that their eyes had been shut, because the opposite would've broken her. She took gradual steps closer, stopping right at the foot of both tables. She stared at each teen's face for a few seconds each. When she felt more tears stinging her eyes, she called out again, "What do I have to do? I want to give them their lives back!"

A voice in her head said, *You can do this. Instincts. It's all about instincts. Focus on what you want, and go for it. Believe in yourself.*

She would have dismissed it as an overactive imagination, but she recognized the voice as male. Didn't sound like anyone she knew, which crossed off Kiran or Skylar. She stared first at Jessi's body, hearing the squeals of delight and feeling the numerous hugs exchanged in the last week. Then, her gaze moved to Kiran, recalling his easily annoyed attitude and his attempts to look like he knew everything when he didn't. Her eyes stung as she thought in her head, *They were so innocent... They didn't deserve to die...*

Her hands coated in a bright white light, ribbons of bleached yellow swirling around her arms, legs, and her whole body. She felt pressure building up in her chest, making her feel almost invincible. She closed her eyes and inhaled deeply. When she released that held breath, she slowly opened her eyes, staring determinedly at the twins' corpses. She took three more steps until she stood equally between them. Then, she stretched out her arms, fingers splayed, and placed one of each twin's chest. The ribbons moved faster, twirling around her body and both of the kids' at untraceable speeds. Both of the twins' bodies slowly started glowing, Kiran's red and Jessi's purple. Jaden felt her fingers starting to fall asleep, her legs shaking under her body weight. Gritting her teeth, she growled to herself, "C'mon, Jaden, keep it together! For them. Keep it together for their sake!"

A few moments later, Kiran's eyes shot open, followed closely by his sister's. Both gasped for air, muscles tensed and eyes wide. Jaden yanked her hands off them and firmly pushed them against the tables themselves to keep herself upright.

Jessi sat up, the sheet over her body rolling into her lap. She held out her hands, twisting and analyzing them. "Are we really…" She looked at the opposite table, where Kiran still stared at the ceiling while catching his breath. "Kir, are we really back?"

Kiran sat up and threw his legs over the edge of the table. "Dunno."

A door slammed open, sending blinding light spilling in from outside of the darkened room. Estelle instantly ran to Kiran's side, grabbing her son in a tight, shaky hug. "My baby boy! My sweet baby boy!"

Kiran's lips started quivering as he tightly held his mother. Voice cracking, he cried, "I'm back, Mama. I'm back!"

Estelle dug her nails into his skull, intertwining in his blonde hair. "Yes, you are, baby boy!"

Jessi hopped off of her table, rounded both of them, and inserted herself around them, a group hug: the first their family had been able to have in six long years.

Jaden's arms and legs decided then to give out. She lost support and crumbled to the floor. Black spots blocked her vision, changing in size and shape and blinking in and out of sight. Her head spun, filled with lightheadedness like she'd never felt. Clearly there was a reason people weren't resurrected regularly around here. It had drained her completely, and she felt herself fading. *Maybe I should have listened to Seth when he said it had been centuries...*

"Jay?" Jessi's worried voice sounded muffled, as if she was underwater. Kiran and Estelle also called her name, but she barely registered them. She vaguely felt someone shaking her shoulders before her world went black.

Chapter 29

"I think she's waking up, Your Highness."

Damn, my head's killing me... Jaden cringed at the sharp headache, almost like a million needles poking in one centralized location to the left side of her forehead.

Someone sat beside her, she could only figure it was a mattress she laid on currently. That someone grabbed her left hand and squeezed it tightly. That urged her enough to open her eyes. She instantly regretted that decision, as light from a large window blinded her.

Her companion snapped, "Curtains, idiots!"

That voice was easily recognizable. "Dove?" she muttered, hating how weak and sick she sounded. When she opened her eyes, now she could see her sister-mother fully, sitting by her side.

Dove flashed her a crooked, slightly comforting smile. "You okay there, Sneakers?"

Jaden nodded slightly. "I... I think so."

"Do you remember what happened?"

She thought for a few brief moments before the memories came flooding back. Arriving at the Second Kingdom, meeting Queen Estelle, witnessing the memory of the twins' murder, their corpses before her, the white and yellow glow... Her eyes widened and darted back to Dove. "Did

I really…" She couldn't even choke out the words from the shock and amazement at what she'd done.

Dove nodded, her smile softening. "Yep, you did. The twins are back amongst the living. And they have you to thank."

Right as the Majora Queen said that, the doors opened with a thunderous slam. Jaden winced. Guess all her senses were sensitive right then. Someone grabbed her in a tight, constricting hug. "Thankyouthankyouthankyouthankyou!"

Jaden patted her constrictor, chuckling, "It's not a problem, Jess. I felt you didn't deserve to die like that. Now, I believe someone once told me something wise." After a brief silent pause, she finished, "She said I needed to breathe."

Jessi released her, plopping on the bed in front of Dove. The wide grin spoke volumes for the happiness and excitement Jaden had given her. "Yeah, that's good advice. Wonder who said it?" She then giggled and gently pushed Jaden's shoulder.

"Jaden?"

All three females moved their gazes to the door to find Kiran standing there, fidgeting, while his mother nudged him into the room. When Kiran lifted his gaze, Jaden thanked Heaven again for his eyes still as blue as they had been as a spirit. She probably would have passed out again had then been the murderous red of demons. "Thank you, Jaden. I don't think any words can equal the gift of life you've given us."

Jaden smiled sweetly and replied, "Kiran, Jess, you guys have helped me loads in the last week or so. While I really didn't like the secrets and lies, all of them have been cleared up by now, enough for me to be satisfied. You made it your mission to bring me home, so it's only fair I do the same for you, and bring you home as well."

Kiran nodded, gaze darting to the floor. "My mother is also eternally grateful. If you ever need anything, she says she will assist." Queen Estelle nodded from behind him.

"I appreciate that." Jaden then gazed around the large room and noticed Kiran was the only male there. "Where's Lukas? And Bri?"

Dove rubbed Jaden's leg, telling her, "They're filling the cars up with gas so we can head back home."

Home. Where the heart is, where people always want to go or return to. This journey had done a lot for Jaden, but one thing felt comforting that wouldn't have a week ago.

She was a Kinetic. She could raise the dead. She could see anyone's memories. Before the twins found her, those qualities would only belong in fantasy novels.

Now, those qualities equaled home.

It felt slightly weird to admit it, but…

I'm finally home.

Chapter 30

Jaden recovered in a few more hours. Her back ached something fierce, compelling her to constantly roll her shoulders. She got back on her feet after a bit of food, plenty of water, and some soda that tasted like Dr. Pepper and Sprite mixed together. You wouldn't think that would be a good combo, but, much to Jaden's surprise, she kinda liked it. The sugar buzz wasn't terrible either.

"Sneakers, are you-" Dove's words cut off as she cleared her throat. Sighing, she said, "Trust me on this, kiddo. Melding two personalities back into one body is no easy task. Like corralling a bull and the Tasmanian Devil into the same barn stall."

Jaden's lip twitched in humor. "I'm going through a similar conflict. I can't decide whether to apologize for fifteen years of sibling torture, or put you in a chokehold on the floor because you hid this from me for that whole length of time."

The warm smile on Dove's face finally resembled a mother's. At least somewhat. Appeared like the Queen was starting to adjust more than she gave herself credit for. She walked up to Jaden and ruffled her black and white hair. "Whatever am I going to do with you, child?"

"Buy me a yacht, a lifetime supply of Cow Tales, and unlimited onDemand of truTV shows, and I'll have everything I've ever wanted out of life."

When Dove shoved her playfully, Jaden cracked a wide grin. "You obviously aren't having any conflicts or crises with your personality," the Queen commented, "You seem just as annoying and unbelievable as ever." Patting Jaden on the back, she added, "I'm proud of you, kiddo."

Cocking an eyebrow, Jaden asked, "Is that gym rat or magical Kinetic Queen talking?"

"Both. But also the proud mother of a remarkable, resilient child. Magic or no." They exchanged grateful smiles, until a few moments later…

"We've got a huge problem."

Both turned to the door of the room to find Lukas and Jessi running in. "What's the problem, Kohei?" Dove asked, a slight worry and protectiveness in her voice. Jaden thought the new maternal instinct was a great new addition to her sister's old personality.

Jessi slammed into Jaden, hugging her so hard Jaden's limbs tingled from weakened circulation. When she realized the girl was shaking, Jaden squeezed back tight. "What's going on, Jess?"

"They-They… They t-t-took him!"

"Took who?"

Sniffling and choking on a sob, Jessi cried, "They took my brother!"

Jaden lifted her head, meeting Lukas' solemn gaze. "Who took Kiran?"

Lukas replied, "Not just Kiran. They got Shalbriri too."

Her gaze narrowed as she firmly repeated, "*Who. Took. Them?*"

Shoulders dropping, he answered flatly, "Keegan, along with some unknown assistance. After we filled up the cars, you still weren't one-hundred percent. So, Kiran and Shalbriri went with me to the gym. We were coming back from there, and the two of them fell behind. They were caught hashing it out in the woods on camera, and that same camera's footage caught the abduction as well. To be honest, I found it weird that Keegan disappeared shortly after arriving to Majora. His Majesty is currently pacing a burning path into carpet while ranting to Queen Estelle, who herself is both fuming and bawling at the same time."

With a weak chuckle, Dove added, "Ladies and gentlemen, I present the leaders of your kingdom!"

Her overexaggerated attempt at making light of the situation easily entered the territory of inappropriate timing, as seen by everyone's glare burning into her. With a heavy sigh, Dove headed for the door. "*Alright*, I'll go calm them down. This'll be *fun*. *Yay* me." The sarcasm and bitterness sounded clearly in her tone and emphasis on certain words.

Once Dove had left, Lukas crossed the vast distance between him and Jaden with very large strides. "Jay, we didn't want Her Majesty to know everything, so we wanted her to leave, even though, obviously, she'd rather have not been bothered."

Sniffling, Jessi murmured, "W-We actually had an Excuse B and Excuse C in case the freaking out of our parents wasn't enough."

Jaden patted Jessi a few times, slowly lowering her to the nearby mattress. "Why don't you sit down? And breathe. Always remember to breathe." When Jessi released Jaden from the constricting hug, Jaden saw she'd cracked a smile. She then turned back to Lukas. "What details couldn't my sister-slash-mother know?"

Lukas reached into his pocket and extracted a folded piece of paper. Holding it out to her, he said, "Read it for yourself."

After eyeing the paper for a few seconds, Jaden accepted it, unfolding the two creases. The note had been handwritten in fancy scrawl:

Dearest Princess,

Despite your best attempts, their resurrections are only temporary. If you desire the safe return of the two royals, you need to meet us where water falls in rainbow ribbons to finish what you started. If you decide against coming, I will not be as merciful to the Prince of the Fifth Kingdom.

Your choice, princess.

"Temporary?" She looked up at Lukas, confusion clear on her face. "What does he mean?"

Lukas heaved a heavy sigh, his shoulders rising and falling with it. "Well, while your actions were pure, your abilities were lacking. Your instincts can use your untrained abilities and raw power to an extent. However, King Cabrera had it right when he said it would take countless time for anyone to master perfect, unflawed resurrections. Your adrenaline and intense emotions gave you a burst of power to make your desire, reality: restoring the twins' lives. And trust me, getting that magic energy yanked out of me caused major pain. All my muscles still ache." As if to demonstrate, he stretched back, groaning until straightening again.

That piqued Jaden's curiosity more. "Why were you in pain? It was my magic." *Feels funny to verbally admit I now have magic...*

With an agreeing nod, Lukas countered, "Yes, your magic, but my seal. I'm your paladin, remember? We are mainly magic containers for our charges, so you all don't accidentally unleash holy Hell at random lapses of judgement. Like a lock to a small storage unit full of grenades. Trust me, you Kinetics are lucky and blessed to have us to keep that mass of strong, world-altering abilities in check."

"Miss Theron?"

All three whipped their attention to the door. Standing in the doorway was a crisply-styled young man. He appeared in his mid-twenties, with a perfectly ironed red dress shirt, slacks, polished dress shoes and… a black fedora?

Who was this guy? A mini Neal Caffrey? A lump grew in her throat as she remembered the countless hours she and her sister spent binging White Collar a number of years ago, one of a lifetime of bonding moments that seemed so trivial now. This new arrival, however, missed two key traits that the ex-con of the television FBI always had: a cocky smirk and a laid-back attitude. This young man had neither, and looked wound tight as a spring, brows furrowed worriedly as he stared at Jessi.

Jessi's eyes widened slightly at the newcomer. "Micha? What are you doing here?"

This Micha walked quickly toward them, practically shoving Lukas out of his path without so much as an 'excuse me' or 'sorry about that'. He got on one knee at Jessi's side. "Princess, I am your paladin. It's my job to protect and serve you."

Well, that explained a bit.

"I figured you'd have been rematched." The whimper in her voice easily told them she'd been hoping that hadn't happened.

Shaking his head, Micha took one of her hands with both of his. "At my personal request, I declined. My carelessness and foolishness got you killed, so I held onto your mother's goal of restoring your life."

Sniffling, Jessi asked, "For six years?"

A warm, caring smile finally cracked Micha's stone face. "Anything for my charge, Princess. Now if I heard correctly…" He stood up, letting Jessi's hand fall back into the girl's lap. Locking gazes with Lukas, he asked, "You realized the glitch in their resurrections?"

Crossing his arms, Lukas snapped, "I knew the second she yanked it out of me."

As he arched an eyebrow, Micha drawled lazily, "Why don't I believe you? Was it the bitter resentment you spoke to me with? Or the knowledge that you had one job to keep an eye on the boys, and, being a sub-par paladin, slipped up." Lukas' face brightened into a rich pink. "Oh, I'm sorry, did I bruise your ego, Kohei?"

Growling softly, Lukas glared at him. "Bite me, jackel!"

Mouth twitching slightly, Micha responded civilly, "Gladly. Though, I'm not sure I'm up for a bitter and sour taste in my mouth."

Lukas had turned as red as Shaggy after eating a hot pepper in Scooby-Doo on Zombie Island. Jaden could envision the steam and smoke shooting out of his ears. With a heavy sigh, she stepped between them. "Knock it off, you two. In case you haven't noticed, we've had two of our friends abducted."

Lukas averted his gaze, muttering, "He started it."

"What are you, six?" Jaden snapped, "I don't care who started it, Wolfe. I'm ending it! I need you to focus on the problem at hand, not your stupid bruised pride."

Micha blinked, as if just noticing her presence. He bowed low. "My apologies, Majora Highness. I regret showing an uglier side of myself in your presence."

Under his breath, Lukas murmured, "Suck up."

Jaden took that quiet insult as an excuse to stamp hard on her best friend's foot. As he cried out, she told him lightly, "You act immature, I'll act immature. It can go both ways, Lukas." As he held his foot and glared at her, she smiled smugly. Then, directing her attention to Jessi and Micha, she asked, "Who's up for a little rescue mission?"

Eyes brightening, Jessi squealed, "Really? You mean that?"

With a nod and a sincere smile, Jaden replied, "One-hundred percent mean it. We're going after them."

"Now, I'm just venturing a wild guess…" Lukas drawled, lowering his foot back to the carpet again, "But I assume you don't want the adults involved?"

Jaden scoffed, crossing her arms, "Who needs them? Besides, His Royal Child-ness would only let me go if meteors were destroying the planet anyway, and, despite knowing everyone would die, he'd still stick to my side like glue. No, we do this our way, and we save them our way. Everybody in?"

Leaping to her feet, Jessi grinned, "Of course I'm in! Who needs 'em?"

As the two girls exchanged hyper hi-fives, Micha placed a hand on Jessi's shoulder. "Miss Theron, I'd normally advise against this, but as this involve young Master Kiran, I will accompany you."

Rolling her eyes teasingly, Jessi responded, "You always look out for me, don't you, Micha?"

Mouth cracking a small smile, Micha told her, "Until the end of time, my Princess. Now, I believe we'll need equipment, won't we?"

It felt good for Jaden to see Jessi's hyperactive, bubbling energy return to the teenage twin. The girl practically vibrated with excitement and anticipation, like a five-year-old hearing the ice cream truck down the road. "Alright, let's gear up!"

As Jessi dashed out of the room like a baby cheetah, Jaden looked at Micha. "Did she mature at all during her six years in Limbo?"

Shaking his head, Micha replied, "Appears not. She's always thought in a mature way, but it's never really transferred to her actions. Everything she actively does is based purely on her wildness of her vast emotional range."

“So, simply put, she’s a loose cannon that can explode with any kind of intense emotion at all?”

The smallest of humored smiles crossed the paladin’s face. “Yes, that is simply put. You’ve got quite a talent for cutting to the chase. I should ask, though, if you’ve crafted a plan to rescue the two royals?”

With a shrug, Jaden replied, “Show up, kick ass, and run back home.”

As she started to follow Jessi’s path, Micha called out, “So, more of a general idea than a detailed, analytical, planed rescue tactic? I thought I was told you were training in business?”

“Someone told me I should take more risks,” she called back without stopping, “Besides, I don’t need more than that idea to win. You all seem to believe I’m helpless and naïve as a baby, like a damsel in distress like other fairytale princesses. It’s rather insulting.” Stopping in the doorway, she finally turned back to the two paladins. “I’m more than my first impression.” With a wink, she stepped out into the hallway. She glanced both left and right. No sign of Jessi.

Until:

“Griffin!”

Griffin. Why did that name sound so familiar?

A boisterous, extremely familiar voice rang through the halls from around a corner, “It’s so good to see you again, Miss Theron!”

Jaden froze for a minute, stopping in her tracks. She definitely knew that voice. And she knew who it belonged to. It seemed illogical and almost a disbelieving impossibility, but she had to have confirmation. As she picked up the pace, she mentally ran through her experiences prior to getting pulled into this new, magic-filled life. Before Jessi and Kiran rescued her from Skylar. Before touching Skylar and getting shocked. In that same room that kickstarted this journey home, she’d interacted with a businessman who'd offered her, an eighteen-year-old college student, guns and weapons should she ever need them…

Turning into the room she'd pinpointed as the source, she screeched to a halt in the doorway. When she caught the man's eyes, he smiled warmly. *Yep, that's him.* "About time, Jaden Walker," said Griffin Valentine, President of ArmsWorth and, at present, someone who had some decent explaining to do.

Crossing her arms, Jaden replied, "Really? That's what you start with, Sir?" Her inner businesswoman always addressed adults, especially bigwigs, as Sir or Madam, but still wasn't sure if those mannerisms still applied in this new life she found herself in.

Griffin answered her internal conflict, as if reading her mind, "Dear Jaden, you are now of a higher ranking than I, as a Princess. No 'Sir' required. Now, I feel compelled to ask…" He cupped his hand around one side of his mouth and whispered loudly enough to show he didn't care if others heard, "How is taking real-life risks treating you?"

Smiling while remembering her brief conversation with the firearm company's CEO back at the Phi Beta Lambda conference, she replied, "I'm riding that motorcycle, and I'm not looking back."

"That'a girl." Dropping his hand, he brushed wrinkles from his ironed, black dress shirt. The only bit of color in his crisp attire was a blood red tie, resting right down the middle of his chest. That splash of color made his appearance much less intimidating, reflecting his laid-back personality he seemed to have. "Now, if young Miss Theron told me correctly, you are planning a dangerous rescue attempt?" When Jaden nodded after a few seconds of hesitation, he arched an accusatory eyebrow. "Without your parents?"

She averted her eyes. "Well, maybe. It's my fault this happened, but-"

"But nothing, Princess," he interrupted as she went silent and continued to stare at her sneakers. Then, his hand came into view, waving a strange-looking pistol. The hole for the bullets was incredibly small compared to its wide barrel size, making her ponder what kinds of bullets came out of that tiny of a hole. Copper pipes looped around various places, and along with the tarnished copper color of the rest of the weapon, gave it a steampunk-inspired appearance. "You'll need this."

"Guess you were serious about supplying me with whatever weapons I might want." Taking the weapon cautiously, she examined it by slowly turning it in her hands. "What does it do? The tip of the barrel looks too small for any kind of bullet I've ever seen."

In a flash, Griffin grabbed the gun, yanked it free of her grip, flipped it in a blur to point at the far wall, and pulled the trigger. After a series of loud, sharp crackles, a bright yellow, almost glowing, bolt of lightning shot out of that tiny opening. When it hit the wall and vanished, a small, singed hole smoked where the shot had made contact.

Griffin held the shock gun by the barrel, handing it back to her. "The switch on the back is for different modes. Choose your attack wisely. Yellow circle is pure lightning, which was that example's mode. Blue is for paralysis. Red is to knock someone unconscious. That red one is funny to watch, though. Like a Taser back on Earth."

Cautiously, Jaden took the firearm back, staring at it in wonder. Finally, she asked, "Is there a safety lock?"

Tapping a button on the right side of the barrel, he told her, "Pushed in is safety mode, stuck out is active, 'Try-Me-Bastard' mode."

After stifling another snorting laugh, Jaden commented, "Guess business here is booming compared to Earth, huh?"

With a hearty chuckle, he replied, "The gun control advocates there definitely keep me on my toes."

Jaden looked up at him and asked, "Why are you here? I assumed-"

"There's your answer," he interrupted, silencing her, "You 'assumed'. In the world you are now a part of, assume nothing. There is only fact or secret, no in-between. But, if I picked up your personality quirks correctly, you seem to like things that way."

Mouth twitching in humor, she countered, "Now who's the assuming one? But, yes, I do like things straight forward. And now, here's an honest fact for you..." She bent her arm up, resting the barrel of her steampunk shock gun on her shoulder. With a cocky grin, she met Jessi's excited gaze, brimming with anticipation as she briefly stopped browsing the weapons that filled this storage room.

"We're gonna save two boys, and kick some traitorous, abducting, Kinetic posterior."

Chapter 31

Between Jaden and Jessi's combined effort, they'd figured out the hint left in the note of where to meet these traitors: the waterfall they'd met Jakob at, and the same one Shalbriri had kidnapped Jaden at a few days ago. It seemed like ages since that day, but obviously not. So much had happened since then, and the one who had abducted her was now not only a companion of theirs, but now he'd been abducted himself. Was it karma? Who knew. Maybe just fate. Or maybe being taught a painful lesson.

They'd commandeered one of the three vehicles they'd come in and drove for an hour, until Micha told Lukas to pull over. "Why?" Lukas snapped, "We're in the middle of a forest-surrounded highway, with nothing for miles."

"Just pull over, Kohei."

With a soft, low, dangerous growl humming in his throat, Lukas did as he'd been told. When the car stopped, he twisted around to glare at Jessi's paladin in the back seat. "Why are we pulled over here?"

Calmly, Micha replied, "This is the closest point of the freeway to the waterfalls. It'll only be a fifteen-minute walk from here."

Once Micha and Jessi had gotten out of the car and shut their doors, Lukas met Jaden's eyes. "Fifteen-minutes of walking with Sir Stiffness?"

Ruffling his hair, Jaden ordered, "Play nice, alright? He wants this mission to succeed just as much as we do."

"Then he needs to stop acting like the stuck-up, bossy A-Lister, alright? He reminds me of the jocks in high school, except more intelligent, half their size, and twice as annoyingly prideful." He practically kicked open his door, slamming it just as forcefully.

Shaking her head in amusement, Jaden got out of the passenger's side. Jessi stood right next to her as the boys already started into the woods, Micha still calm but tense, and Lukas still red and glaring like a cartoon character. "Which one do you think is more wound up?" Jaden asked the younger teen.

"Hmmm..." Jessi pondered, watching the two males get deeper and deeper into the forest. "Not sure, to be honest. I think it's a close race. What about you?"

"Yeah, too close to call."

"But, I think we're almost like parents for them," Jessi commented, "It's like dealing with two young children that don't get along."

Jaden's mouth tugged into a small, humored smile, as she added, "More like two toddlers that are bickering over who gets a gold star on their report card."

Jessi's mouth mirrored Jaden's as she input more, "And the chore they're trying to get credit for ended up more messed up than when they started, because they fought the whole time." A trademark snort with Jaden's laughter shot out, her hand clapping over her mouth. She continued to giggle from behind her hand though, along with Jessi, whose laughter howled way more than Jaden's own.

After a few moments of shared humor, Lukas called back to them, "Get a move on, Jaden! We don't got all day!"

Exchanging smiles with the girl, Jaden called back, "We're comin', we're comin'! Take a chill pill!"

Lukas' voice echoed back, clearly pissed off, "You try taking a chill pill while walking with this stiff!"

Giggling again, the two girls jogged after them. Once reaching them, Jaden placed a hand on Lukas' shoulder and leaned into his left ear. Softly, she growled, "Behave yourself, Wolfe. I need you focused and ready, alright?"

Lukas nodded and responded, "Yes, I know. Sorry. I'll reign it in."

Patting his shoulder a few times, she said, "Good." Hand dropping back down, she looked over at Micha. "Now, how away far are we?"

"Little over ten minutes."

Sure enough, ten minutes later, they arrived at the waterfall. It still fell in rainbow ribbons, just as the note described. The sun shining through the trees shone light onto the crystal-clear pond, glimmering as the water circulated. However, something was missing.

Lots of somethings.

"Where are they?" Jessi whimpered, clutching her arms to her chest.

Then, a loud shout of pain shot through the calm air. Jaden had never heard him in pain before, but he was easy enough to identify. "Bri…" she murmured. The sound had come around the hill the waterfall dumped over. She jogged around it and spotted a cave. When another roar echoed out of it, she knew she'd found them.

The other three had followed after her, and they all looked at each other hesitantly. As quietly and cautiously as they could, they crept into the cave. As they made their way down the darkened tunnel, they heard Keegan speak up, "Seems the famed invincible Prince of the Fifth Kingdom isn't so invincible after all, is he?"

The sound of spitting reached their ears, followed by Shalbriri's strained voice: "Do your worst, Kelly."

"Ha! You haven't even experienced the tip of the iceberg, Princey."

Jaden heard the want to sound intimidating in Bri's voice, but his attempt wasn't worth the effort: "I am not afraid of you."

"Well, you should be," came Keegan's answer, "Because I'm not just following orders from my King. I'm acting on my virtues and facts. And the fact of the matter? Your family is scum!" That last sentence had been delivered so darkly, Jaden could hear the poison and resentment in it.

"Shalbriri, you asked for that one."

Jaden stopped in her tracks, frozen. Her eyes darted over the rocky cave floor, comprehending that voice that had just spoken to Bri. She had only heard this individual say a few words, and just in a single dream, but she knew who it was.

"Raiden..."

Jessi's hand rested on Jaden's shoulder, directing her attention to her. "Jay, are you alright?"

"No," Lukas answered for her, "She's not."

Brow furrowing, she asked, "Why not?"

Jaden sucked in a shaky breath, the image of the wheat field spattered in blood, the garnet irises, the sword plunging into her gut... Squeezing her stinging eyes shut, she whimpered, "We just heard your dad."

"Dad?" Jessi asked. Jaden could hear the slight confusion in her voice. "Are you sure that was him?"

"Looks like Jakob was right then..." Lukas commented, gazing at his three companions, "King Raiden did elect to stay in Limbo."

Jessi's wide eyes darted toward the back of the tunnel. Jaden acknowledged conversations further in, but the buzzing and pounding in her ears muffled them out. However, she could hear her group's talking loud and clear. "So… That's why they took Kiran."

"How so?" Micha asked.

After sucking in a deep, shaky breath, Jessi answered, "Because he doesn't know who killed him."

Jaden's head jerked up at this new information. "What?" she hissed, hoping their voices weren't carrying to the torture room awaiting them.

Fidgeting with her hands, Jessi continued, "My dad hit him from behind. When Kiran tried to see his attacker, my dad evaded his line of sight. Once my brother went down, a mercifully quick death, he moved on to me. Once we were done, I saw a slight pang of regret in his eyes for a few seconds until he growled, squeezed his eyes shut, and dashed back toward the complex. When Kiran first reached Limbo, he spotted Shalbriri running in the same direction as our dad. He ran after them, and watched Bri and our dad duke it out in the blood-spattered, massacred ballroom. And… well, I'm assuming you know the rest of what happened..."

"So that's why he hates Skylar and Bri," Lukas commented, "Because he thinks Skylar killed his father in cold blood."

Jessi nodded. "Exactly." She started taking deep breaths, the shakiness of it slowly calming. Then, after a few moments, she looked up at them again. "My brother watched them die. That means he can see our dad. He can hear him. He can acknowledge him. But, I know for damn sure my father hasn't told him the truth. Otherwise, Kiran would have at least attempted to get free. We've got to tell him."

They all nodded in acknowledgement.

"Miss Cabrera? It's so nice of you to arrive. Why don't you come join us?"

Raiden's echoing voice sounded soft, gentle, unthreatening. Some part of her felt compelled to walk into the open, while her logical side screamed, *No, stay silent. Act like you're not there.*

"I know you're there, Princess. Come of your own free will, or I will send somebody to assist you."

Swallowing past a hard lump in her throat, Jaden started forward. When the others followed, she stopped and held up a hand. *No...* she mouthed, *Stay hidden.* After getting silent, agreeing nods, she sucked in a deep breath and kept walking. That pinpoint of light at the end grew rather quickly, eventually breaking open into a wide cavern. The ceiling and floor had multiple stalactites and stalagmites jutting out, the upper ones dripping drops of water into puddles on the cavern floor.

Off to the left, Shalbriri sat in a chair, hands tied behind it. He had been beaten hard. Blood dribbled from his lip, with a black eye, bruises and cuts decorating his exposed legs. His gym shorts had been sliced up a bit, while his blue tee had been styled with Do-It-Yourself fringing along the bottom. Blood stained that shirt, making the soaked spots a dark, rich purple-black. Keegan stood nearby, a bloodied knife in one hand, with the knuckles on both of his hands cut up, raw, and tainted red. "Dear Miss Jaden," he drawled, the hunger in his eyes apparent. It seemed the training instructor had lost *some* of his sanity since she'd last seen him. "Did you come to participate?"

Okay, he'd lost *all* of it.

Glaring at him, Jaden asked, "Where's Kiran?"

Keegan waggled the damp knife lazily. "Well, he's in another room over there..." He jerked his head toward a metal door in far side of the cavern. "But, he's asleep. Wouldn't want his first bout of living sleep to be interrupted, now do we? Oh, and that door is sound-proof, so you can scream all you want, but…" His wide, wild grin unsettled Jaden. "He would never hear you."

Jaden crossed her arms, glare sharpening. "Let both of them go."

"Well, Kiran seems to be enjoying his stay here, so I doubt he'll leave. This one, though…" Keegan placed his dagger at Shalbriri's throat. His eyes shined with a sick, twisted, sadistic gleam. "I'd rather keep him around. He's such a fun plaything."

"What happened to you?" she asked, buying time, "Were you always like this?"

Keegan's smile softened. He let the knife drop to his side. "My revenge has always burned bright, but when you cut yourself off from most of society for as many years as I did, you tend to grow soft. Once we got you home, I was reminded why I ran. For my safety. And for a chance to dole out revenge for my cousin's undeserved murder."

An arm wrapped around Jaden's stomach from behind, clutching her firmly to his body. She yelped at the sudden, paralyzing shock shooting through her body and angled her head to meet warm brown eyes. However, despite the eye color difference, the rest of his features screamed the truth.

"King Raiden…" she growled.

With a small, soft, almost regret-filled smile, Raiden said, "In the spirit. It's so nice to see you, Princess. You've grown up so much, haven't you?"

"Enough to kick your demonic posterior across a highway."

His mouth twitched. "Quite the wit. Just for future reference, humor won't help you. At least, not right now."

A sharp pain shot through her pinned arm, and her gaze jerked away from her restrainer's face to see him slowly sliding a letter opener down it, slicing open the skin. It burned and stung like she'd never felt before. Well, wasn't as bad as what she'd felt from his sword in her gut from that horrific dream, but that injury would go away once awake. No injuries that she might get here would go away. And, she had a sickening feeling she would come out with a lot of them.

If she came out at all.

"See, I hold all the cards. I've got your precious Fifth Kingdom Prince restrained to a chair, my son greeting me with open arms, and my wife no longer burdened with the pain of her two children being taken away from her. However, that burden is now on me. Even though your intentions were pure, you didn't finish the job. Another Channeler can just as easily send them back to Limbo. Not all the threads keeping them in Limbo have been severed, making it quite simple to reverse your efforts." He jerked her, and another shocked yelp shot from her vocal chords. Her body started shaking while blood ran down her arm and dripped to the stone. "You care to help out with that?"

That stupid lump in her throat had grown, making even swallowing excess saliva painful. "What do you propose, Your Majesty?"

When she looked up at him, his smile was warm but also victorious and confident. "That'a girl. It seems like you have a good head on your shoulders, despite your human upbringing."

With a quick bark of a chuckle, Jaden drawled, "Yeah? Blame my sister. I think she's the unfortunate reason I had to be the mature one. After all, it appears all the royals on this dimension have uncontrollable emotion spans and the maturity of a five-year-old. I assume the same goes for you."

She practically felt the anger radiating of his ghostly skin from behind her. He quickly swiped the switchblade across her wrist. Pain shot through her arm, and she gritted her teeth to balance the pain. "Watch your mouth, Princess. It could get you into more trouble than you desire."

"How do you know how much trouble I desire?" she asked. She banked on sparking his anger to give her an opening. "For all you know, I might be suicidal, and I'll just allow you to do the dirty work yourself."

His grip on her stomach tightened. He leaned his mouth closer to her ear and whispered, "Careful, Princess. You have no idea how easily that can be arranged."

Suddenly, shocks convulsed through Jaden's body. They stopped when Raiden released her. She whipped around to find Raiden now on the floor, twitching slightly. His eyes gazed in disbelief and betrayal toward the entrance to the cavern. Jaden followed his gaze and saw Jessi standing there, the shock gun Jaden must have dropped held at arm's length, aimed in their direction. "Well, didn't realize that would work in Limbo."

The girl shook, eyes swimming with tears as she lowered the weapon. Her voice cracked when she spoke:

"You lost control. I know you couldn't help that. But…" She choked on a sob. "But seeing you cut Kiran down like you did has haunted me for six years. The worst part? He didn't know you did it. He glorified you our whole time in Limbo, and I restrained the truth I desperately wanted him to know. I hid it for your sake. Then you do this." She waved a hand toward where Shalbriri had been sitting. Jaden looked over there to find Lukas and Micha untying a slightly-aware Bri, while Keegan was nowhere to be found.

Jessi cringed as she continued, "I spent six years letting him believe you were a saint, while knowing that the demon that twisted you could also twist him. And, you know what? When we get out of here, I'm telling him. I'm telling him everything! And, if you try to interfere otherwise, I will not hesitate to have Jaden send you to the Hell you seem to channel in your actions. The devil must love you right now, right?"

Jaden walked up to Jessi and pried the weapon from the girl's hand. As Jaden held her tightly, Jessi cried, "I didn't know what to do, Jay."

Squeezing her comfortably, Jaden told her, "You did the right thing. Looks like you've got good instincts too." A few moments later, she asked, "I thought you said only Kiran could see him?"

Jessi sniffled, then answered, "I said Kiran saw his death. I didn't say I wasn't there too."

With a soft chuckle of comfort, Jaden responded, "And I assumed you were an open book."

"Remember what Griffin told you?" Jessi pulled back and smiled at Jaden. "Assume nothing."

Epilogue

"So, he's in Limbo?"

The soldier nodded from where he knelt before a glorious throne, where a woman was seated. "Yes, Your Majesty. Prince Shalbriri wanted you to be aware."

The woman's lip twitched. "Did he now? Keep eyes on him and the Majora Princess. If anything out of the ordinary happens, contact me immediately."

"Yes, of course, Your Majesty."

With a wave of her hand, she ordered, "General, you are dismissed."

After another nod, the General stood up and dashed out of the room. The woman slouched in her chair, sighing heavily.

"Mother?"

The voice of her youngest daughter, a mere eight years old, made her straighten. "Yes, Laraine?"

Laraine hesitated, but took more steps toward the throne. The braided bun of the girl's blonde hair had taken an hour of her mother's time, and ten minutes after handing the job over to the young girl's ladiesmaid. She'd had no idea how difficult to was to style hair, as she had chopped off her own golden locks years ago. "I heard BriBri was hurt. Is he okay?"

With a warm smile, the woman nodded. “He is a little bit beaten up, but recovering.”

Laraine smiled with an innocent giggle. “Goodie! When is he coming home?”

The woman’s smile faded slightly. She stood up, walked over to her daughter, and got on one knee in front of her. A strand of the child’s bun hung down, loose from its tight updo, and she tucked it behind the girl’s ear. “I don’t think BriBri can come home just yet.”

Laraine pouted. “Then make him! I wanna see my big brother!”

“Queen Keira?”

With a small eyeroll and soft sigh, Keira kissed the top of her daughter’s head. “Sweetheart, we’ll talk later, okay? Go play with your siblings.”

With a curtsy, Laraine replied, “Of course, Mommy. I love you.”

Keira smiled warmly back. “I love you too.” Once the girl ran out of earshot, she stood up again, staring toward that hallway Laraine had run down. Fingers digging into her palms, she growled to herself, “He can’t come home because his job isn’t finished yet. If he wants that peace like he’s preached, he’ll get the job done. He’s like his father.” With a small, wicked smile, the Queen of the Fifth Kingdom gazed at the line of thrones to her right. Her eyes landed on one colored midnight blue and turquoise.

“He never leaves a problem unresolved.”

Other Works

Tales of Terrara Vikos saga

eBook only::

#1- *Cross of Faith*

#2- *Trees In the Storm*

#3- *Blood of a Broken Hand*

#4- *Warped Destinies*

Available in eBook or print::

The Protektor's Reality: a Trials of Terrara Vikos prequel

The Vikan Quartet: a Tales of Terrara Vikos collection (Stories #1-4 above)

The Chaos Accounts

eBook only::

#1- *Account of Anxiety*

#2- *Account of Unrest*

#3- *Account of Friendship*

#4- *Account of Secrets (Coming Soon!)*

KINETICS series

eBook for Instafreebie subscribers only::

Kinetic Tragedy (a Kinetics prequel)

Available in eBook or print::

Kinetic Rebirth (*Kinetics,* Book One) (Available October 2017)

C. McDonnell

Born in Schenectady, NY and raised in Richmond, VA, Christine has always had a love of reading and writing. She didn't become aware of her gift for crafting stories until fifth grade, when she made it her dream to one day see her works on a bookstore shelf. Her love in the literary world has always been fantasy novels, because they allowed her to leave this world and venture into another. She devoured books growing up and still does in her free time.

Christine lives in Virginia, balancing her day job (working with numbers and Excel) and her creative endeavors.

You can find more about her and her works at::

terraravikos.com

AND

Help support her journey at::

https://www.patreon.com/discoverywritin

Made in the USA
Middletown, DE
18 March 2022

62756685R00159